BURN AND BLAZE

THE AZAR TRILOGY : BOOK TWO

GRACE MCGINTY

For the readers who reach out.
You make the hard times and the never ending hustle
worth it!

G x

Hell's Redemption Trilogy

The Redeemable: The Complete Novel

The Unrepentant: The Complete Novel

The Fallen: The Complete Novel

The Azar Nazemi Trilogy

Smoke and Smolder

Burn and Blaze

Rage and Ruin

Stand Alone Novels and Novellas

The Last Note

Bright Lights from a Hurricane

Castle of Carnal Desires

Treasure

BURN AND BLAZE

CHAPTER 1

Azar shifted back to avoid the fist hurtling towards her face. She felt the wind brush across her cheek as the swing missed her by a hairsbreadth. Her body shifted to the side, muscle memory kicking in as she spun and aimed a vicious blow to her opponent's kidney. Her assailant turned barely in time and her fist only grazed his hip. He twisted and was suddenly behind her, his arms like chains around her torso, locking her arms to her side.

She swung her fist backward, aiming for his groin, but he loosened his hold and danced his lower half away. She twisted in his grasp, raising her own arms to push against his chest, but her opponent entwined one leg behind her own and dropped her unceremoniously to the ground. She whipped a foot out to kick the front of his knee as she tumbled, and the connecting blow sent his body hurtling down after her. He landed on top of her, his weight crushing the air from her lungs. She locked her leg around one of his and tried to position her hands under his chest to tip his body off hers, but he was too heavy.

Her assailant leaned forward and nuzzled her neck.

Azar sighed. "We always go so well until we get to the floor work," she grumbled halfheartedly. The only response she got was a mumbled agreement as his lips nibbled her earlobe. She ran her hand through silky, golden hair as a tingle ran up her spine, making her let out a little moan.

There was an uncomfortable cough from the other side of the gym.

"I'm unsure how Huzin trained you in combat, Bast, but I'm fairly sure it wasn't using those techniques," came Mira's amused voice.

Mira was the acting commander of the Adel, the combat and investigative force of the Djinn, or genies as Westerners referred to them. The Adel were like the human Delta Force, but with bonus features. They investigated rule breakers and traitors and then, if they felt it was necessary, summarily executed them.

Azar gave Mira an innocent smile. "I'm trying to learn, but he keeps finding a reason to get me into these compromising positions and then take advantage of me."

Mira laughed and shook her head. Azar and Mira had become close friends during the months of her compulsory servitude. Mira was a powerful Marid, a long lived race of Djinn with an affinity for water, and the sea in particular. Mira could draw the moisture from a person's body, or freeze it in their veins. It was said that a Marid controlled the ocean and the tides. Azar wasn't sure about that. She had lived as a human firefighter for a very long time, and the science behind the lunar cycles and the tide seemed pretty solid to her.

Sometimes she thought more like a human than a Djinn, but that was to be expected; she had lived in solitude from her own people for over a century to avoid having to do the compulsory servitude.

However, like all good things, that had come to an end. She'd been caught, and given fifty years of slavery, but only because she'd voluntarily tracked down a rogue Djinn that had planned to destroy

New York City. The way she saw it, fifty years was a small price to pay to save the lives of her friends.

Bast poked her in the ribs. "You can try that innocent act in my room later," Bast whispered saucily in her ear and Azar held back a laugh.

Mira just threw her hands in the air at the exchange. She wouldn't have been able to hear what Bast had said, but it wouldn't take a genius to guess. "When you two are quite finished canoodling, can you please come to the Comms room?" Her voice held mock disgust but she was chuckling as she turned and left the gym.

Bast's lips continued to make their way across the sensitive skin of her neck, and then down her collarbone. "Do you find my training methods unsatisfactory?"

He nipped at her chin and Azar fought back another moan. "I don't think you do anything unsatisfactorily. I doubt it's even in your vocabulary," she purred back and then let out a frustrated sigh. "But we need to get up. We can continue this later." She winked at him and gave him a gentle shove. He rolled onto his back with a groan.

She pushed her aching muscles into an upright position and walked over to towel off the sweat that coated her body. Bast had been training her in the basics of hand to hand combat almost every day for the last three months, since the first day of her compulsory servitude. To this day, Azar thanked her lucky stars that she had met Bast, otherwise she would have died a slave. The Council had spared her life in deference to her father, even though she had broken several of their strictest rules. But they had still insisted that she complete her one hundred year servitude. Bast had volunteered to complete fifty years for her, on the proviso that they both served under the Adel. Apparently, two slaves had been better than one.

She still shook her head when she thought about him voluntarily getting back into a life he'd deplored, unable to believe what he was willing to do for her.

One hundred years of compulsory servitude was one of the founding principles of Djinn society. Every Djinn of full or half-blood was born with a slave mark on their bodies; a brand imbued with magic that, when coupled with Anadari bracelets or slave cuffs as she liked to call them, allowed the Djinn to be controlled by a third party.

When the Djinn Council assigned a Djinn to their Master, an ancient magical contract was entered and a Djinn was under his or her Master's command for the term. Once the servitude was over, the slave cuffs fell off, the mark disappeared overnight and the Master's control was voided. It helped keep all the parties honest. People, and by people she meant other Supes or even very powerful humans, paid huge sums of money to have a Djinn slave. They used them as mercenaries, emissaries, luminaries and a multitude of other roles, sometimes even sex slaves. Servitude could be unpleasant for the Djinn serving it.

Azar pulled a shirt over her sports bra and stepped into her sweatpants. She'd baulked at the tiny training outfit Bast had presented her with on the first day, which was basically a sports bra and little boy shorts that cupped the bottom of her ass cheeks. But she found it gave her complete ease of movement, so it could have been worse. She could have been running around naked for some oozy Troll King.

The whole ordeal with the rogue Ifrit had resulted in her having night terrors for months, each night showing her the outcome of her life if a single factor had been different. If she hadn't responded to the fire and seen the Djinn symbol seared into the floor. If she hadn't confided in Keenan Reilly, the arson detective, about what she really was. If she hadn't met Bast. If she hadn't been successful in defeating the Rogue Ifrit. If her father hadn't been a Councilor. The what-ifs crawled around her mind like a virus.

Darkness clouded her vision as her lungs constricted and she mentally berated herself for her weakness. Panic attacks were another leftover symptom of the experience. She took a deep breath in and pushed everything that happened three months ago to the back of her mind.

She felt Bast's large hand come down on her shoulder and pull her close to his side.

Azar smiled up at the tall Jann beside her. They really couldn't be more different. Of the six Djinn races, the Jann and the Ifrit had the least in common. They were like two ships moored in the same harbor, but at opposite ends. They had no ancient rivalry, or benevolent camaraderie.

The Jann were Djinn of growth, creation and beauty. They made dreams come true and provided oases of good to those in need. The Ifrit, on the other hand, were a race of pure destruction. All Ifrit had the ability to control fire, but such an ability had few uses that didn't result in wholesale destruction.

The only passive use of her powers, the ability to read and control fire in emergency situations, had

GRACE MCGINTY

been taken away from her when she had been forced into fifty years of servitude. Up until last month, she had been a firefighter, and a damn good one at that. But the Adel had slowly been easing her out of the fire house, until no one even noticed her reduced hours.

She'd told her partner, Joe that she was getting burnout, but she knew Joe didn't believe her. He just thought she was suffering from post-traumatic stress disorder after the whole thing with the Rogue. He didn't know the details, and he never would. The truth could be dangerous, especially to humans, and she'd already caused enough problems on that front.

Bast leaned down and kissed the top of her head, a sure-fire way to get her out of her own twisted thoughts, before walking over to his duffel bag and grabbing his shirt. Azar appreciated his physical beauty. She often thought of him as nature's greatest symphony in gold. He was tall, easily six and a half feet, with a permanent sun kissed tan and golden hair that shone so brightly, haircare models would be jealous. His honey colored eyes could draw you in so deeply that you never wanted to escape, and all the physical perfection was balanced by the littering of scars on his body from his previous days as an Adel foot soldier.

Her feelings for Bast scared her to death. She definitely cared for him, but she was all messed up inside, her thoughts tangled like Christmas lights in November. Sometimes she thought she might never get it all straightened out.

Bast had given her the space she'd asked for, always giving but never pushing her further than she wanted to go. But Bast was under her skin, his searing hot presence wearing her down and she knew that one day soon she was going to give into her attraction for him, regardless of whether her head was ready or not. Her body and her heart had voted, and her head could just play catch up.

"Are you ready?" Azar startled as Bast's words mirrored her thoughts. She thought he might have a touch of telepathy, but if he did, he'd never let on.

She saw him standing near the door and breathed a sigh of relief. He meant was she ready to go to the Comms room. She hefted her gym bag and strode over to the door. Bast took it out of her hands and carried it easily with his own.

They headed along the narrow stone hallways of the Adel compound. The compound was actually underneath the Djinn Council headquarters, which occupied the top three floors of an old stone building in Lower Manhattan. There were three subterranean levels that had been added after the Djinn had taken possession of the building, and those levels housed the Adel headquarters. Some of the Adel lived off-site, but anyone who was still in their servitude lived in the dorms on one of the upper levels. The public front of the building masqueraded as a private brokerage firm, complete with security and a well appointed secretary in case any humans ever wandered in.

They came to the huge double doors of the Comms room. The Communications Hub was the epicenter of the Adel Intelligence Branch. They could find anyone or anything from within these walls. They could even hack the most sophisticated servers in the world; they'd actually hacked into the Homeland Security's personnel database and created a false terrorist attack, complete with special agents, to assuage her Chief when she'd been abducted. It was a terrifying amount of power to be possessed by a race that cared nothing for humans.

Mira and Joia, Mira's Sila partner, were both sitting at the large conference desk waiting for her and Bast.

"I'm glad you two could finally join us," Joia quipped.

Joia was not amused, but then the Sila was rarely

ever amused. She was born without a funny bone, and hundreds of years of service with the Adel had made her so serious that Azar had never seen her face crack a smile. The Sila were the Djinn's only all-female race. They were highly intelligent, wily and could generate lightning. They were great politicians and could be cryptic enough to make you want to strangle them from time to time.

Mira smiled at them as they took their seats. In comparison to her partner, Mira was happiness personified. But Azar never fooled herself that all her happiness wasn't wrapped around a core of pure, ruthless steel.

"Let them have their fun, it's not as if this information is of an urgent nature." Mira winked at them. "But now you have arrived, I have some news." Her face took a serious but sympathetic turn, like she was about to tell Azar that her goldfish died. "Killian is arriving tomorrow."

"Who?" Azar really hated it when she was the only person in the room out of the loop. It happened a lot of course; a person couldn't run away from Djinn society for her entire life, and then magically know everything there was to know in three months. She'd been studying the books given to her by Mira on Djinn history and laws, but it didn't stop her from feeling out of her depth ninety percent of the time.

It was Bast who answered. "Killian is the Director of the Adel, and probably the most highly decorated Adel soldier who has ever held the position. He's also a full-blooded Ifrit." He gave her the 'dead goldfish' look too. "He's also your brother." Bast winced a little, obviously hoping to break the news with a little more tact, but there was no subtle way to insert long lost siblings into a conversation.

"I have a brother that is the leader of the Adel." She gave a dazed shake of her head. Her life was a circus and she was only the first act.

Joia obviously interpreted her statement as a question. "There are very few positions of power within our society that a member of your family cannot be found." Her tone said she wasn't overly pleased about that fact.

Azar wasn't sure how she felt about it either. Her father was the Councilor for the Ifrit, and now her brother was the Director of the Adel. She had at least nine more siblings roaming around, apparently doing important things with their lives. Apparently, she'd been born into the Djinn version of the Vanderbilt's.

"Why is Killian coming? Last I heard, he was positioned in Europe," Bast inquired warily.

"Given the activity within our domain in the last few months, he wants to personally ensure we have everything under control. Plus, we have a little situation building that he wishes to oversee personally."

That caught both Bast and Azar's attention. Bast motioned for Mira to continue, but she merely shook her head.

"It's on a need to know basis, and it's being handled by other members for the moment. We will brief everyone on the situation if and when we feel it is necessary." Mira shuffled around some folders that sat on the conference table in front of her. "I assume Killian will want to speak to you personally, Azar. He may also wish to undertake some of your training while he is in town. I suggest you take the opportunity to learn from an accomplished soldier of your race. But as your friend, I feel I should warn you that Killian can be..." Mira searched the air for a politically correct term.

"Obnoxious, blunt, arrogant?" Apparently Joia had no problem filling in the blanks for her.

Mira grimaced. "I was going to say remote, but unfortunately Joia is not wrong. Killian is a determined man and a solid leader, but he didn't climb to his position in the hierarchy by making friends. However, he is the Djinn's most ardent protector." Mira's tone softened. "What I'm trying to say is don't expect too much familial warmth from him."

Azar nodded, not feeling overly worried that her brother was cold. She wouldn't know how to receive familial warmth any better than Killian knew how to give it.

Once they were dismissed, they took the elevator up a floor to the dorms. Bast wrapped an arm around her shoulder and squeezed her close. She loved the smell of Bast, like the warm summer sun and the sand dunes of her homeland. She turned her face so she could press her cheek against his hard chest. He bent forward so he could see her expression, his eyes clouded with worry. She gave him a wan smile and he squeezed a little harder. Her world had been so much chaos for so long that now chaos felt semi-normal to her.

They stepped out of the elevator and into a large hallway lined with doors. She and Bast had separate rooms, but it didn't stop Bast treating hers like his own. He stayed over most nights, and even had a spare uniform in her closet.

Bast was close on her heels as Azar unlocked her door and walked into the small room that had now become her home. The rooms were nothing grand. A double bed took up most of the floor space, except for the galley kitchen and bench that ran along one wall, a small grey stool pushed in the crevice underneath. A large mirrored built-in robe ran along the opposite wall and a single bookshelf perched above the double bed.

Every time she walked into her dorm room, she missed her little apartment. The homesickness had been unbearable at first. After a life on the run, her well-ordered little life as a FDNY firefighter had meant a lot to her. She'd had standing lunch dates with friends. The guy at the convenience store had kept a New York Times behind the counter for her to pick up after work everyday. She'd revelled in the little intimacies of that life. The only thing that had saved her from completely breaking down during her first few weeks in the compound had been Bast's soothing presence.

The sexy Jann in question came up behind her and pressed his warm, hard body into hers. His hand slipped under her tank top to the smooth flesh of her stomach, making the skin burn beneath his caress. He came to her bed every night and just held her in his arms. Sometimes he teased her until she was sure that her body would ignite beneath his skilled hands, but they were yet to do anything more than third base. But her response to his touch was getting stronger and harder to deny.

"I have to shower," she murmured as Bast kissed the sensitive hollow just behind her earlobe. Even though Bast's kisses distracted her mind, her body still ached from the training session. Her muscles now groaned when she walked.

She had been in peak physical fitness as a fire-fighter, but the demands of daily combat training made her body feel as if it were coated with lead. She needed a cascade of hot water to loosen her muscles and make her feel half human again.

"Mmm, that sounds like a great idea. I'll come and wash your back." His throaty suggestion made heat pool low in her body. Bast's hands hadn't stopped their intimate exploration of her torso, his nails scraping up the sides of her hips.

"If Joia catches you in the women's bathroom again, she will probably fry you until you are extra crispy," Azar said laughingly.

She was only half joking; the angry Sila had threatened to do exactly that the last time she busted Bast in the women's bathrooms 'helping' Azar shower. They'd come so close to finally making love that day, only to be interrupted by Joia pulling back the shower curtain. She had gotten a good view of Bast's naked body pinning Azar against the shower recess wall. Azar had never felt so embarrassed, but Bast had just laughed when Joia had threatened to put a bolt of lightning somewhere unpleasant if she'd ever caught him in there again. Not much rattled Bast.

Now, he held her hips, pulling her back against his body so she could feel the hard shape of him against the curve of her backside.

"It'd be worth it," he purred in her ear.

Azar wanted to take the extra step so badly that it was an actual physical ache. But she was still floundering in this world, and deep down, she knew she wanted her first time with Bast to be beyond perfect. If that meant waiting until the time was right, then she would find the mental fortitude somewhere to take it slow. But boy, did he make it hard for her.

"I promised Oliver I would go to Onyx tonight for the official reopening." She shook her head to clear her lust addled mind.

"Fine," Bast sighed and slapped her on the butt. "But you are going to be in big trouble when we get back." His eyes said he was serious, and she took him at face value.

When they did eventually make love, she was

going to pay for this delay with excruciating plea-sure. As if to seal the promise, he gave her a soft lingering kiss, the kind that made your knees weaken and your insides melt like chocolate.

"I'm going to my room to change. I'll be back in ten," he whispered against her lips.

She watched his ass as he left, and wondered if it shouldn't be illegal for a man to have an ass like that. It trashed all her sensible thoughts.

Knowing that Bast would be back in exactly ten minutes, he wasn't a man prone to exaggeration, she stripped off her clothes, put on her fluffy robe and rushed down to the women's bathroom.

Azar wasn't surprised when the room was empty. There were only two dozen female Adel in the United States, of which there were only seven in New York City, including herself. She speculated that like most antiquated institutions, there was an underlying belief that women weren't strong enough to get the job done.

Standing beneath the pulsating needles of water, Azar wondered if the lack of female Adel had less to do with sexism and more to do with a far greater problem within the Djinn race. When she looked back on her trial, there were far more males than females, even within the civilian population who had come to be spectators to her possible execution. If you ruled out the females from the Sila race, which were all females, the men outnumbered the women at least three to one. Turning off the water, she made a mental note to ask Mira about the issue. If the birthrate of females was dropping, it could be signaling the early stages of extinction for full-blooded Djinn, and that was a problem for everyone.

Vigorously drying herself, she looked at the clock and realized she'd been standing under the shower for longer than she expected. She marched double time back down the hallway to her dorm room, still not passing anyone.

In her room, she stood in front of her closet and pulled out her favorite black skinny leg jeans and a deep red tank top. Stuffing her feet in combat boots, she put on half a dozen wrap bracelets to hide her slave cuffs. It was perfect attire for The Onyx, which exclusively played metalcore music and catered to the disillusioned and probably the partially deaf. It was owned and run by Donovan, a half-blood Shaitan she would hesitantly call a friend. She had a minor case of fatal attraction to Donovan. He was tall, scary, and set her body on fire. Not that she would ever tell anyone that. That was one forbidden crush she was never going to act on.

The best thing about The Onyx in her opinion was that the security were an all Were outfit that Donovan employed from a local Werewolf pack out in Sterling Forest. She would definitely call most of them friends. Especially Oliver, a werejaguar who was somewhere between best friend and a wet dream. She hadn't really worked out how Oliver had fit into a Werewolf pack; dogs and cats usually weren't a great mix, but she'd seen first hand that they loved him unconditionally, as if he howled at the moon once a month just like the rest of the pack.

She was swiping lip gloss on her lips when there was a knock at her door and Bast let himself in. He was dressed similar to herself in black, bootcut jeans, combat boots and a tight, black tshirt. The unrelenting black set off his golden skin. He literally took her breath away.

Azar swallowed hard and clenched her fist to stop herself from reaching out and peeling him out of his clothes. She had less control over her libido than a teenage human going through puberty. She needed to snap out of it. Bast's half smile and hooded gaze meant that her internal struggle wasn't remaining so internal. Smug bastard.

"I just have to do my hair, give me a minute." Bast nodded and laid down on her bed.

Azar turned back to the mirrored door of her closet and ran the brush through her dark hair. Her Persian heritage, combined with the agelessness of an extended lifespan, allowed her to get away with not wearing make-up. Her olive skin was flawless, and her eyes were framed with naturally thick eyelashes. Tying her hair back in a high ponytail, she shot a look at her bed, and the giant hunk of lean muscle that was currently dwarfing it.

Bast had picked up the book on Djinn history that had been resting open on her nightstand. His tshirt had crept up a little, baring the hard muscles of his abdomen, and the delicious V of his obliques. Looking at that V, she struggled to remember why she hadn't jumped his bones yet. Tendrils of lust curled tightly in her abdomen, and she knew that if she didn't leave now, her body would take control, regardless of what her head said.

She finally found her voice. "Let's go."

It came out an octave higher than normal, and her cheeks heated. She all but ran for the door, Bast's chuckles echoing behind her. It was going to be a long night.

CHAPTER 2

I t hadn't taken Donovan long to rebuild The Onyx after the Rogue had burned the place to the ground. Two construction crews and three months later, The Onyx was bigger and better than ever. Looking at the outside, you would never have guessed that it had been a pile of sooty rubble less than twelve weeks ago. Aesthetically, the club remained basically the same, right down to the surly security guard manning the door.

The last time Bast and Azar had visited, Bast had had to sweet talk his way through the door. This time, the wall of muscle that passed as a bouncer smiled so brightly at them that it probably would have eclipsed the sun.

"Azar! It's so good to see you." John, at least she thought that's what his name was, reached over and wrapped her in a tight hug. Now she really felt bad that she didn't know his name.

In her defence, there were a lot of Weres and they all looked basically the same; tall, broad, and so muscular that they seemed to have no necks. They all wore permanent scowls for anyone but pack, and apparently now Azar. She had become kind of an honorary pack member when she'd saved the life of one of their younger wolves. She maintained that Aaron, the young wolf, had saved her life, so there was no blood debt or anything along those lines, but the wolves were a stubborn bunch.

She greeted the Were just as warmly, asking after the pack and generally making polite conversation. Eventually, John ushered them through the velvet ropes, informing them that Oliver was behind the bar for the night. She thanked him again and gave him a quick goodbye hug before they melted into the crowd.

Bast looked down at her from his six foot five height, one eyebrow raised.

She shrugged. She liked the Weres, and she also liked that they considered her to be one of their pack. There was a sense of family and community within the pack that Azar had never had up until now. Within Djinn society, it was every race for itself, and even within the individual races there were strict rules and protocols to follow, a level of stiff formality that was maintained even with blood kin. Not so with the Weres. Their passions ran high and they were never short on affection.

Bast led them through the crowded club, and the masses seemed to part for him. Azar didn't know if it was just his height and breadth, or the leashed wildness that seemed to permeate from his body, that cleared the people from his path. Perhaps he did it with his Jann abilities; she'd seen him clear this very club in minutes using mind control. At the time, Azar had been awed and scared in equal parts as she'd watched on. Now she just considered it rather convenient that they could be at the bar within seconds of entering the room.

Oliver looked up from where he was pouring shots of Patrón and a smile lit up his classic beach boy features.

"Azar!" he yelled as he jumped the bar effortlessly, making all the humans around them gape. She barely had time to frown at his reckless behavior before he swept her into his arms and dipped her backwards to nuzzle her neck. The sensation of his lips against her skin made her heart race a little, but she pushed it down. She had Bast, she didn't need more trouble in her life, especially the hunky man kind. She repeated this to herself, hoping her lady parts listened.

"I've missed you! When are you going to leave the dusty old guy and run away with me?" He asked the question loud enough for Bast to hear and she just rolled her eyes.

"Well, I'm kind of tied up for the next fifty years or so, but I'll pencil you in for about 2069," she replied laughingly.

"I'll be waiting," he purred, and her heart flip-flopped. Oliver was playful by nature. He liked to rib the other alpha males who seemed to crowd her life, and tease her until she blushed.

The women around them eyed her enviously, but she was determined to ignore anything but the platonic feelings she had for him. She needed a best friend more than she needed another love interest. Her life was not her own for the next fifty years. There was no space for the all consuming heat that would be sure to happen with Oliver. Plus, she had Bast. She didn't need anyone else, right?

Oliver finally righted her back into a vertical

position and leaned across her to shake Bast's hand. No one was more self-assured than Bast, so he played along with Oliver's teasing with a mock scowl, but there was laughter in his eyes. They'd become fairly close as well in the last couple of months.

Oliver returned to the bar, but through the door this time, much to the disappointment of the crowd. He poured a round of drinks for them and waved away Bast's money.

Azar took a sip of her scotch, straight up, no ice. "Why are you behind the bar tonight instead of doing what you normally do?"

She actually had no idea what Oliver's role was in the club. There was plenty of Were muscle, and while Oliver had a lean musculature about him, like the jungle cat he was, the wolves won the award for pure intimidation.

Oliver shrugged. "New girl called in sick. I think Donovan scared the crap out of her the other day. So they stuck me behind the bar because I'm prettier than Jerry."

Azar couldn't help but nod in agreement. No one would call Jerry, the head of Donovan's security, pretty. "What do you actually do for Donovan?"

Oliver wiped down a spot where a drunken girl

had spilled something pink and strongly alcoholic on the bar. "Normally I just float around and keep everyone happy and calm. I dance with the girls, mosh with the guys. If someone spills their drink on someone else, and it looks like it's about to get ugly, I give them a free drink card then call Jerry to kick their drunken asses out. If two guys look like they are about to come to blows over some girl, I step in, escort the girl to the bar and get the other two kicked to the curb."

He grinned that devilish grin and Azar could see him waltzing into the middle of a fight, wrapping his arm around a woman then waltzing back out again. Oliver was more attractive than 99% of the population and the female gender were drawn to him like flies to honey. The other guys wouldn't even stand a chance.

The Onyx had both human and Were employees, and it bothered Azar that some of the human staff were skipping shifts because of Donovan's temper. Donovan was half Shaitan and by definition, the Shaitan were petrifying. But normally, Donovan had control over his Shaitan abilities, and was able to tone it down enough not to scare away employees and customers. If he was involuntarily terrifying the bar staff, then Azar's gut said something was wrong. She downed the rest of her drink.

"I'm going to see Donovan," she told the guys. Oliver gave her the thumbs up and moved down the bar to serve a waiting customer, and Bast nodded but made no move to follow her. He was good like that. He didn't feel the need to hover over her like a shadow. He respected the fact that she could take care of herself, unlike Keenan.

Like usual, thoughts of Keenan made her stomach clench into knots. Keenan Reilly was an arson detective, human and her ex-lover. He'd been caught up in the whole Rogue Ifrit drama and as a result had almost been sentenced to death by the Djinn Council. Bast had managed to talk them out of a summary execution by expounding his worth as an informant, and now he was basically sentenced to a life of being balanced between two worlds, on a knife's edge of usefulness and obsolescence. He would remain in that precarious position until the day he died.

She waded across the dance floor, through the gyrating bodies, towards the hallway that led to the back office. The little hallway contained the women's and men's bathrooms at one end and a red door at the other. Behind the red door was Donovan's cramped little office.

As soon as Azar stepped into the hallway she could hear raised voices coming from the office. She discerned Donovan's booming yell and the distinctive screech that could only mean a woman screaming. Azar picked up her pace but relaxed a little when she saw Jerry leaning up against the darkened wall. Jerry was gruff, rude and had the manners of a barnyard animal, but his sense of right and wrong was well honed. He wouldn't let Donovan terrorize an innocent woman.

Azar stopped dead in her tracks when a small head peeked around the side of Jerry's tree trunk sized thighs. However, it wasn't the fact there was a child in a nightclub that had her stopping mid step, but the little girl's uncanny resemblance to Donovan.

The girl had Donovan's jet black hair and bottomless dark eyes, as well as the pale alabaster skin that made them both so ethereally pale. Of course, her skin was free from the multitude of tattoos that graced almost every inch of Donovan's pale flesh, apart from his face. She speculated about whether other places were tattooed, but she was too frightened to ask. Not because she was worried

Donovan would take offense, but because he'd probably show her first hand.

She estimated the girl to be about seven or eight, and already she had Donovan's long, lean build. Azar moved so she stood across from Jerry and the girl, a friendly smile plastered over her shock.

"Hey Jerry. Long time no see." She bent forward and gave Jerry a quick peck on the cheek.

"Not long enough," he growled, but there was amusement in his eyes.

She and Jerry had gotten off to a rocky start; she'd actually threatened to barbecue him. But like the other Were, Jerry had forgiven her and accepted her as one of his own. She turned to the child. "Who's your friend?"

He gave her a stern look that basically told her to mind her own business, but Azar just continued to smile. Minding her own business didn't really come naturally to her. If it had, she probably wouldn't be doing fifty years of enforced servitude. The little girl saved Jerry from answering.

"I'm Freya." Her voice was a squeak that threatened to get lost in the cacophony of metal music and domestic disturbance. Her big black eyes were solemn, her face too serious for a little girl who's most pressing thought should be what to dress her Barbie in now.

"Hi Freya, my name is Azar. It's nice to meet you." She gave the girl a warm smile. "Have they been at this long?" She directed the question to Jerry.

"About thirty minutes," came his gruff reply, as if he was parting with information under extreme torture. Chances were he was probably just sick of babysitting duty. Azar could hear snatches of the fight through the red office door.

"She's been kicked out of three schools in the last twelve months. The kids don't even want to sit near her in class. What am I supposed to do with her?" The voice was a thready screech, as if she'd been yelling for hours.

"I don't know Trina, how about take care of her like a mother is supposed to?" came the angry retort.

"I don't want her. She's nothing but trouble. She was cute as a baby, but now all she does is sit around staring at me with those creepy eyes. She doesn't do anything normal kids are supposed to do. Quite frankly, she weirds me out..." Azar shot a look at Freya, noticing the expression of hurt on the little girl's face before she quickly concealed it.

Anger bubbled up in her chest. How could a

mother be so cruel? She felt the fire beneath her skin start to simmer. It was time to stop this.

She took the girl's hand and Freya's little fingers threaded tightly into her own, even though she was basically a stranger to the girl. Azar looked over Freya's head at Jerry.

"I think it's time to interrupt this conversation, don't you?"

Jerry nodded, and she could see the anger simmering in his eyes even though his face was a perfectly neutral mask. Azar pushed open the red door and two sets of eyes turned to stare at her, one set Djinn and the other human. The human woman was wearing a pair of denim cut-offs and a lace racerback tank in pink. She was pretty, in a Midwestern stripper kind of way. And as Azar expected, she didn't look at all like Freya.

"What do you want?" Donovan snapped, and Azar quelled the urge to run away. She had to give it to the human woman; she must have balls of steel to stay in the same room as Donovan in his current mood. In fact, Trina seemed to be impervious to the threatening anger that was pouring off Donovan in waves, too caught up in her own vindictiveness. Azar had heard that the Shaitan could inflict pain telepathically, but she was in no hurry to see that first hand.

"Well, I was just introducing myself to your daughter and I couldn't help but *overhear*," she emphasized the latter word and nodded towards Freya, "so I thought I would come in and check if everyone was okay." She shot Donovan another pointed look.

Trina glared at Azar, but when she turned back to Donovan, the look she gave him was downright scathing. Donovan gave her an equally savage look in return.

"I was just telling Trina that Freya would be in danger if she came to live with me."

She could tell Donovan was working hard to moderate his tone and the effects of his ability, but she was unsure if it was for her benefit or Freya's. Not that his current mood seemed to phase the child at all.

Trina leaned over and picked up her handbag. "I don't care, she is your problem now." With that she strode out of the room, careful to avoid Freya's eyes. Azar's hand lit up almost involuntarily. How could anyone abandon their child so coldly? She was going to burn every hair on that woman's head, just to teach her a lesson.

"Don't Dad." Freya's tiny voice resonated around the room and Azar looked over to see a deadly gleam in Donovan's eyes, power glowing behind the onyx orbs. The kid must have been able to sense her father's intentions, because the power faded and he just looked at his daughter sadly.

Azar retracted her flame, but she heard Jerry growl as Trina strode past him. Abandoning your cub was one of the worst crimes within the pack. Donovan didn't take his eyes off Freya, but he ordered Jerry to ensure that Trina left the premises unharmed.

Donovan slumped down onto his desk and for the first time since Azar had met him, he looked utterly bewildered. She guessed parenthood could do that to a person. She wrapped her arm around Freya's shoulders and cuddled the girl close. Freya resisted for a moment, before eventually melting into Azar's side.

"We'll figure something out. Between us all, we must be able to find one acceptable solution, right? Until then, I bet Freya is hungry." The little girl nodded solemnly and Azar gave her a warm smile. "How about we order pizza and chocolate ice cream then? There's no problem in this world that can't be at least momentarily solved with chocolate ice cream." Her tone was too upbeat, but if she didn't put on a happy facade, anyone who walked into the room at that moment would confuse it for a funeral.

Donovan caught on to Azar's happy act, and pasted a half-hearted smile onto his face when he looked at his progeny. Azar was dying to know how Freya came to be. Well, not the mechanics of the act, she'd had those techniques mastered for quite awhile now, but the situation that led to Donovan knocking up a human. It kind of begged a very important question.

"Does Trina know about us? The collective us, I mean."

If the human woman was privy to the secret of their existence, it would make everyone's position a little more tenuous. The Djinn council were very harsh in the punishments handed out to Djinn who disclosed the Forbidden Secret of what they were. Most of the time, that meant death for everyone involved. She'd been an exception to the rule, given the circumstances, but she still lived with the crawling fear that one day she'd wake up and they'd change their minds. Then it will be poof, off with her head.

"I'm not an idiot. Trina has no idea. I told Freya, of course. She had a right to know, but I stressed to her the grave danger of revealing that secret to anyone, even her mother."

Another solemn nod from the girl. It would be tough being so young and having to keep such a big secret from the one person with whom you are meant to be able to confide everything.

Donovan shook his head. "She's only one-fourth Djinn, I didn't think her abilities would present so strongly. Hell, I didn't think they'd present at all. She wasn't even born with a slave mark." He held up a hand. "And before you ask, the Council doesn't know she exists. The Shaitan are purists, they believe in keeping the bloodlines strong. They barely accept me; there was no way they'd accept Freya. The Shaitan have rather final ways of disposing of things they don't accept. Completely deniable of course." Donovan's sardonic sneer returned to his face and for some reason it made Azar feel more comfortable. Touchy feely Donovan wasn't someone she'd ever had to deal with before. Normally, getting information out of him was like pulling teeth from the mouth of a piranha.

Azar looked around Donovan's cramped office. He wasn't exactly an interior decorator, so the room was cramped and depressing, the only furniture was a desk with a stack of distributor catalogs resting on the corner, a large filing cabinet and two chairs. There wasn't a plant, photo, painting or knick-knack in the place. The overall effect was claustrophobic. They needed to get out of here and Azar knew exactly where they should go.

A knock sounded at the door, and she knew who it was even before Bast stuck his head around the door jamb, his face relaxed but eyes alert.

"You didn't come back so I thought I'd come check…" His voice trailed off as his gaze fell upon Freya, then Donovan and then back to Freya. He looked at Azar and grimaced, and she thought he must have accurately surmised that they were about to become neck deep in someone else's problem.

"Bast! Just in time. I was about to propose a trip to Coney Island," Azar said brightly.

Bast lifted his gaze heavenward and shook his head. Freya squealed in delight at the mere mention of Coney Island, and it softened Bast's features as he threw the girl a quick smile. For those who were strong enough to get past the instinctual fear permeating from the tiny little Shaitan, she was really cute.

Donovan bent down to lift Freya and the little girl wrapped her arms lovingly around his neck. He squeezed her tightly in return, and Azar blinked rapidly to try and mesh her perception of big bad

Donovan with the doting Daddy before her. Life was truly strange.

Bast nudged her in the ribs. "If you don't stop thinking so hard you might accidentally set them on fire," he joked and wrapped an arm around her shoulder, leaning in to kiss her temple.

She wondered if Bast was really thinking that she was more trouble than she was worth. The sad thing is, he'd probably be right.

CHAPTER 3

Azar demolished another slice of pizza and washed it down with a gulp of beer. The pizza was now cold and the solidified cheese squeaked against her teeth when she chewed. It wasn't a pleasant sensation.

Sitting around amongst the broken amusements in Bast's warehouse, they'd talked and Freya played amid the wonderland of boxes, broken carousel horses and decommissioned bumper cars. Bast had created a pit out of boxes for her, and emptied a dozen huge bags of sideshow toys into the middle. It was like a stuffed toy ball pit, and even Azar had to hold herself back from diving in. The draughty old warehouse was heaven for a seven year old. The adults watched her childish glee with their own amused expressions, every tiny giggle making them grin involuntarily. Her joy was infectious. Donovan watched his child with parental diligence, ready to save her from any hurt.

Now, Freya was asleep in the stuffed toy pit, curled up as if she were a baby bird in a fluffy nest, her tiny face angelic as she sucked her thumb. Bast had his hands interlaced in front of his face, his index fingers steepled against the tip of his nose, giving Donovan a perplexed expression. Azar didn't know if he really was perplexed, or just using his hands to hide the grin on his face. She was going to go with the latter.

"So let me get this straight. You knocked up a stripper in Reno, she ended up on your doorstep nine months later with a baby, so you put her up in an apartment, sent the kid to a private school, visited every Sunday but somehow forgot to inform the Council you had reproduced?"

Donovan gave Bast his signature expression of homicidal irritation.

"We've been over this. I thought she'd be mostly human. I couldn't have predicted her powers would develop to this extent. She doesn't even have a slave mark. The Shaitan would definitely have had her killed."

Azar speculated that it wasn't just the Shaitan who would have disposed of Freya as a problem. Her level of power, while small in comparison to a full or half-blood Shaitan, was still considerable enough to be wielded against humans. Her lack of a slave mark would present all sorts of problems for the Djinn. Someone like that, who couldn't be immediately pigeon-holed, would have no place in the Djinn's archaic system. The system, and its Council, were like most outdated systems of governance; they scorned anything new that could threaten their ancient laws and understandings. Speaking of ancient understandings, there was another thing that niggled at the corner of Azar's mind.

"Why didn't Trina wet herself when you went all big bad Shaitan in there? Even I wanted to run away, and I am far more immune to your abilities than a human."

"Maybe I'm losing my touch? Or maybe I'm just misunderstood and deep down I'm actually a nice guy." She knew he was being sarcastic, but after tonight she wasn't so sure it wasn't the truth. Donovan was never going to be citizen of the year, but seeing him with Freya was proof enough that he wasn't all bad either. He just shrugged. "She hasn't been susceptible to my abilities since she became pregnant with Freya. It's like the baby gave her some kind of immunity. Frankly, I don't know and I don't care. The bitch is lucky she isn't dead."

Azar was pretty sure that if his abilities had failed, he would have jumped across the room and strangled Trina the good old fashioned way.

In all honesty, she knew that she shouldn't be getting involved with Donovan's problems. She was already on the Council's shit list. She had barely got out of her last reprimand with her head. But she felt sorry for the little girl. Freya didn't fit in anywhere and it was a familiar feeling for Azar. So against her better judgment, she wanted to help if she could.

They all sat in silence for a while, thinking and planning, hoping and scheming for a solution.

Azar chewed her lip. "The way I see it, you have two choices; you can tell the Council about her and hope she gets integrated into Djinn society, if she isn't killed on the spot." She grimaced. Not her favorite idea. "Or you can stash her somewhere that the Djinn will never look and hope that she grows into her powers enough that she can hide them and enjoy a reasonably normal human life."

Bast took a thoughtful bite of cold pizza, screwing up his nose at the squeaky cheese too. "She can use my apartment if you need it. It's going to be sitting there empty for the next fifty years anyway."

Azar patted Bast's leg affectionately. He mightn't like getting mixed up in other people's business, but once he was in the mess, he was right in the thick of it. Bast always had her back, and it made her heart swell. But Donovan shook his head.

"Thanks for the offer, but I don't think hiding her in the apartment of a Djinn known to flaunt the law is going to work. It'd be too risky for the both of you."

Donovan ran his fingers through his already tousled hair. All the tattoos that littered his body danced in the overhead lights. There were two skull tattoos on his arms that were messily shaded red and blue, where Donovan had let Freya color them in with markers earlier in the night. To Freya, he wasn't a scary demon of Hell, a near immortal who could kill people with his mind and strike fear into the bravest of warriors. To her, he was a giant coloring-in book and her Dad. It made him appear far less menacing. Donovan was quickly losing his Shaitan cred.

The coloring-in book in question let out a frustrated humph.

"Get on with it, Azar. You obviously have a place

in mind." His coal black eyes glittered with anger and she knew right then, even watered down and clucky, Donovan was still one scary mofo.

"The Sterling Forest Pack has offered me a life favor for saving Aaron. It wasn't something I asked for and I really had no intention of using it, but it might be the best alternative for Freya. If I could convince them that the blood debt would be met if they were to raise Freya as one of their own among the wolf cubs, she might be able to live a semi-normal life. As you know, the Weres are less susceptible to our abilities than humans and some other supes, and given the weakness of Freya's abilities, they should be able to live reasonably harmoniously." She chewed her lip as she thought. "That being said, she'd need to have full control over her abilities first. I'm not setting her amongst the cubs so they can live in fear within their own dens, purposefully or not."

The Shaitan had the ability to instil strong emotions within their prey, such as fear, rage, passion, hatred and any other negative emotion. In turn, the Shaitan fed off the energy that pervaded from their victims when they were in the throes of those emotions.

Before the Council had been introduced, and

strict laws put upon the Shaitan, they used to torture their prey before they killed them, milking as much negative energy as they could. Azar had read that on special occasions, the Shaitan would gather an entire town together for an orgy on the sand dunes. When the lust energy started to wane, they would cause them all severe mental pain, before finally running them down individually to slaughter them like animals. Azar hadn't slept for a week after reading that passage in her Djinn history books.

They had garnered such a bad reputation, even amongst the malevolent Djinn, which also consisted of the Ifrit and the Ghul, that the Council had set up strict laws for the Shaitan, with summary execution for anyone who broke those laws. The result of this zero tolerance policy was that there were very few Shaitan left in the modern world. Not really such a loss, except when you remember that the Djinn system was based on balance. If the Shaitan were wiped out, then their benevolent counterpart, in this case the Sila, would have no checks on their power, and could essentially rise up to rule the Djinn. No one wanted a world run purely by the Sila. The PMS alone would be a killer.

Bast had tested Freya's power earlier, when the little girl had been playing on a large slide that had fallen out of favor in the amusement park, to get an accurate reading of her abilities and their strength. Freya's powers were nowhere near as strong as her father's, let alone a full-blooded Shaitan, but she could still instil low level feelings. She could make a person angry enough to punch a wall, but not so angry that they would tear apart their own family with their bare hands. Her abilities were also largely uncontrolled, which was why she had frightened the human children in her class.

Bast turned to Donovan. "Yes, she'll need to be in control of her abilities, but time is of the essence. The longer she is in your care, the more time there is for someone to let it slip to the Council. Maybe you can teach her to channel positive emotions like love and happiness?" he joked.

Donovan scoffed. "Love? I don't think there has been a Shaitan in history who has wielded either love or happiness. We channel the things we are capable of feeling, and love and happiness are not amongst them. The Shaitan are cold."

And apparently also blind, Azar thought to herself. He loved his daughter, even if he didn't recognize the feeling.

But Azar had to agree. The chance of a Shaitan being able to switch tracks was unlikely, but it couldn't hurt to try. "I'll go and see Anton to request this as my favor, as soon as you can assure me she has her powers suppressed or at least under control." Azar gave a theatrical sigh. "I was going to use my favor to get the pack enforcers to rough up a couple of my ex-boyfriends, but I guess this is more noble." She smiled at both Bast and Donovan. "On that note, we better return to the compound. I am a slave you know, wouldn't want to displease my masters."

She was joking, of course. As far as forced slavery went, she'd gotten pretty lucky. Plus technically Mira was her master, and she knew the woman had a big soft spot for her. Bast stood and stretched, and then passed a set of keys to Donovan.

"Use my place while you are getting organized. The security system is good and the building tenants are entirely human. Just put the keys in the ficus plant out the front of the warehouse when you don't need the place any more. It'll protect them until I can pick them up."

Azar was no longer surprised by Bast's creepy plants that seemed partially sentient. It was part of his Jann abilities; he could grow greenery even in the harshest of environments, and summon water from underground. He could also shape your subconscious mind to see an internal oasis of your own making. When Azar had been dying aboard the Staten Island ferry, the pain so unbearable that she thought that death would be a sweet release, Bast had created an oasis in her mind, soothing her and almost making love to her. It had been a comforting display of power. If the Djinn ever went mainstream, the Jann would make quite a killing as anesthetists.

Donovan waded into the teddy pit and picked up Freya. She didn't even open her eyes, just snuggled into the comfort of her father's strength. Donovan looked down at her and the expression on his face made Azar laugh. The Shaitan can't feel love, her ass!

She raised her eyebrows at him and he frowned. The guy had looked perpetually confused and frustrated all night. Well, welcome to parenthood buddy, you better get used to it. She walked them to the door as Bast went to turn out the lights. Donovan laid the girl on the back seat and drove off.

The lights behind her were all turned off and Azar felt Bast's arm snake around her waist, pulling her back tightly against the warmth of his body. She ran her fingers along the hard muscles of his forearm and let out a gentle moan as she felt him kiss the base of her neck. He drew her back into the complete darkness of the warehouse, shutting the door with his foot and spun her around so he could kiss her, pressing her back against the cool metal.

His kiss was deep and sensual, his tongue exploring the surface of her lips, pushing past her teeth to stroke her tongue with his own. Her arms had snaked around his neck, threading his slightly too long hair through her fingers.

Due to the total darkness of the room, her sense of touch heightened. The sensations were doubly intense, the feel of his fingers running over the soft skin of her back, the taste of him in her mouth, the intoxicating scent that was purely Bast, each more potent from the deprivation of her sight. She felt her body and its overwhelming need push her protestations to the back of her mind. She needed Bast, and no amount of self-flagellation and retrospection was going to change that fact.

The decision made, she sighed against his lips and let her body melt into his, no longer two bodies but one, seared together by heat and need. Bast sensed her surrender, and his kisses became more demanding, more intense. He peeled off her tank top, his hands running up her rib cage as his thumbs reached across to stroke her nipples through her delicate lace bra. She let out a breathy moan that seemed to echo off the high ceilings of the warehouse.

She tugged at Bast's shirt, needing to feel his hard body under her hands and he ducked his head down so she could pull his shirt off. His mouth was so close to her breasts, his tongue flicked out and licked one of her aroused nipples, sending shock waves to the hot place between her thighs. He trailed kisses across her collarbone to her other breast, his hands skillfully undoing her bra and discarding it into the darkness.

He took her nipple into his mouth and sucked it hard, and her hands tugged painfully at his hair, pulling him closer. He slipped his hands under her butt, and lifted her until her breasts were face level, and she wrapped her legs around his waist. He moved them as his mouth nibbled and teased at her breasts, his hands massaging her ass. He kicked something with his foot and then she was falling into a mound of soft synthetic fur.

"Are we really going to do it for the first time on a pile of stuffed toys?" she laughed, but the sound ended in a moan as Bast hummed his affirmative on her nipple. He broke off his attentions on her breasts to wrangle them both out of their shoes and jeans. When he rejoined her, his body pressed into hers as he kissed her neck, his hard shaft pressed against her thigh.

"Wherever we make love for the first time will be magical, but perhaps this will help. Close your eyes." He pressed his forehead to hers, and the scene bloomed before her.

She was lying on the softest grass she had ever felt, under a large palm that only let in dappled sunlight. Bast was there, his body leaning over her, the golden shade of his skin too perfect, gleaming in the warm desert sun. Over his shoulder she could see undulating hills of sand and she knew she was home. She remembered this place from the last time Bast had taken her into an oasis, when she was writhing in pain on the deck of a boat.

Today there was a light breeze dancing over the waters of a calm, crystal blue lake. The sun warmed her skin. She ran her fingers lightly down the muscles of his back, barely touching his skin, and watched his body shiver with delight.

"Aren't you a romantic," she teased.

There was something about this place that made her feel languid, effortlessly sultry. She arched her back so her breasts rubbed against the light golden curls on his chest with delicious friction. She gazed at him in wonder. "How can any man be so beautiful?" Even the scars that crisscrossed his body, tokens of long ago fought battles, were beautiful imperfections.

"You do not know real beauty, *Jaaneman*. Real beauty is what I see when I look into your eyes," he whispered back. *Jaaneman* was a Persian word, meaning 'soul of me'. "Let me show you." The scenery slightly shifted, and instead of staring up at Bast, she was staring down at herself. "This is what I see when I look at you." His voice was like a calm water.

What she saw was an impossibility. It wasn't like looking in a mirror, where all you saw was faults and flaws. Looking at herself through Bast's eyes was like seeing the most perfect version of herself. Her dark eyelashes fluttered slowly against her olive cheeks. "This is what I feel when I touch you." Her neck was soft as silk beneath Bast's lips, her hips fitting perfectly in his hands. Her skin, her breasts, her hair, it was all perfect through his eyes. She felt his touch as he traced a line down her torso, but also the feel of her abdomen through his sensations, how he revelled at the suppleness that was so inherently female. The dual sensations threatened to shatter her mind, and when his hands ran up the backs of her thighs, readying her body for him, she had a moment of panic. Would it be too much? Would the dual sensations splinter her heart? Make her lose a little piece of herself that she feared she could never get back?

"Are you ready, *Jaaneman*?"

She swallowed hard, but she wanted to know how he felt. She nodded, stretching up to softly kiss his lips as he slowly drove his cock into her. She let out a low moan as he filled her, felt the sweet stretching of her muscles, combined with Bast's glory as he buried himself in her. She moaned as his pace quickened, the feel of him inside her from both of their minds and bodies, the pleasure that was rolling through them both. It crashed down on her like a tsunami. Her body moved to meet him, matching him thrust for thrust.

They came together so completely, that Azar didn't know which were her sensations and which were his, as pleasure rolled through her body like lightning. Her hands ran over his body, her fingers digging into his hard muscles to anchor herself in the storm of feelings.

He pressed his body to hers, chest to chest, heart to heart, driving deep inside her until she could hear her screams echoing around the warehouse. She felt his climax climb with hers and then they were both standing on the precipice together. Pleasure threatened to shatter her soul.

The oasis fell away as she opened her eyes, her breathing hard, every inch of her body tingling and coated in sweat.

Bast was a dead weight on top of her, his strong arms holding her so tightly, as if she were anchoring him too. Eventually he rolled to the side, his breathing evening out, his body still pressed closely to hers.

"I fear you've shattered me, and then remade me, but somehow I don't think I'll ever be the same," Bast said, his voice was heavy with emotion.

"Then you are more beautiful for having been broken, *Jaaneman*." She used his endearment for her, and she truly believed it. He had worked his way into her very soul.

CHAPTER 4

The radiant warmth of Bast's body woke her the next morning. She looked around her dorm room, trying to judge the time of day. They had straggled home in the early hours, sneaking through the halls like a couple of teenagers. Bast had laid her down on her bed and made love to her for the rest of the night. It had been the most romantic, electrifying thing to happen to her in all her long years.

Azar stretched and yawned, turning in Bast's arms so she could gaze at his sleeping face. His lashes fluttered on his cheeks, and soon she was looking into the warm gold of his eyes. She opened her mouth to say something, anything, that would help express how she felt right now, but she was interrupted by the chirping of Bast's phone.

Bast had once been a well decorated Adel member, centuries before he had met Azar. From what she had gleaned through compound gossip, and their interactions, Bast and Mira had been partners. That was until Bast had become so disillusioned with the system that he'd left the Adel.

He'd bought Coney Island from Mira's father, Mosel. It was whispered in the halls that he had been one of the best soldiers the Adel had ever had, which was why the Council had been so eager to barter fifty years of her servitude to have him back within their fold.

When their servitude had started, Bast had been given his old rank in the hierarchy, but slightly below Mira. It had definitely burned Joia that she and Bast now had the same level of command, which amused Bast to no end.

He lazily leaned over Azar's body to reach for his phone, the stubble of his chin scraping deliciously across her nipple. He pressed the answer button and rested his head on her breasts.

"Bast. Yes. Okay, we'll be right there. ETA two minutes." He hit the hang up button and threw his phone back on top of his jeans, turning his face to nip the side of her breast. Azar sucked in a breath. "They want us in the Comms room. Killian has arrived."

Bast didn't make any move to rise from the bed, instead running his hand across her abdomen. Azar ignored the flood of sensation that traveled in the wake of his extremely skilled fingers and sat up.

"And you said we'd only be two minutes?" She shot out of bed.

She pulled on a pair of jeans and a t-shirt, feeling the heat of Bast's gaze as he watched her bend over to wiggle her feet through the skinny bottoms of her jeans.

She threw his t-shirt at him. "Get up! It's my first meeting with my brother and my big boss. I want to make a good impression."

She splashed her face and brushed her teeth in the tiny little kitchen sink, wishing she had more time. She turned, pulling her hair into a quick braid down her back, and saw Bast unhurriedly dressing. She jammed her feet into her boots and gave him a scowl.

"If you don't hurry up, I will literally light a fire under you to get you moving." A little flame formed in her hand to back up her words.

Bast just laughed and gave her a pacifying

gesture, sliding into his jeans sans underwear. The room got a little warmer but she kept her mind on the job. She'd thought that making love to him would ease the burning need that seemed to plague her every second of every day, but it had just made it worse. It was an ache in her soul now.

He finished tying his boots, and the look on her face made his own soften. He came over and wrapped one arm around her body, the other cupping her cheek. He kissed her, the sensation so consuming, she briefly forgot the pressing deadline. When he broke off the kiss, a smile lit up his face.

"We're going to have to sprint, or we'll be late." He gave her a quick peck on the forehead and then bolted out the doorway, leaving Azar to chase down the hall after him.

When she finally caught up, he was waiting for her outside of the Comms room. He gave her arm a quick squeeze of support and then pushed open the heavy doors, standing to the side to let her enter before him. She knew he would give her space, so her brother would see her as an independent person, rather than half of a matching set. He waited until she was halfway across the room before he followed her in, and purposefully sat down at the opposite end of the conference table. A little part of her wanted to scrabble onto his lap and hide behind his self assurance.

She took in the people at the conference desk, a polite smile on her face. Mira and Joia were there, of course, and next to them were two more Adel that she'd only met briefly when she'd moved into the dorms. She wasn't even sure of their names; none of the Adel members spent a lot of time in the compound, so she barely had more than a passing acquaintance with the majority of the Adel members. However, next to them was a familiar face. Danian had been assigned as Keenan Reilly's handler, the liaison between informant and the Adel Intelligence Department.

Azar had to physically fight the urge to ask after Keenan. Danian seemed to sense her turmoil, because he gave her a small smile and nodded. Keenan was okay, and that fact lifted her heart a little as she turned toward the head of the table, to the last unknown person in the room. Raw power emanated off the man in waves, and she knew he could only be one person.

Killian.

Azar bowed her head in deference. She didn't know if it was the right thing to do, but she was a slave, and he was her master, irrespective of their blood relationship. She studied him quickly beneath her lashes. They looked fairly similar, and that came as a shock. They both had square cut faces, olive skin and remarkably similar noses. Azar's lips were a little fuller than Killian's and his face was littered with scars, much like Bast's. But the most startling difference were their eyes. Killian's were a blue grey, like a thunder cloud before a snow storm.

She stood straight, and found Killian regarding her with just as much interest. Apparently he was equally as curious about his long lost sibling, irrespective of Mira's warnings.

"Azar, I am Killian. Please take a seat." His voice was commanding, and Azar found herself complying without thought. Six months ago she would have told him to stick it; she'd never been good with authority. She looked at the intricate gold bands on her wrists. Killian, and to a lesser extent Mira, were her masters. If either one of them told her to do a handstand naked, she would have to comply with a smile.

The loss of free will grated against her nerves, but she held it back. She'd made a choice, and she could rail against the consequences all she liked, but it wouldn't change anything. Killian spoke again, softly, but the authority in his voice was unmistakable.

"I am temporarily assigning myself to this branch of the Adel. Given the recent events, I believe that the Central North American branch could benefit from my presence. A Rogue, a Great Weapon and recent events have set a disturbing trend in this city, and it concerns me. Therefore, I shall be the Commander until I feel that the threat to the Djinn has passed."

Azar's eyes flew to Mira, but she seemed unconcerned about her sudden demotion to Second-In-Command. Joia next to her looked a little more peeved, but she hid it well.

The great weapons were meant to be an urban legend, lost to time and generally forgotten about. They were powerful weapons forged to kill the original Djinn. The original Djinn were to modern Djinn, what Godzilla is to a gecko. The Rogue that Azar had taken on months ago had found the weapon to be wielded against the Ifrit, and had used it to try and release Balraka, the original Ifrit. That was a story for another day, but needless to say, the re-emergence of the great weapons threatened to create upheaval within the supernatural world. One touch from a great weapon had the potential to kill a

Djinn instantly, whether you stabbed them in the heart or gave them a glorified paper cut.

Each weapon was targeted at a particular race, and could be wielded from the strongest of the Adel to a human child. If someone got their hands on the weapons and decided to take out the Council, or even some of the stronger bloodlines, the resulting upheaval would throw everyone back into the dark ages; Djinn, Supes and humans alike.

Bast's voice cut into her thoughts. "What recent events are you referring to exactly?"

Killian smiled, his white teeth flashing in the overhead light. "Ah Bast, it's good to see you. Probably not the most ideal of circumstances," he threw Azar a quick look, "but fortuitous regardless. I shall let you know if the situation requires your involvement, however at this moment it is being handled by Kouros and Lida." He indicated the two Djinn in the room she didn't know. His tone was hard to read, and Azar was unsure if he was antagonizing Bast or was actually happy to see him again.

Bast's face was unreadable, his usual neutral mask firmly in place. There was definitely an undertone between the two men, and Azar couldn't put her finger on what it was.

The two other Adel in the room, Kouros and

Lida, gave her a steely eyed look, bordering on disdain. It was a look she was becoming all too familiar with. A look that said they didn't like her, but they were keeping that opinion to themselves because her Daddy and Big Brother could make their life hell. Azar doubted her relatives would bother, and that was fine with her. She'd been fighting her own battles for over a century, so she didn't need anyone patting her head and putting a band-aid on her boo-boos.

Killian was still addressing Bast while the other two were giving her the stink eye. "I shall take over Azar's training for the duration of my stay. I am sure that Mira has something of a more critical nature for a man of your skills." Stormy blue eyes met golden ones.

Well, that confirms it, Azar thought. There was definitely tension between them. Enough to kill a horse. Hell, there was enough tension between them to kill a whole herd of horses.

Finally, Bast inclined his head as if the very motion caused him pain.

"Good. Everyone else knows what to do. Azar, I shall meet you in the gym in five minutes." With that, Killian stood and swept out of the room, taking all the air with him. Lida and Kouros left straight away, but not without sending her a chilling look on the way out.

She let her shoulders relax. "Well, next time you guys want to call an early morning meeting, I think I might go skinny dipping in Siberia instead." The words came in a relieved whoosh. Mira shot her a sympathetic smile.

Bast kissed the top of her head and then shooed her out the door. "In case you missed it, that was an order. The Anadari Bracelets won't react kindly if you're late."

She'd been lucky so far. For the last three months, she had been reasonably compulsion free. Mira had assigned her training over to Bast, and had given her very little by way of direct orders. Somehow, Mira knew how to phrase a request to bypass the slave cuffs.

So, she hadn't really experienced the full compulsion of the master/servant relationship. However, she now found herself walking quickly along the halls without consciously deciding too, and even when she tried to force herself to slow her pace, she couldn't. She let out a yell of frustration. She hated having no control over her body. She pushed through the double doors of the gym and felt the compulsion stop as soon as she stepped across the threshold. But her anger burned and her eyes blazed as they settled on Killian across the room.

She held up her cuffed wrists. "Flexing your might already? If you'd given me ten minutes, I could have got my gym gear."

Killian just smiled enigmatically. "You won't need them. Today we are working on your Ifrit abilities. I'll show you how best to wield it to bring down threats to Djinn society, including other Djinn. Now change."

"Change into what? I just told you I didn't get my gym clothes." Killian raised an eyebrow and she blushed a little. "Oh."

He wanted her to go full Ifrit. She'd spent her life avoiding the full change, sometimes to the point of pain. She'd only really done it two or three times in her life, and the sense of loss after turning back to her human form was nearly unbearable. Like feeling the sun's warmth on your skin after hiding in a cave for half a century.

Even during the last three months of her servitude, she hadn't changed to her true form. It wasn't training that Bast could teach her and no one else had offered.

"Can you turn around? Getting naked in front of a stranger is a little weird. Getting naked in front of a stranger who happens to be my brother is even weirder." Killian rolled his eyes but turned towards the wall obligingly.

So what if she had the morals of a human? She knew the supernatural world had a rather blasé view on nakedness, especially those who could change forms. They'd spent most of their lives being naked in a crowd, from their first change as a kid. It was like growing up in the world's most deadly nudist colony. Azar held her breath and moved away from Killian. She exhaled and just let herself go.

Within seconds, flames encased her body, spreading down her limbs to the very tips of her fingers. She felt like a hypocrite, because there was no way to be anything but naked in the Ifrit form, but the flames covered her modestly. Each strand of her hair turned into an individual flame, rising up from her head like a candle flame. Azar yelled as bat-like wings burst from her back and unfurled like a hellish flower. She flapped them twice to activate the muscles. Then it was over, and she stood there as the fire embraced her skin like an intimate lover's touch. She'd never felt so alive, so happy. To be able to do this any time was almost worth the fifty years of slavery.

Killian turned and looked her over with a critical

eye. "Very nice, if a little slow. You will need to practice changing forms until you can do it in less than
three seconds. If you are in a fight, even three
seconds can be the difference between life and
death." He moved across the room so there was a
good ten feet of distance between them. "I will stay
in my human form for today's lesson, but next time
we will both train in our true forms." The hard fist of
worry loosened in her stomach.

A full Ifrit in its natural form was a terrible sight
to behold. They looked like the human visage of
Satan. When a full Ifrit transformed, their faces
elongated until it was bestial, their feet turned into
cloven hooves, little horns sprouted from their head.
Not to mention the flames and the bat wings. The
fact that Azar still had nightmares from seeing the
Rogue Ifrit in his true form was a testament to the
horrifying nature of it, even for a fellow Ifrit. It was
one of the only plus sides to being a half-blood that
she could see; when she transformed, she kept her
human form, apart from the wings. It was a disad-
vantage in a fight, but it allowed her to look in the
mirror and not shudder at what was looking back
at her.

Killian clasped his hands behind his back, and
walked in a circle around her. "Sun Tzu said 'know

thy enemy and know yourself.' I don't have a lot of time for the thoughts and whims of such a fleeting species, after all, what grasp could a human have on the bigger picture when their lives are but a single speck? However, that being said, as a military strategist, I find the writings of Sun Tzu quite poignant. Useless outside of human wars of course, but sometimes they accidentally bumble onto something quite profound.

"To defeat your enemy, you must know not only their strengths and weaknesses, but your own as well. So first, we shall see how well you know your enemy. Imagine that I am a Jann," a small twist of his lips that could have been a smirk, "and it is your job to destroy me. Show me what you would do. Go." He braced his legs apart, but he looked no more than mildly alert.

He obviously didn't think her capable of any real damage. As he was a full-blood Ifrit, it was probably true. Even in his human form, his body would just embrace the flames. Pretending he was Jann, she did the only offensive move she knew how to do. She made a huge fireball. It started as a small orb in her hands, and her fire fed its flames as it grew larger and larger. When it was the size of a beach ball, she tossed it at Killian. He thrust one hand out and as the fireball touched his palm, it shrank back in on itself until it was the size of a golf ball. The whole thing took less than fifteen seconds.

"That was not a bad sized fireball for a half-blood. But I would expect nothing less from someone of my bloodline." He gave her a small smile. "However, a fireball is too slow to use as an offensive weapon, unless you are using it as a sneak attack. This also shows a glaring lack of knowledge about the strengths and weaknesses of the other Djinn races. I want you to tell me what you know of the Jann, while you run laps around the gym. Your body does not have the benefits of self-healing like that of a full-blood, so you will need to keep it in peak physical condition if you don't want to die on your first mission."

Azar's feet moved before her mind had even processed the order. She gritted her teeth at the commands that laced his every word. Killian probably didn't even realize he was doing it, he was in a position of power so he would give commands to everyone. Or maybe he did, and he was testing her. Either way, being in slave cuffs pissed her the hell off. She absently wondered if she'd just keep running around the gym, even if Killian left the room. Would she run until she died of exhaustion, unable to stop? She cleared her throat and recited what she knew.

"Historically, the Jann are known for creating oases in the desert for those they consider worthy. They are benevolent Djinn, with the ability to grow flora in any environment, and can call water from the earth. They also have the ability to enter people's minds. They are vulnerable to fire, as they are essentially creatures of air." Another lap, and not a bead of sweat. She'd remained in peak physical condition as a firefighter, especially where her physical strength had to equal the man next to her. Naturally that wasn't a problem for her; she would be able to lift more, run faster and for longer than any man at any firehouse in the world. However, it helped to lift some weights and run on the treadmill to keep up appearances.

"That's good, but it's to be expected considering you are dating a Jann." His tone was derisive and it set her teeth on edge.

She didn't consider there might be a stigma about interracial dating, given how few Djinn were left in the world. 'Get it where you can' should be their motto. The number of Djinn in the world numbered in the tens of thousands.

She dragged her attention back to Killian.

"The Jann are also incredibly quick, which is why your fireball would never work. What you have to do is essentially trap them in a ring of fire. It's quite simple really, a child's trick. Come here and try to surround me in a ring of fire."

Azar jogged towards him, a small ball of fire flying from her hand onto the ground in front of him. She closed her eyes and tried to command the fire to circle around his feet. Eventually, she had a tube of fire, six feet tall, around Killian.

Again, Killian waved his hands and the fire melted away. "Too slow. In that time, the Jann would have been in your head and you would have been on the ground writhing in pain, remembering every beating you'd ever taken in your life. I want you to practice these rings repeatedly, until they form almost immediately. Now, more laps, and tell me what you know of the Ghul."

On and on it went, Killian filling the gaps in her knowledge of the Djinn races strengths and weaknesses, and the best way to combat them. The Ghul were creatures of decay, and fed off corpses and blood licked from the soles of human feet. They could spread decay to anything, and once they had hit you with necrosis, it quickly spread unless the area was cut out or treated by Djinn healers almost immediately, otherwise it would be fatal. They were malevolent Djinn, and were ruthless, sneaky and brutal in their methods. However, they were physically weak and could be overcome with strength or by covering their bodies in high temperature fire. They also had very weak mental barriers, making them exceptionally vulnerable to the Jann.

Azar remembered her run in with the Ghul. She very much wished she'd had the opportunity to set the Ghul in question on fire at the time. Actually, she'd still like to set her on fire, if she ever got the chance. Lila had 'forgotten' to warn the Council about the Rogue Ifrit, and that had almost resulted in Azar being killed. As it was, she had to undertake her servitude. So Azar paid special attention to Killian's teaching about the Ghul. Even if she never used the knowledge, it would add some realism to her homicidal fantasies about Lila.

Killian was pushing her harder than she'd ever gone before, making her fly around the room on basically unused wings. She was starting to get a light sheen of sweat by the time they got to the defensive moves against the Sila.

The Sila, one of the benevolent races, were an all female race who were highly intelligent and strategic. They were neither strong nor fast, but usually kept a stable of paranormal bodyguards. They also had control over lightning, and could call up a lightning strike powerful enough to wipe out half an army. They also had nearly impenetrable mental barriers, making them almost immune to the psychic powers of the Jann and the Shaitan. However, it isn't an instantaneous offensive weapon, and can take at least ten minutes to call up. They could also be defeated by encasing their bodies in high temperature fire, but you better do it in ten minutes or less, otherwise you'd be electrocuted like a possum in a power station.

Azar's wings felt like they were about to fall off. The muscles were weak and ached as if someone was trying to hack them from her body with a rusty knife. She landed, panting hard, and her wings dragged along the ground, singeing the floorboards.

"Why have you stopped?" When he told her to fly around the room, it mustn't have been an order, or she would have kept going until she fell out of the sky. She was very grateful for that small mercy.

"I can't fly anymore," she croaked out of her bone dry throat. He threw her a bottle of water from the fridge in the corner of the gym, and she chugged it down so quickly, that it dribbled down her chin.

"You can run more laps then, but keep your

wings off the ground," he ordered unsympatheti-cally. She took off at a slow jog, her muscles protesting angrily. She let her wings drop a little, and they brushed the ground.

"Every time your wings touch the floor, it's ten more laps. Keep them up!"

Azar grimaced and flipped him the bird, making him laugh. He had a nice laugh, like a deep rumble. "You'll thank me one day. Now tell me what you know about the Shaitan."

The Shaitan were a problematic race, as they would feed on the battle rage, fear and adrenaline that came during a fight. They had the ability to cause pain, fear, lust, anger and other negative emotions in their opponents, and as the intensity of an opponent's emotions increased during battle, it fed their own strength, making them harder to defeat as the fight progressed. They were also scary looking monsters with eyes like black pits of death.

However, they were loners by nature, which meant it was very rare to have to fight more than one at a time. They had no tangible physical abilities, so a speed based attack was necessary. The Shaitan were resilient like cockroaches, so unless you ensured they were well and truly incapacitated, they could feed off their energy reserves and heal. Therefore, they needed to be speared through the heart with a Sila lightning bolt, which would cremate their bodies to ash. There was no coming back from that. The best an Ifrit could do is keep them incapacitated until a Sila Adel came to execute them.

"Five more laps, and tell me what you know of the Marid. This is the most important knowledge of your life, so you better know it so intrinsically that you can repeat it in your sleep. Now go," Killian yelled across the room.

The Marid were the Ifrit's natural opposite, and the Ifrit would always be sent out to take down rogue Marid. Not that it was a big problem, as there weren't many Marid left in the world. The Marid had power over water, in all its forms. They could pull moisture from the air and the bodies of their victims, could create ice and control the sea. Killian scoffed at the latter point. It was merely a rumor, but it was one that the Adel treated seriously, unfounded or not.

"If you have to fight a Marid, it will be the toughest fight of your life. There is a fifty-fifty chance you won't survive. They will try and freeze the water in your bloodstream, snuffing out your fire in the process. You must try and cover them in fire, and ensure the fire enters their bodies through their nose, mouth, eyes, wounds, however you can, so you can evaporate the water within their body. Without water, the Marid shrivel and die, turning to dust in the wind. Whoever can complete their offensive move first will be the victor, so you better work on your speed."

Azar breathed a sigh of relief that there weren't many Marid left, and the chances of her personally having to battle one in the next fifty years was slim. As long as Mira didn't go rogue, she'd be fine. Actually, if Mira went rogue, she wouldn't even stand a fifty percent chance. She would be dead.

"Last is the Ifrit. You have no advantages against another Ifrit, and a full-blooded Ifrit has an advantage over you. They will be faster and stronger, and their ability to heal will be almost instantaneous. At best you have hand to hand combat, so I suggest you continue working on that with Bast, until you can fight an opponent who outmatches you completely. But I guess you have already experienced that." There was a hint of respect in his eyes.

He walked to the fridge and grabbed out another bottle of water and threw it to her. Somewhere around the Sila lesson she had started to lightly perspire. Now, sweat was pouring off her body, not from the running, but from the use of her Ifrit abilities, which were almost completely unused muscles. It was like learning to walk.

"Go have a shower and report to Mira. We are done for today." With that Killian left the room, and she collapsed onto the polished floor of the gym.

She was desperate to return to her human form, so she could lose the weight of her wings dragging at her back. She crawled towards her clothes, changed forms and then flopped naked on the ground. She didn't care if anyone walked in and saw her. Maybe this is why everyone in the supernatural world was so relaxed about nudity.

CHAPTER 5

The following day, Azar was really feeling her half human side. Her muscles ached and she was physically and mentally exhausted. She had stumbled down the hall like a zombie to the Comms room for a briefing. She stuck her face in a bowl-sized cup of coffee, and hoped her core muscles would be strong enough to keep her upright in her chair. She may have dozed off a little, until Killian's voice cut through her self-pitying haze.

"There have been two attacks against Djinn within the region, where members of prominent Ghul and Sila houses have been found torn to shreds and then set alight. Their bodies were unrecognizable. Kouros and Lida have pinpointed it as a Were attack, but the packs have been unforthcoming with information, except to deny any involvement."

Azar's mouth fell open. The Djinn were more powerful than most other supernaturals, including the Weres, and it would have taken almost an entire pack to take down a single Djinn. But it could be done.

Killian continued after everyone had absorbed the news. "Both of the deceased were young, less than one hundred years." His face turned into a hard mask of cold rage, and it was terrifying. Even Donovan would have turned tail and run.

The Djinn were long lived, but it varied between races; some lived to be ancient, like the Marid and the Jann, and some had lives of less than five hundred years. It halved again if your bloodline was watered down with human blood, like her own. As such, anyone under a hundred years was considered a child within Djinn society.

"Danian's informant tells him that the human police are baffled, and they consider it to be a serial killer. The case is being handed over to the FBI. A copy of the case file has been given to the Adel." Azar knew that must have been hard for Keenan. His loyalty and integrity were what made him a good man and a great detective.

Killian turned those stormy eyes in her direction. "Mira tells me you have connections in the Were community. I would like you and Bast to meet with them and gather whatever intel you can. Keep it civil, Bast; we do not need an inter-species war on top of everything else."

Even as he said it, she felt herself rising involuntarily. She gritted her teeth at the compulsion of the Anadari bracelets.

Peeved off, Azar stood and saluted Killian mockingly. "Yes, Sir." She saw Mira wince and she mentally face-palmed, the practical side of her nature chastising the rebellious side for antagonizing a man who could make her life hell for fifty years.

However, instead of reprimanding her, a small smile tugged at Killian's lips. "Obedience. It's not a trait I thought would ever be exhibited from someone of my bloodline."

It was only a tiny admission of the connection between them and Azar gave him a small smile in return. Someone scraped back their chair and Azar noticed that every set of eyes was looking at them warily. Bast shook his head, grabbed her arm and marched her from the room.

"I think that went well," she said, a grin stretching its way across her face. Bast just rolled his eyes.

"I think one day you are going to give me a heart attack," he grumbled. She just patted him on the arm.

Azar made several calls on the way to Sterling Forest, the woodsy home of the Sterling Forest Pack. First, she called to make an appointment with Anton, the Pack's Alpha. She got permission for Bast to come within Pack grounds, which was just good manners. Bast was a benevolent Djinn, his abilities not inherently destructive, but he could probably "suggest" the entire pack take a walk off a cliff if he wanted to. But Anton had met Bast several times, and they had developed a mutual respect.

After making an appointment for midday, Azar's next call was to Donovan. She wanted to check on Freya. She was going to kill two birds with one stone, and request that Anton take the girl in exchange for her blood debt.

Donovan informed her that Freya was fine, and they had begun training on how to control her abilities. Donovan sounded stressed, but she could hear the little girl laughing in the background of the call.

"Promise whatever you have to, I can cover it. Money, connections, anything. Freya needs this chance, because I have no Plan B up my sleeve." She could tell it pained him that his daughter's very survival was riding on a conversation that he couldn't control, or even witness. Control was important to Donovan. Azar reassured him as best she could. She only wanted what was best for the little girl too.

She directed Bast off the main road, down what appeared to be a fire trail. Last time she'd ventured onto pack lands, she'd been in her prized Shelby GT and every pothole had made her grimace in pain. She loved that car. The Adel had given them use of a hulking SUV, so she could relax and really enjoy the scenery around her.

This part of the forest looked untouched, like the bustling metropolis of NYC didn't even exist less than two hours away. Wildlife ran from the noise of the car as it bumped over the uneven track. The den was twenty miles down this road, and she felt herself starting to doze in the warm dappled sunlight, only to jolt awake every time they hit a large pothole. She was in the doze stage of this cycle when Bast's voice roused her.

"We're almost there. The welcome wagon has arrived."

Azar pried one eye open to see Tao standing just off the road, twenty feet ahead. Tao was a Were

Sentinel/Enforcer, and the man was as big as a barn. He was easily the biggest Were she had ever met at just under seven feet tall, and she would estimate three feet across the shoulders. He was a solid wall of muscle. He made Jerry and the other Onyx Werewolves look like the weaklings. He didn't try to stop them as they drove past, just gave them a small nod. Azar waved back, and was suddenly glad that she was considered Pack. Tao wasn't a particularly violent man, but he'd probably be able to flip the SUV if the need arose. She wondered what his Wolf looked like, if it would be as brutally scary as Tao. Even as she wondered this, a part of her hoped never to see it firsthand.

They pulled the SUV into a clearing in front of what appeared to be some ranger cabins sitting in front of a jagged cliff face. If you were an unsuspecting hiker, who'd managed to get pass the sentinels by some freak accident, you would just think that you'd stumbled upon a remote ranger outpost, not a fully-fledged Werewolf Pack, with upwards of fifty members. There was a crack in the cliff face, barely four feet wide, which was the entrance to the dens. From a distance it looked jagged, but from experience she knew that the edges of the opening had been worn smooth from time.

Azar wondered how Tao even fit through the opening as she climbed out of the SUV and started towards the chasm. She'd barely taken three steps when a tiny body launched itself at her legs, knocking her off balance and landing her flat on her back. She looked down to see a Werewolf pup cuddling her legs.

"Azar!" she squealed as she crawled up her legs to wrap her arms around her neck. She sat up and hugged the girl back.

"Hello Kayla. Wow, I think you've grown a foot since I last saw you. What have they been feeding you?" Azar asked as she set the little girl on her feet, and climbed up from the grass. She had once fixed the little girl's toy truck after it had been destroyed by another one of the pups, and had become Kayla's hero for all of eternity. Kayla bounced around until she caught sight of Bast. She quickly hid behind Azar, her head poking around the side of her hip.

"Kayla, this is Bast. He's my..." she trailed off. Did she call Bast her boyfriend, partner or what? "...friend," she finished rather lamely. Bast raised his eyebrow at her.

"Like your boyfriend?" Kayla asked, her childish curiosity getting right to the heart of the matter.

Bast squatted down and shook the little girl's

hand, "Yeah, just like her boyfriend." His smile was warm, and the little girl smiled hesitantly back, before her brow knitted in confusion.

"Like Mr.. Oliver?" She chewed on her lip, trying to make sense of the situation.

She laughed and ruffled the little girl's brown curls. "Only in Mr.. Oliver's dreams."

And maybe sometimes in mine, she muttered internally.

She turned and saw Dotty standing off to the side, her smile friendly but alert. Azar might have been considered Pack, but Bast held no such standing. He was treated with good manners, but the Were would be on guard, just in case.

Dotty was elderly, the Matriarch of the pack, the mate of a former Alpha. It was a position that demanded respect, even from the Alpha. As the Matriarch, it was Dotty's job to greet guests.

Azar walked over and kissed Dotty on the cheek, and received a fond pat on the arm. She introduced Bast and the old woman's smile grew wide.

"He's quite a handsome one, isn't he? If I was a few years younger, I would give you a run for your money." She waved a finger in Bast's direction, and there was a spark of mischief in her eyes. She imagined Dotty was pretty wild in her younger days.

"I doubt I would have been running," he joked, winking saucily. Dotty cackled and slapped Azar on the back.

"Child, you are in so much trouble."

Azar knew it, and as she followed Dotty through the crack in the cliff, she realized that she and Dotty were probably the same age.

They eventually navigated the sloping pathways to a large oak door, with a brass handle shaped like a wolf's head. Dotty knocked and walked through the door without waiting for an invitation. She ushered Azar and Bast into the room, and then left.

Anton rose from a leather wing back chair and Azar bowed her head out of respect, the proper courtesy to show to an Alpha. She slid her eyes across at Bast to ensure he was doing the same. The raw power that emanated from Anton was completely unlike Djinn power. It was earthy and raw, like the crackling air during a lightning storm. The feel of it so wild that she wondered if Anton harnessed it, or if the power rode Anton.

She raised her head, and walked across the room to shake Anton's hand, a genuine smile on her face. She had total respect for the Sterling Forest Alpha. He would do anything to care for those under his protection, and that protection now extended to her.

Not that she needed protection, she was more than capable of looking after herself, but the feeling of belonging was a gift she'd never imagined she would ever possess.

"It is lovely to see you again, Azar. You look well." His eyes were subtly scanning her for mistreatment. It was common knowledge in the supernatural world that Djinn slaves didn't always receive humane treatment from their masters. She wasn't sure exactly what Anton would have done if he had discovered she was being abused, but it was nice to know he cared.

"It is wonderful to see you too. I'm sure you remember Bast?" Anton nodded and shook Bast's outstretched hand.

Azar looked around the room, and she could see it was a library. Two chesterfield lounges sat facing each other, a well-polished coffee table sitting between them. The rest of the room was floor to ceiling books, a rolling ladder was set on a gleaming gold rail that circled the edges. A beautiful chandelier fashioned from sticks and twigs to look like a birds nest cast intricate shadows over the walls. Azar and Bast sat on one lounge, and Anton reclined into the other.

A younger female wolf that Azar had never met

arrived with coffee and set it on the table between them. She cast a warm smile in their direction and quickly took her leave.

"So, what can the Sterling Forest Pack do for the Djinn?" He lifted his latte to his lips and took a sip, a sigh escaping as he swallowed. Azar picked up her own mug, and took a sip. It was fantastic. Bast was happy to let her take the lead.

"You've probably heard that there has been a couple of attacks on the Djinn, where the victims were torn apart and set on fire. The Adel have narrowed it down to a Were attack. We were hoping you might have information that would allow us to track down the perpetrators and bring them to justice."

Azar decided she had to cut back on the Law and Order reruns. She sounded ridiculous.

Anton merely nodded. "Yes, a couple of Adel tracked down our pack liaison a few days ago to request information. Unfortunately, I'll have to tell you what he told them. The Pack would never sanction such a cowardly and vicious attack, especially not on Djinn so weak in their powers. It would go against our pack laws. We protect the young, even those not of our species."

The silent jab there was that the Djinn did not

have such scruples. The sad fact was, it was true. Aaron, a teenage Were, had been taken by the Rogue Ifrit and tortured for days. The Djinn did not have the morals of the Weres, unless it directly related to other Djinn, and sometimes not even then.

"I'm also unaware of any Pack within our region who would order such a thing. To start such a war would be suicide for a Pack, and ruin a truce that we've had with the Djinn for a millennium. We run our own affairs and the Djinn run theirs; it is a harmonious balance that wouldn't be trifled with lightly. Everyone with half a brain knows that if it came to a war between the Djinn and the Were, it would be bloody and both sides would suffer more losses than either species can afford."

And the Were had no chance of winning. It was left unspoken but the knowledge was common. A single, average Djinn could overcome at least ten Were before falling. An Adel could take on triple that.

Azar had no doubt Anton spoke the truth, and nodded her agreement. "I'll tell the higher ups." She sat forward on her chair a little. "On a more personal note, I would like to call in my favor, if I could." Anton rose both eyebrows in surprise. Obviously he didn't think she'd ever call in the favor either. "It's not really for me, but for a child. It will be a lot to ask, even considering the blood debt."

The Alpha motioned for her to continue and Azar took a deep breath. "Freya is a one-quarter blood Djinn. She is Donovan's daughter, I'm not sure if Jerry has told you about her?" Anton shook his head. "She was abandoned by her human mother, and is in great danger if she tries to enter into our world. The Shaitan would kill her like a pest. They have been pretty vocal about their thoughts on Djinn purity." Azar couldn't keep the disgust out of her voice. "So, she needs a place to live, somewhere the Shaitan and the Council will never think to look. She is weak in her powers, and Donovan is working with her to control them. She would pose no physical threat to the pack, and I'll ensure she has control of her power before she is brought to the dens. Donovan is willing to offer you anything you desire if you would take her."

Azar had practiced her spiel several times on the way to the Pack's territory. Anton looked thoughtful, and Azar held her breath.

"It is not a decision I can make lightly, even in fulfilling a blood debt. The wellbeing of my pack always comes first." Azar nodded, her stomach sinking. He wasn't going to go for it. Anton sighed as he thought it over. "She would be raised as a Were, and follow our laws. Donovan must never know the location of Pack grounds, and the girl will be taken to see him by one of the Wolves already in his employ, or yourself. And, of the utmost importance is that she must be able to control her abilities. If she risks the safety of this Pack, I would have her punished in the way of the Were." That meant she'd be executed. Killing another member of the pack was an instant death sentence for a Were.

Azar nodded eagerly. She couldn't imagine Freya harming anyone on purpose. "I'll think on it and give you my answer within forty-eight hours. I understand time is of the essence."

Azar agreed readily. It was a positive result for Freya, and Azar had been ready for a straight up refusal.

"Thank you for considering it," she said sincerely. She stood and so did the two men in the room. "We've taken up enough of your time, Anton. Thank you for seeing us." She inclined her head again in deference, as was custom. She could kiss Oliver for his crash course in Were etiquette

"You are welcome in our dens at any time, Azar," he replied warmly. "Perhaps as you leave, you should seek out Aaron. I know he is anxious to see you." He sighed deeply. "That boy will be Alpha one day, I can tell. But there are many hard lessons left to learn before he is ready."

There was an underlying message in Anton's tone, but she couldn't puzzle it out. As they stepped through the door, the girl who brought the coffee was standing on the other side, leaning casually on the wall. She straightened up when she saw Anton.

"I'm sorry I can't take you to him myself, but my next appointment has just arrived. Beth, could you please show our guests to one of the empty sitting rooms and then fetch Aaron?" The girl nodded, and indicated they should follow. She set a quick pace through the maze of halls, and they turned left and right, up and down several times until Azar was well and truly lost. The dens were a labyrinth that she would never be able to navigate on her own.

Finally, she led them into a little room with an overstuffed couch and two recliners, a large oil painting of a wolf stalking a rabbit on a green field. A bookshelf filled with bestsellers was arranged beside a laptop that sat on a desk in the corner. Beth motioned for them to sit and was gone in a flash.

The decor in this room was just as lovely as the Alpha's library. The only thing Azar couldn't deal with in the dens were the lack of windows. It made her claustrophobic. Beth returned equally as quickly with Aaron. A huge grin stretched across Azar's face.

The boy looked good after his ordeal, his scars had healed and he'd put on weight. She jumped out of the recliner and skipped over to wrap Aaron in a huge hug. Adversity and fear had bonded them for life.

"You don't know how happy it makes me to see you looking so good," she enthused. Aaron laughed and hugged her again.

"I'm happy to see you too. Come and sit down." He led her to the couch and sat next to her, Bast relegated to one of the recliners. "What brings you to our neck of the woods?"

"In my new role as Adel badass, they've sent me out here to investigate a case where a couple of Djinn kids were murdered by Weres," Azar told him.

Shock transformed Aaron's young face, all evidence of the carefree kid that had been there moments before disappearing in an instant. It was more than the natural horror about hearing of a gruesome murder. Bast leaned forward in his chair, picking up a vibe as well.

Azar rested her hand on Aaron's knee. "Do you know something about this?" A shadow passed over his face and his brow knitted. She could see him fighting an internal war of loyalty.

"Kind of." He shifted on the lounge and turned to look at the painting on the wall. "I think it's W.A.D.," he murmured after a minute.

"Wad?" Azar asked, confused. What the hell was a wad?

"Weres Against Djinn. They formed after I was..." he hesitated, "taken by the Rogue. It's mostly a group of young radical Weres, going to meetings and dissing the Djinn. From what I've heard it's just a few kids from lots of different groups, not just wolves. They asked me to join, but I told them I owed my life to a Djinn, that I wanted no part in their hate group." Aaron's nostrils flared a little. The kid had been at the other end of such hate, and had come out stronger on the other side. Azar couldn't help being proud.

"Who asked you exactly?" Bast asked, and Aaron looked at him suspiciously. He obviously didn't want to rat the person out, knowing the Adel wouldn't treat the person kindly. "They killed two kids in the most brutal of ways and then set their remains on fire. People like that do not deserve your loyalty." Bast's soft voice seemed completely reasonable and non-threatening.

Aaron sighed, seeming older than his years. He'd obviously been struggling over this dilemma. "Her name is Becca. She was my girlfriend before I was taken. I think she was one of the founders of the group. When I said that I didn't want to join, she told me that I was weak, broken, and that no female wanted that in a mate. I told her that in comparison to you guys, we are all weak." His solemn tone broke her heart.

She held Aaron's hand tightly and looked him dead in the eye. "Where it counts, you are the strongest man I have ever met. You helped save millions of lives, including mine, and defeated a creature that was riddled with hate, who was easily the deadliest being I've ever had the misfortune of encountering. You did this while being extremely physically and mentally injured, against all odds. You are a hero." She squeezed his hand tight, and Aaron gave her a half smile. "Besides, the bitch is obviously crazy. It's better to have loved and lost, than to live with a psycho for the rest of your life." That put a smile on his face, and she hugged him close again. "So, where can we find this Becca?"

Azar was going to tear the girl a new one for hurting Aaron.

"She's not here. She told her parents she was

going on a road trip with her college friends. She's an anthropology major at NYU." Aaron shook his head, "But she came to see me before that. She told me she had found a way to ensure that we were never the weak one's ever again. She told me she'd found one of the Great Weapons, on eBay. She was going to Canada to collect it."

Azar was speechless. Bast seemed equally as shocked.

"She found a Great Weapon on eBay? Are you sure?" The idea was preposterous.

Aaron nodded. "She'd become obsessed with them after they discovered Drakhul. She researched them, found every scrap of information she could, no matter how farfetched. She was sure."

Azar finally found her voice. "Fuck."

CHAPTER 6

"Seriously, eBay? The humans are selling our greatest relics on eBay?" Killian ranted at the room, and Azar rolled her eyes and nodded. For the tenth time. To say that the Adel were shocked that an ancient relic, which they'd assumed was lost to antiquity, had resurfaced in the hands of a middle-aged Canadian man from British Columbia, would be something of an understatement. "Are we certain that it is authentic?"

Mira shuffled more papers. "We have our historians looking at the images from the eBay entry as we speak, but they seemed pretty positive that it was the real deal. It's Ibsali."

Joia sucked in a shocked gasp, her eyes wide with fear. Ibsali was a Chakram, a metal ring originally designed for Djinn warriors in ancient times, and later appropriated by the Sikhs in India. However, it was made most famous by a leather-clad *Xena, Warrior Princess* on human television. That funny ring of death thing she flung around, which always managed to kill ten men in one throw; that was a Chakram. It was the Great Weapon used to destroy the Sila, and Azar felt pity for Joia. She knew what it was like to come face to face with an urban legend, the stuff they scare little kids with to make them behave.

Everyone was looking at Joia, and she finally came out of her shocked stupor for long enough to stand up and excuse herself from the meeting. Mira watched her leave, concern marring her usually serene expression. Azar could tell she'd like to go after her partner, to comfort and reassure her, but she couldn't.

Instead, Mira cleared her throat and got back to the issue at hand. "There is another problem, Sir. British Columbia is the known territory of The Green Man."

Killian sighed and dragged a hand over his face. Azar wondered who or what the Green Man was? It sounded like a hippy music festival in California. She looked around the table to see if anyone else was as confused as she was, and the varying reactions of the group perplexed her even more. Mira looked concerned, and Killian looked stressed. But Bast looked almost nostalgic. She knew she should wait and ask Bast or Mira later, to hide her ignorance from Killian, but she couldn't help herself. She had to know.

"Who is The Green Man?"

It didn't help when three eyes turned to look at her with incredulity.

Bast covered her hand with his. He knew her lack of knowledge was a sore point for her. "The Green Man is a powerful Fae, more specifically Tuatha Dé Danann. He is intrinsically connected to the earth, to nature and the spring. He has elemental magic and a solitary nature. The Djinn do not mess with the Fae without good cause. Their magic is old and powerful."

"And they are sensitive as hell," Killian muttered.

Azar knew about the Fae of course; she might have been cut off from Djinn society, but she'd still roamed in the supernatural community over the last century. The Fae encompassed a lot of different species of creatures, some humanoid, most not so humanoid. There were three branches of the Fae; the Tuatha Dé Danann, the Seelie Court and the

Unseelie Court. They all came from separate regions, but had united under the title of Fae for who-knows-what reason. They were also supposed to be tied to the soil of Europe. Because of that, Azar had met very few Fae in her time. As far as she knew, there were none in the Americas. This brought up an excellent question.

"What is a Fae doing out of Europe?" From what she heard, the Fae were literal creatures. When they said 'tied to the soil of Europe', they meant they could not set one foot outside of the ancient boundaries.

"From what we have gathered from our interactions with the Green Man and other Fae, he is a law unto himself, a force of nature if you will. He makes his own rules," Mira explained.

Azar could respect that. To be able to live outside the strictures of a preordained society would be a dream.

Killian rubbed his temple, like he was getting a headache, but she wasn't sure full-blooded Djinn could get headaches.

"This is a problem. The Green Man has to be treated with tact and respect. He abhors unnecessary violence, so we will have to retrieve Ibsali and leave the rebel Weres to be punished another day."

Azar cleared her throat nervously. "I have a suggestion, if I may?" Killian nodded. "I think it would be best for everyone if we can capture the W.A.D members and return them to the Packs for discipline. As you know, Were discipline is rather, uh, brutal by nature, so I am fairly sure the rebels will be punished in a very final manner, and we will not cause further unrest between the Djinn and the Weres. It's win-win."

She peeked out from under her eyelashes at Killian, and she could see him considering her idea. There was even a small glint of what looked like pride in his eye, but that could be her inner child desperate for the approval of her older brother. Who knew the inner workings of her mind? She was a therapist's wet dream.

"That seems like the most diplomatic course of action. But we must make it clear to the leaders that further acts of violence against the Djinn will be considered acts of war and responded to in kind." He nodded to himself absently. "We must go to Canada and collect Ibsali before the Weres. Mira, you will be lead, Lida will be your second. A Sila cannot go on this mission, for obvious reasons, so I shall send Danian as back up. Also, Azar will go. This will be a good first mission. You four will go to the address of the human in British Columbia and convince him to give you Ibsali. I'd prefer peaceful methods, but by force if necessary. If you can get in and out without coming to the attention of the Green Man, all the better. Any questions?" He looked at each of them.

Azar couldn't believe that she was being sent on this mission and not Bast. By the angry look on Bast's face, he wasn't happy about it either. Bast opened his mouth to protest, but Killian put a hand up to stop him. "Bast, you have been requested by one of the Councilors to conduct a special assignment in Europe. You will be briefed when you get to Stuttgart. You leave in two hours. The rest of you leave at 0600 tomorrow, by private jet. Meet me here at 0500 for a briefing. I shall inform Danian."

With that, Killian stood and strode out of the room. Bast eyed his departing back with suspicion, before standing and walking out. Azar followed and no one tried to stop her.

When they were back in Bast's room, Azar allowed herself to feel fear. This was the first time she would be without him acting like her security blanket. Her anxiety ratcheted up several notches and her breathing hitched. The panic must have shown on her face, because he sat on the bed and pulled her into his arms.

"It'll be fine, *Jaanaman*. Mira and Danian will look after you, and I will be back from Germany before you know it. I'll visit you every night in your dreams while I'm away." He laid down on the bed and shifted her to the side so he could curl his body around hers.

"Why does he hate you so much anyway? It can't be because of me, he barely knows me."

Bast sighed and nuzzled into her neck. Silence reverberated through the room, and she was beginning to think he wouldn't tell her.

Finally he sighed again and rolled onto his back.

"Before I quit, I was in line for his position, Director of the Adel." Azar rolled over so fast, she almost bounced off the bed. Bast smiled and ran a finger under her chin to click closed her gaping mouth.

"We were always competitive, but I was always a little faster, a little stronger. I have a longer lifespan and could have led the Adel for centuries. But I decided to quit instead. So, Killian got my position, but he never forgot that he was a second choice, and it burns him on the inside. The fact that I'm dating his sister probably only makes it worse." He gave a mirthless laugh. "But I didn't think he'd send me away out of spite." His face hardened into its mask of neutrality, and he sat up.

Azar watched him pack his things and thought how much she would miss him. She didn't know when she'd become so dependent on a man, but she didn't like it. She was Azar Nazemi, lone wolf, badass Ifrit, who didn't need any man to shield her from the world. She didn't realize she'd become so pathetic. She sat up and straightened her spine. She would get a grip and do her job, not pine away like some love sick puppy.

She walked over and gave him a long, hot kiss, and he returned it with equal fervor. It was the kind of kiss that haunted dark nights when you were alone in your bed.

"I better get back to work, I don't want Mira to crack the whip." She wrapped her arms around his waist, and rested her ear against his chest, listening to the steady thump of his heart. His hands ran over her back and he kissed the top of her head. "Please be safe," she whispered.

He just squeezed her tighter and walked her to the door. "Don't do anything crazy while I'm gone," he warned, and even though he said it jokingly, there was a thread of truth to the statement.

"I can't make any promises," she joked over her shoulder as she left the room. She rushed down the hall before she did something really pathetic like burst into tears.

THE BREEZE off the snow capped mountains was touched with ice, and it whipped around the small group standing on the tarmac like a cold embrace. The Djinn didn't actually feel hot or cold unless they were extremes, so the group probably could have stood there in their underwear and only felt mildly uncomfortable. But they were rugged up in quilted jackets, caps and snow boots, just to keep up appearances amongst the humans.

A black SUV pulled up in front of them, and the woman who slid out of the driver's seat was of medium height with soft, rounded curves. She had a classic beauty that had fallen out of fashion in the last hundred years or so, but renaissance artists would have begged to paint her. The black cargoes and black tee, the unofficial uniform of the Adel, hugged her curves. The woman shook hands with everyone as she introduced herself.

"I'm Beth from the Vancouver compound. I flew here last night with supplies. I brought enough resources to set you up with whatever you need. Come on, I'll show you to your hotel."

Azar smiled warmly at the woman. There was something about her that was infectiously happy. Beth shook Azar's hand enthusiastically.

"I'm Azar, nice to meet you."

A look of recognition crossed Beth's face. "I've heard a lot about you. I was part of the team tasked with finding you when you disappeared a century ago. I have to tell you, you did a great job hiding your tracks. We looked everywhere for twenty years. It's nice to finally welcome you into the fold, even if it was under somewhat dire circumstances."

Azar just blinked at her dumbly. She was obviously another Ifrit, and reasonably old as well. Definitely a voluntary Adel recruit, as opposed to being assigned for the term of her servitude. Beth gave her one more big smile and then moved back around the SUV to the driver's seat. Everyone loaded their packs into the back and climbed into the SUV. She got squished in between Danian and Lida.

She had discovered that Lida was Ghul on the flight to Canada, and it kind of explained the obvious disdain she felt for Azar. The last Ghul she had met was the owner of a swingers club called 'Blue Smoke'. Lila was a little blonde Barbie doll with the temperament of an evil weasel. Azar had hated the bitch on sight. Even more because Lila and Bast had some kind of romantic history, which just made her stomach roll in disgust. Come to think of it, there were a lot of physical similarities between Lida and Lila. Azar turned to the Ghul next to her in the car.

"So, do you know Lila at the Blue Smoke Club?" she asked, with as much politeness as she could muster.

"We're half-sisters," came the clipped response.

Well, that explained the waves of loathing that poured off the woman.

"Oh, I see. Now that I think about it, I can see the resemblance. In the scowl, and those wrinkles on your forehead," Azar said pleasantly. "I bet family holidays are a blast at your house."

Lida shot her a look of hatred, but Azar could feel Danian's body shake with contained laughter. Though his face was perfectly blank. That mask of neutrality look must be a Jann trait.

The rest of the trip was conducted in silence as they drove through the streets of Dease Lake, and Azar was secretly glad it was spring. Snow and the Ifrit weren't comfortable companions, and even though it was desperately cold, at least it wasn't sleeting. The town was one of those blink-and-you'll-miss-it sized towns, but the streets had a fresh exuberance about it, free from the corruption of smog, gangs and the other trappings of New York City. Azar liked it on sight. Not enough to move there of course, even if she wasn't in her servitude. The minus twenty degree weather they experienced in winter sounded horrible, even if she wouldn't feel it as badly as a human.

Beth pulled into a small hotel off the highway and parked in the almost empty lot. They all piled out of the SUV like it was a lamp.

Beth opened the door to one of the rooms. "I got two double rooms under your assumed bounty hunter names, paid upfront for a week just to be on the safe side. I stowed all your equipment under the bed. There's a map on the night stand. I have to fly back tonight, so I'll leave you guys to it." She handed the SUV keys to Danian and left with a wave. Another black SUV picked her up in the parking lot.

"Azar, Danian, you can have the room next door. Go stow away your stuff and we'll meet out the front in ten minutes. We'll walk down to the diner we just passed, and I'll brief you on the plan over lunch."

Azar looked at Danian but he was already walking out the door to their room. Their room. She wasn't a prude by any stretch of the imagination, but she has assumed she'd be sharing a room with Mira.

Maybe Mira wanted to keep a personal eye on Lida, the Wicked Witch of the East? She picked up her duffel from the rear cargo area of the SUV and walked into her room.

Danian had taken the bed closest to the door. The motel rooms were exactly like every other budget hotel room in the western world. Two single beds with peach covered bedspreads from the seventies, two bedside tables with a Gideon bible in the top drawer, and a little Formica table pushed into a corner was hugged by two ripped vinyl chairs. She flicked the knob on the big old box TV and discovered that it didn't work. Surprise, surprise.

There was a tiny bathroom, not even wide enough for her to spread her arms, with a shower over bath, a bowl sized vanity and a toilet that probably came off the assembly line during Nixon's term in office. Just your average hotel room. Azar just hoped the sheets were clean and the bedbugs were friendly.

She didn't think they were going to be in Dease Lake for that long, so she didn't bother unpacking. She went into the closet sized bathroom and splashed water on her face, the tiny mirror mocking her with her reflection. She looked damn tired, and her eyes were bloodshot from a sleepless night without Bast. Her hair was mussed and her clothes were crinkled. She looked like a bag lady.

She went back out to the room and pulled a fresh t-shirt from her bag, along with a pair of tight blue jeans. Danian was sitting on the bed, sharpening a knife. They hadn't brought small arms into Canada, just in case the Customs guys got extra curious, which was why Beth had delivered them their care package personally. Apparently, Danian had no such qualms about human government officials, and brought his own arsenal of throwing knives.

She didn't want to have to try doing contortionist exercises to get changed in the bathroom. Maybe if she was fast enough, she could get changed in the room, and Danian wouldn't even notice. He seemed pretty intent on the task at hand, his body turned away from her. Azar turned her back to him as she stripped off her shirt and pants, quickly throwing on the clothes from her duffel bag. When she turned back again, Danian was looking at her appreciatively, one eyebrow raised. Azar's cheeks flooded red, but he just turned and went back to sharpening his knives, never saying a word. The silence was awkward.

Azar cleared her throat. "How's Keenan?" She

never thought she'd see the day when Keenan Reilly would become a safe topic, but here they were.

"Reilly is fine." He didn't even lift his head.

"I know he's physically fine. I mean, how is he emotionally?" Danian threw her an incredulous look. She guessed from his position, trying to speculate on the emotional well-being of another man, let alone a human, would be slightly like asking a snake to judge the emotional well-being of an ant.

He shook his head. "Uh, he doesn't cry if that helps?"

She rolled her eyes. Danian was useless as a source of information. She grabbed her toiletries bag and went into the bathroom to freshen up.

When she walked out five minutes later, all the knives had magically disappeared from Danian's bed, and the man himself had changed. He was in jeans and a cable knit sweater. A knit cap was pulled snugly down around his ears. He looked like modern day Captain Ahab. She would bet all her hard earned money that most of his knives were now hidden on his person somewhere. There was no telltale lumpiness of holsters or anything else beneath the sweater though.

He jerked his head towards the door. Azar pulled

on the down jacket that she'd thrown across the bed and she followed him out.

Mira and Lida were already out the front, and together they walked across the road to a homey little diner. A colorful sign out the front advertised that breakfast was served all day. The outside had been hammered by the weather, its paint faded and peeling, but the inside was warm and cozy. They grabbed a booth near the front windows, and a young waitress came over to take their order. She eyed Danian with something close to desperation.

Azar turned to him, and appraised him impartially. It was hard to judge the looks of the long lived against that of a human. Supernaturals tend to have their rough edges smoothed out over time. If you coupled that with rapid healing and immune systems that were all but impenetrable, they were all almost attractive by default. Their bodies physiology was completely different to that of humans, and the fact that their human forms were more like a suit than something they were stuck with, meant that their physiques were always reasonably attractive, even in the half-bloods. The only thing that set them apart from each other were their physical features, which varied just as often as that of humans.

However, a Djinn could have a nose the size of a

bratwurst, but they would still be attractive to humans. The Djinn emanated a sense of otherness that humans seemed to find so appealing and scary simultaneously. It was the buried natural instinct of a predator and prey, like insects to a bug zapper. She'd never be able to put their finger on exactly what it was, and would likely put it down to charisma or mystique.

Danian was a prime example of this. He was an average looking guy. Dark hair, dark eyes, the physique of a man who had a manual labor job. His mouth was a little too wide, and his eyes a little too far apart to be GQ handsome. But he had a mysterious air about him, coupled with a dark, brooding look that accented the wildness that oozed from his pores, and it attracted women like honeybees to a big, yellow flower.

The waitress finally found her voice. "What would you like?" she squeaked out, and Azar saw the girl grimace. Danian gave her a megawatt smile, and Azar thought the girl might pass out in a dead faint.

"I'll have the Lumberjack breakfast, and coffee." The girl smiled and scrawled something on her notepad. She went to turn away, then realized she hadn't got anyone else's order yet. Her cheeks flaming, she took the rest of their orders. Azar felt sorry for the girl as she pushed through the doors to the kitchen.

Mira muttered something about men and shook her head. "Alright, let's get down to business. This should be a simple retrieval. For those of us who were operating without caffeine this morning during the briefing, here's the highlights. The owner of the eBay account selling Ibsali is Troy Davis, a middle aged divorcee from a speck town called Hearne Creek. He's a seasonal tour guide during the summer, and makes 'rustic' furniture during the winter. No criminal history and lives alone. I expect this to be a very easy retrieval. We get in there, offer the man a ridiculous amount of money, get Ibsali and we can be on the road home by tonight. Danian and Lida, I want you guys in the forests around Davis' house, keeping an eye out for W.A.D. We don't need any surprises. Azar and I will approach Mr. Davis." When Lida scowled about being relegated to support, Mira shrugged. "Let's face it, of the four of us, Azar is the most human. We will tell him that we come on behalf of a private collector from Dallas, hand over the cash and leave. No muss, no fuss. Any questions?" Everyone shook their head.

The food started to arrive, and Azar watched Danian eat in awe/horror. The man could fit a ridiculous amount of food in his mouth before he needed to chew. Like an entire pancake.

She screwed up her face at him. "Didn't your mother teach you table manners? I grew up a street rat, and even I know better than to try and fit a whole plate of food in my mouth at once." She shook her head in disbelief.

Danian merely grunted. "I didn't touch a fork until I was at least three hundred. God put the perfect utensils on the end of our wrists; who am I to argue with practicality?"

Food flew out of his mouth as he spoke, and she cringed. He stuffed an entire sausage in his mouth to make a point, and she decided that this was a battle she would never win. If only the waitress could see him now.

She dragged her eyes away and focused on the huge club sandwich in front of her. Everyone ate in silence, and a lot more delicately than Danian, but she still noticed several of the locals giving them strange looks. They devoured their food swiftly and Mira tipped the waitress a twenty as they left.

They crossed back over the icy road, and retreated to Mira's room to suit up. She handed each of them a gun, a knife and a mobile phone from the huge portable lock-boxes Beth had stored under the bed. Lida and Danian both got changed into camouflage gear, and tucked extra weaponry around their bodies. They all had their own abilities of course, but why go through the hassle when you could just shoot a guy and be done with it?

Mira twirled her finger in the air. "Let's roll out!"

CHAPTER 7

The trip to Hearnes Creek took two and a half hours, but at least she didn't have to sit in the back with Lida. That dubious honor went to Danian. But Azar could still feel Lida staring daggers at the back of her head.

Mira drove the SUV with ease along what was essentially a gravelled forest service road, but the trip was filled with indescribable beauty. Spruce and birch trees lined the road, spreading down towards the Strikine River canyon, creating a great blanket of greenery as far as the eye could see. Mountain goats skittered up and down the sheer cliff faces of the canyon with gravity defying ease. Caribou scampered away from the sound of the SUV's engine, while the moose merely raised their heads from grazing beneath the low branches, and then turned away. They saw two black bears playing in a shallow part of the river. It was so beautiful that she just knew Bast would have loved it here.

The river's current was swift, but where the water spun out to calmer areas, the water was so clear that it created the illusion that it was glass. Mira looked longingly at the water, and at one stage Azar was convinced that the Marid was going to pull the SUV over and dive off the side of the canyon into the crisp water below.

Eventually, they made it to the township of Hearnes Creek, if it could be considered that. Nestled in the embrace of a mountain and the Strikine River, there were essentially four buildings that made up the town. There was a petrol station on the way into town, a general store, that doubled as the post office, as well as the camping and adventure sport outfitters. There was also a bar and grill with several pickup trucks out the front, and a quaint two story Tudor style house that boasted it was a B'n'B on a sign out the front. There were several more shop fronts, but by the look of them they had been empty for a long time. Paint was peeling off the exteriors and there were cobwebs across the doors and windows. A dozen houses dotted the slopes behind the main street of town.

Mira briefed us as we pulled into town. The Adel techies had pinpointed the IP address of the eBay account that had posted Ibsali to a satellite mounted on the roof of the general store. That meant they were going to have to ask for directions to Troy Davis' house. Resistance from townspeople was expected, and getting them to disregard their general distrust of strangers would be incredibly difficult. They drew straws for the job, and Azar had come out second best.

Mira pulled up in the small lot to the side of the general store. Azar grimaced as she slid out of the car and into what could only be described as a muddy bog. Thank god she was wearing her boots. She squelched her way up the porch steps and vigorously wiped her feet on the welcome mat, pushing open the heavy front door.

A small brass bell tinkled above her head as she stepped back in time to the nineties. The floor was polished hardwood, and a large counter with a timber top ran right along the wall opposite her. To her left stood a large double fridge and freezer, and to her right was a single computer, with a sign that stated hire charge was only two dollars per hour. It was old. She was actually surprised you could get the internet on the old box computer. The wall to her left was floor to ceiling shelves, stocked with dry goods and household essentials, and the wall to her right was filled with camping, hiking, hunting and fishing products. Two large free-standing shelves stood in the middle of the room, and held everything from hardware to fresh vegetables, and one side had a small library of books and movies for hire. Everything a small town needed was jammed within these four walls.

She walked up to the counter and a man in his late forties came out from a back room, a smile on his face.

"What can I do you for?"

She put on her most winning smile and hoped she didn't look like she had a bad case of indigestion.

"Hi there. This is going to sound so strange, but I'm looking for my cousin Troy's house. Troy Davis? You see, I've been trying to get a hold of him for months to tell him that my Grandma died, his great aunt, and she left him some money in her will. But the lawyers can't track him down." The man nodded sympathetically. "I'm the heir to most of her estate, but I felt that I should at least try to find him first. I know he lives in Hearnes Creek, but for the life of me I don't know where." She put her best innocent Mary Sue expression. She spoke quickly so the guy behind the counter didn't have time to process too many details. "You sure have a nice place here. Cold though," she said in a simpering voice, wrapping her arms around her waist and pushing up her breasts.

His eyes involuntarily took in her figure, and a stupid grin lit up his face. She guessed they didn't get many single women through here. Maybe she should have just worn a lower cut shirt. That way the guy wouldn't have been able to pick her face out of a police lineup. Her boobs would be another matter though.

Dragging his eyes from her chest, he cleared his throat. "I didn't realize old Pete had a sister." The man's brow lowered.

"Yeah, she left as soon as she turned sixteen, went to New York to be a dancer," she fibbed on the fly. The man nodded sagely. She guessed a lot of the youngsters from around here would try and escape this backwater town at the first possible chance.

"Yeah, I can see that. The Davis family have been here since forever. There isn't much here for a woman though. Troy lives about fifteen minutes out of town. You take the main road north, and then you'll see his mailbox after about ten minutes. Turn left there, and follow the road down about five minutes. You can't miss the place. Big log cabin, wrap around porch. Tell him I said hi."

"Of course I will." She smiled in relief. "You've been so helpful. It's true what they say; chivalry isn't dead, it's just hiding in the country," she practically purred as she grabbed a chocolate bar and threw a dollar on the counter. The man laughed, like she'd said something outrageously funny. There was definitely a lack of estrogen in this town.

She turned and waved, sauntering out of the store with a definite swing in her hips. May as well give the poor guy something to dream about on those long mountain nights.

She skipped out the door towards the SUV, the cold wind picking up her hair and tangling it in her mouth. She slid into the passenger seat again, and the conversation in the car came to a dramatic stop. It was a bit like her years at the orphanage, when the mean girls would stop talking when you walked past, so you just knew they were talking about you.

Lida looked even angrier than usual, and even Mira looked disgruntled. Danian looked amused, and that was never good.

"Ten minutes north, mailbox on the side of the road."

Mira just nodded, and reversed out of the lot. They drove in silence, and turned off at a rusty white mailbox, right where the store owner said it'd be. Two minutes down the long winding driveway, they stopped to let Lida and Danian out of the car. They melted into the forest like ghosts. Mira continued down the dirt road, and it finally opened up into a small clearing.

A picturesque log cabin perched in the middle of the house yard, looking like an honest to goodness Bob Ross painting. Fire curled from a chimney and an Alaskan malamute stood up on the porch, suddenly alert. Deciding they weren't friends, it barked loudly. Azar eyed the dog warily, and only got out of the car when a man walked out onto the porch.

He looked like something out of a lumberjack commercial, with a face like the side of the canyon. Despite how badly the sun and harsh wind had aged him, he had an earthy kind of appeal. His voice boomed over the top of the malamutes strangled barks.

"Sit down, Blue!"

The dog immediately stopped barking and sat next to his owners legs, but his eyes never left her and Mira. Animals could sense the otherness of paranormals far better than humans could. There's no mainstreaming amongst the animal kingdom.

"Can I help you?" the man's gruff voice boomed out over the distance between them.

She and Mira stepped away from the car, and walked towards the porch.

"Mr. Davis. My name's Miriam and this is my colleague Ally. We are here on behalf of a private collector regarding an item you placed on eBay. Could we come in and talk?"

The man eyed them suspiciously, and then decided they didn't look threatening. That was probably a mistake. He nodded and beckoned them inside.

The dog made no such mistake and gave them a low growl as they walked past, but he was too well trained to nip at their heels.

Troy Davis showed them through to a living room, with big comfy leather couches arranged around a log fire. "Would you like a coffee? Maybe a brandy?"

Azar shook her head, but Mira asked for a glass of water. The man disappeared for a second, and the sound of pipes rattling resonated through the house. He returned holding a tall glass of water. Mira took a sip and smiled. She was truly beautiful when she smiled. It was as if her whole face glowed.

Azar watched a stunned look cross Troy Davis' face, and for a second he looked like a deer in the headlights. It was unlikely he would ever see anyone even half as beautiful as Mira again in his lifetime. Azar cleared her throat, and Troy dragged his eyes from Mira's face.

"Mr. Davis, our employer would like to buy the Chakram, the metal ring, you put on eBay. We know from the listing that it is already sold, but we are willing to offer you twelve thousand dollars to break that agreement," Azar offered.

All the blood rushed out of Troy Davis' face when he heard the figure, and she quickly continued. "He is a private collector, and he is most enamored with this Chakram. We are prepared to negotiate."

Troy Davis sat down heavily on the armchair and dropped his head in his hands. Azar thought the man was about to cry.

"I don't have it. The guy came and picked it up yesterday."

Her heart sank and she felt like putting her head in her hands and crying right along with him. W.A.D already had Ibsali. Things just got a little more difficult. Mira interrupted the man's internal self-flagellation.

"Could you tell us who the guy was? Perhaps we can persuade him to part with the Chakram. We'll throw in a finder's fee for you if we can track him down, of course." Davis' eyes lit up.

"I didn't catch his name. Big guy, brown hair. Quietly spoken. Good manners. It was a quick transaction, I gave him the ring and he gave me five hundred bucks. Only strange thing is, he must have walked here, because there wasn't any car."

Definitely W.A.D. The Weres would have run across the border, probably so there was no trace of their entry or departure from Canadian soil. Plausible deniability was important for a hate group.

Mira stood and thanked Troy for his time. Azar smiled reassuringly at the man and followed behind Mira. She was about to step off the porch, when she changed her mind. She pulled out her money clip and handed the man five hundred dollars. He tried to wave it away but Azar pressed it into his hand.

"No, I insist you take it. I feel bad you got shafted out of the proper price of the Chakram." She winked conspiratorially. "We'll just write it off as a business expense anyway." Troy Davis beamed at her and waved as they left. Azar smiled back, but her face fell as soon as they were back in the privacy of the SUV.

"So much for being out of here by tonight," Azar sighed as Mira started the car. "If the pack is a day ahead of us, we are going to have to either beat them to the border or wait for them back at the dens, and there's no way the Pack Alphas will allow that." Mira was nodding, and dodging potholes in the winding driveway.

They stopped when they got back to the spot where they dropped Lida and Danian. Mira leaned out the window and whistled like a black bird, the predetermined sign to return to the meeting spot. They waited for two minutes, but neither Lida nor Danian returned. Mira whistled again, but another two minutes passed without either of the Adel returning.

"We'll go look for them. The W.A.D members should already be gone, but it can't hurt to be cautious. Take your gun." Mira nodded to the glove compartment where she'd stowed their guns before going in to talk to Troy Davis. "Signal if you find them. Twice if there's a problem." Mira faded into the woods on the left side of the SUV, and Azar went to the right side.

She moved slowly through the woods,

attempting to use the stealth moves that Bast had taught her during training. However, every footstep yielded almost deafening noise in the silence of the forest. She scanned the trees for any sign of Danian or Lida.

The birds fluttered noisily overhead, and every so often she would see a rabbit bounce through the undergrowth, but there wasn't any sign of trouble. She was turning back when she heard Mira whistle. And then whistle again.

Azar took off through the trees as fast as she could in the direction of the sound. She sprinted over the driveway and into the forest on the other side. She hurdled a fallen log, and dodged around a large birch tree, before running smack bang into Danian. Azar bounced off his chest and hit the ground with a thud, her head snapping back against the hard earth. She rolled to the side and cursed, lights flashing in her vision as she scrunched her eyes closed against the shooting pain in her head. When she opened them again, she was inches from Danian's face. Except he was upside down. She rolled onto her back and realized he was hanging from a tree by his feet. So were Lida and Mira; both women were squirming around and cursing a blue streak. Azar jumped to her feet, as her brain snapped back into working order.

If Danian was hanging from a tree, then who did she run into?

She whirled around and came face to chest with a man. His own face was silhouetted by the sun and she took two or three quick steps back. Far enough away, she got a good look at the guy. He was tall, and ordinary looking really, except for the pale, pale skin, tinged with green, like frost on the grass during winter. Azar backed away until she really bumped into Danian.

"The Green Man," she whispered, mostly to herself

"Call me Jack. I guess these belong to you?" He indicated her fellow Adel members hanging from the tree by vines. They reminded Azar of angry Christmas ornaments.

"Uh, yeah." She looked at Mira. "Killian is going to be pissed."

Mira just groaned.

CHAPTER 8

The Green Man, er Jack, cleared his throat and she turned back to him.

"Are you going to hang me up there too?" She was sidling closer to Danian, trying to subtly stand on the tips of her toes so that her knife would be at the right height for Danian's tied hands.

"Oh no. I was just waiting for everyone to arrive."

With that, he waved a hand and the vines unraveled, dropping the captives on the ground with a thud. Danian grabbed Azar's knife out of her belt pouch on the way down.

Jack's eyes swiveled to Danian. "There's no need for that, Brother. I mean no harm to those who don't intend to hurt the forest. I quite abhor violence. It is part of my blessing but is also a curse. I can't raise a hand in violence unless someone intends to hurt the balance of nature. But that itself is balanced by the fact that even if you were to stab me until you could no longer lift your arm, I would not die." He smiled serenely. "If you were to cut down this tree, or kill a creature you didn't intend to eat, we may have a problem though."

Danian put the knife back in her holster, though she knew he probably had enough knives on his person to start a culinary school.

Azar took the time to study the man in front of her. His skin wasn't just pale, it was translucent. His eyes were a moss green, but they were different to any eyes she had ever seen. Their irises were so huge that no whites showed, like a wolf's eyes. His hair was shaggy brown tufts, and stuck up from his head haphazardly.

She bit her lip thoughtfully. "I thought you'd be leafier, or greener."

Jack raised an eyebrow and Mira groaned. Azar figured that they were in about as much trouble as they could actually get, so there was no harm in honesty now.

Jack just shook his head and chuckled. "I thought you'd be hotter, Ifrit. I guess it was a day for being underwhelmed."

Danian laughed. He whispered something that sounded like 'burn', but seeing how he wasn't a frat boy, she decided she was probably mistaken.

"I can get far hotter, but I don't think you'd like the consequences." She turned over her palm and a little flame perched in her hand.

Jack stepped toward her, and everyone went into defensive stances. He waved them away and took her hand in his own. Azar had expected his skin to be cold, like marble, but he was surprisingly warm. He cupped her hand in his left, and put his right over her palm, extinguishing the flame. Azar was too shocked to even try and rip away her hand.

He'd just put out her flame. She didn't think that was even possible unless you were another Ifrit.

"I'm not scared of a little fire, Ifrit. In fact, some things must turn to ash in order for new life to blossom."

He removed his hand from her palm and Azar just stared at the little flower that was nestled where her flame had been. He smiled at her, and she now had an intimate understanding of how Troy Davis must have felt in the presence of Mira. He didn't just seem luminous, he *was* luminous, as the sun glinted off the crystalline quality of his skin. She couldn't breathe. She looked at the flower, and at the Fae, her gaze bouncing back and forth between them. His wide eyes stared down at her intently.

Danian grabbed her shoulder and pulled her back to stand beside him, and it broke the spell. Azar swallowed the lump in her throat.

"We'd appreciate it if you didn't try and mesmerise members of our group." There was a hard edge to Mira's polite tone.

Azar knew that some of the Fae, especially the Seelie and Unseelie courts, could entrance a human, and lead them into Faery to entertain the Courts until they grew old and died. He must have been trying to entrance her; it made a creepy kind of sense.

Jack just grinned smugly. "Unfortunately mesmerism isn't one of my abilities." He winked at Azar and she scowled back. "Let's go back to my place, I believe I have something you'd like to see."

She felt a guilty blush creep up into her cheeks. She mentally berated herself as she followed the group back to the SUV. Mira looked hesitant; torn between not causing a Fae political incident, and getting the hell out of dodge so they could track down W.A.D.

When they got to the car, Azar got stuck between

Danian and Lida again. As they bumped down the dirt road, Lida leaned over and whispered in her ear.

"I don't like you. The Ghul don't like you. You won't always have your family, your stupid boyfriend, or even the weak Marid around to protect you, and then we'll be coming for you." A chill ran down Azar's spine, but she didn't let it show. She just turned to Lida, both eyebrows raised incredulously.

"Bring it on, Rot Breath." She didn't whisper.

Danian turned to her, a frown on his face as he looked between the two women in the backseat with him. His hand touched hers ever so gently, and Azar knew that Danian had her back. He may not really care what happened to her, but he was Bast's friend. Plus, he had an inborn hatred of the Ghul, the exact opposite of the Jann.

Further conversation was halted as Mira stopped the car out the front of a tiny log cabin, half the size of Troy Davis'. Jack got out of the car and waved for them to follow. Mira looked at him, and then at the cabin, before ordering them all out of the SUV.

"Lida, stay out front and keep watch for any unwanted surprises." Lida nodded and took post next to the door. The rest of them followed Jack into the house.

The cabin was surprisingly roomy on the inside. It was an open plan, just one large area except the bathroom off the back. A fire burned to the left, but it was starting to smolder. Azar waved a hand at it, and it roared back to life. Jack grinned. It was a nice place, if a little rustic.

The cabin was split into two, an invisible line between them. On one side, a bed and a clothes chest sat in one corner, two big bookcases filled with old books in another, and the fireplace nestled between them. A big old couch perched in front of the fire and an oil painting of a woman, writing at a desk hung above the mantelpiece. A galley kitchen ran along the other wall, with a small scarred wooden table sitting in the middle of the room.

Jack indicated the couch. "Please, have a seat. I'll make coffee."

Mira narrowed her eyes. "We're fine, thank you."

Actually, Azar could use some artificial pep right now, but she kept her mouth shut. Mira knew what she was doing.

"I promise it is not spelled. All sustenance in my home is freely given and without expectation. On my honor." He bowed at the waist. She could have kicked herself. How could she forget that little nugget of fat folklore?

The Fae were tricky creatures, and liked to think they were smarter than everyone else. They conducted their lives as a series of favors and agreements. If they could get you to eat their food, through temptation, trickery or just stupidity, they would. And once you'd consumed a single mouthful, you owed them a favor. Doom on you if they decided the favor they requested was a lifetime of entertainment in the Unseelie Court. It was why it was drummed into paranormal children never to accept gifts, food or anything from strangers. That lesson had even trickled down into human folklore, but most just thought it was an old wives tale. Except in the Emerald Isle, where the Fae were most prevalent. There, those lessons stood as superstitions. Because so many of the Fae interactions involved bargaining and agreements, honor was paramount amongst their people. Therefore, they didn't lie.

They could omit the truth as much as the liked, but they never lied. Talking to a Fae was like walking on a knife's edge. It was better to listen to what they didn't say.

Mira gave Jack a hard look, judging his honor. Finally she shrugged, "I shall leave it up to my people. If they wish refreshment, it'll be on their heads." Danian shook his head and politely declined.

Azar would have preferred a direct order. In the end, she shrugged. "Sure, I'd love a coffee. But I'm under servitude for fifty years, so if you are being creative with the truth, you'll have to put off spiriting me away to Faery until after then," she joked. Jack laughed, and the sound came easily to him.

"I can assure you, Ifrit, I haven't spirited any beautiful women anywhere in the last millennium." He pulled two mugs from beneath the sink. "I grow my own beans around back. I hope you like your coffee strong and intense, Ifrit."

Coffee wasn't the only thing she liked strong and intense. She watched him turn towards the kitchenette, and squashed the thought down. *Stop it,* she growled to herself.

"My name is Azar," she found herself saying despite her internal chastisement. He threw her a sultry look over his shoulder and inclined his head.

She bit her own lip hard to snap herself out of it, and went to look at the bookshelves in the far corner of the room. She glanced up at the rows of books. There seemed to be a variety: some very old hardbacks, some paperbacks from the General Store in Hearnes Creek, a magazine or two. She touched a first edition set of *The Lord of The Rings* reverently. They were in beautiful condition, and would easily be worth fifty thousand dollars.

"They are signed as well." Jack's voice was right behind her and she jumped a little. "Your coffee."

She mumbled her thanks, finally sitting down. "If you come and live with me in my cabin, you can have them," he teased. She knew he was joking, but she was half tempted. She really liked Tolkien.

He leaned on the mantle, his coffee leaving a ring on the beautiful polished wood. His skin glittered like crushed diamonds, their sheen hiding the green tint to his skin. He waved a hand in front of the painting above the mantle, and it shimmered, dissolving. A glamor. What was left in its wake drew a gasp from Mira.

It was Ibsali.

"I think you may have been looking for this," he said as he took it down from the wall. Its bronze sheen glowed in the firelight. "I felt its energy as soon as it arose in my territory. I left it in the hands of Mr. Davis for as long as possible, but when I heard he'd put it onto the World Wide Web, I thought it might be best to intervene."

Mira reached out to take it from him, but he

moved it out of her reach. "Unfortunately, this does come with a price."

Mira's eyes narrowed and Azar slumped back in her chair. She didn't know whether to be relieved or terrified that Ibsali wasn't in the hands of the Weres. At least they could have just taken it by force from them, like stealing candy from a baby. But to take it from Jack, the Green Man, a Fae unto himself? That was quite a different story.

"What do you want?" Mira's tone was terse; the politically correct niceties were slipping away. Jack just shook his head.

"It is not a deal I wish to make with you, but with your Councilors. I shall travel back to New York City with you, to address them personally." He screwed up his nose with distaste. As a creature of nature, he would probably be appalled by the smog, the traffic and unnecessary violence of her concrete jungle home. "Trust me when I say I have no nefarious designs. In fact, the topic I wish to discuss with the Council is of an extreme importance to both our people."

Mira stared at him in a way that would have made a normal man uncomfortable, her eyes measuring his worth. Finally, she threw one last longing look at Ibsali, and nodded.

Everyone sat in awkward silence until it became unbearable and Azar had to speak. She cleared her throat. "So, Jack, what brings you to Canada?"

Azar Nazemi, master of small talk, savior of awkward silences.

The bemused expression returned to Jack's face. "Ah, North America is the last refuge of true wilderness. There are very few of the great forests remaining in the old country, and I despair that within the next two hundred years, there will be none left anywhere." The sadness on his face broke her heart. She wanted to reach out and stroke his arm, to tell him that it would be alright. Instead, she made a soothing noise, but he didn't seem to hear her. He was gazing off into the distance, a wistful smile on his face. "If only you could imagine the magical things I have seen in my long life, the things that have been lost to the destruction of progress or become forgotten with the steady march of time. It's almost unbearable. But progress must go on, and soon nature in all its forms will be damaged beyond repair, and so will I."

Azar didn't know for certain, but she had a suspicion that the fate of the world rested squarely on the shoulders of the Green Man. She'd heard Mira and Danian talking on the flight about the powers of the

Green Man. It was rumored that if he died, so too would the world. It was why he was virtually indestructible. He could not be killed by mortal weapons, or by mortal hands, a rumor he'd confirmed himself. Mortals would certainly be the cause of the Green Man's demise, if the science behind the rate of global warming was correct.

Jack shook himself out of his reverie and smiled. "It is getting late. You are welcome to remain here, of course. I would not suggest driving the road back to Dease Creek. The road is treacherous in the daylight hours. At night, it would be certain death. Or there is the B'n'B in Hearnes Creek. Quaint little place, the owners make a fabulous continental breakfast."

Mira politely refused his invitation to stay at the cabin, but assured him they would check into the B'n'B for the night. Azar was secretly glad. She didn't want to spend the night deep in the wilderness with Mr.. Tall, Green and Handsome.

A wolf howled in the distance. Not such a strange sound in the wilderness, but Jack cocked his head to the side.

"There are Weres on my territory," he murmured thoughtfully.

A scream from outside the door chilled the blood

in Azar's veins, and she rushed towards the door, right on the heels of Mira and Danian.

When she stepped outside, time slowed. It was a bloodbath, an undulating mob of animals all attacking a single target.

Lida.

CHAPTER 9

Everything slowed, the clarity of battle taking over as she jumped the rail of the cabin's tiny porch, wading into the mass of Weres. Some were transformed. Large wolves, bears, big cats and even snakes were in the mass of bodies. Eagles swooped down from the sky, and part of Azar was vaguely aware of their sharp talons slicing at her skin. She heard Mira yell to incapacitate not kill unless necessary. Oh yeah, the Green Man didn't like violence.

She lit the bear's fur on fire. It wouldn't kill him, but it would sting like a bitch. But as soon as the Werebear ran off, several wolves took its place, circling her and biting at her legs and ankles. There was only one thing to do.

Azar released her inner Ifrit, trying to do it as quickly as she could. The fire traveled up her body at astonishing speed, her wings bursting from her back like a hot knife through butter. She didn't restrain the flames that leapt from her body, instead letting them burn as high and as hot as they could.

The wolves backed away from the searing heat. She flapped her wings once, pushing herself above the mass of bodies, and flew over to the middle of the group to where Lida lay prone in the center. Careful to pull the flames on her lower body close, she stood over Lida's body, shielding her from the vicious onslaught of claws and teeth.

The ridiculousness of the situation penetrated her brain. The woman had threatened to kill her less than an hour ago. But her basic instincts were to protect, something honed from being a firefighter for most of her life. Regardless of her personal feelings about a person, nobody deserved to die like this.

She spread her wings out, the flames dripping off them and onto the flesh of the animals still standing too close. She created a ring of fire, eight feet tall around the group, like Killian had taught her. She confined most of the Weres inside the ring of flame with her. She pulled the fiery ring towards herself, shrinking its diameter, forcing the Weres to inch closer and closer to her molten heat. Some of the closer ones began to whine loudly.

"Enough!" she boomed over the cacophony of noise. "Lie down and surrender, or cook in your own skins. The choice is yours."

Apparently, turning into a fiery beast gave her a flair for the dramatic.

The fighting stopped, as the animals who had ferociously been attacking Danian realized they were trapped. Of course, Danian was also trapped, and a brief look of panic crossed his face. Jann and fire were not good friends. He schooled his features back into a battle mask, his stance tense in case the Weres attacked him again.

To make her point, Azar sent out her flames a bit further, licking at her enemies like tongues. The ones immediately around her dropped to the ground, and slowly the ones further out followed suit.

"Return to your original forms," she shouted over the noise, that had quickly changed from battle cries to scared whimpering. The air around her became blurred, as the Weres switched forms en masse. The changing of so many Weres distorted the energy around their bodies, messing with the light refraction. It was kind of like watching a wolf change into a man beneath the surface of a swirling river. If they weren't trying to kill her, it would actually have been a pretty magical moment.

The birds of prey above her screeched and took off, but a freak hail storm came down, the golf ball sized stones punishing their small bodies until they were forced to land, broken on the ground. Mira ran to where they fell, taking them into custody.

Danian waved a hand. That was it. But the results were immediate. The faces of the Weres around her got euphoric, the ones that were still shifted switched back to human. They all stood in unison, blissful smiles on their faces, every single one of them naked as the day they were born. Danian's eyes glowed perfectly white and it gave her the jeebies. Azar turned to Jack, who still stood on the porch, looking on.

"Is there somewhere we can put these guys for the night?"

Jack tipped his head towards the cabin. "They can stay in here with me, so they don't freeze to death."

Danian started herding them through the doors. That's exactly what it is, herding. The group were docile as lemmings now. Mira followed behind, with a naked guy and girl, their hands locked behind their backs with hunks of ice. Danian waved a hand at them, and warm smiles spread across their faces. They followed their compatriots into the cabin. Azar counted twenty-seven naked bodies. It seemed like overkill for a simple retrieval.

The only people left outside were the injured. One boy, he wouldn't have been more than twenty, was still lying to her left, a huge gash in his side, blood pooling around his body. A woman a few feet over was curled in a ball, moaning in pain from the burns on her body. Another man sat against a tree, a long dagger pinning him to its trunk, like a butterfly to a board. Beneath Azar's feet, blood bubbled from Lida's mouth as she gurgled out a moan. She let the Ifrit recede, until she was standing in her human form. Her naked human form. If Lida wasn't dying at her feet, she was sure she'd be completely embarrassed.

"Mira!" Azar yelled. Mira was next to her in a blink of an eye.

"Look after the boy, staunch his wounds," Mira said firmly, and Azar leapt towards the boy.

The gashes were deep, and his eyes were wide with fear. Panic overtook her, her mind flashing back to the last time she was leaning over a boy who was bleeding out in front of her.

Her breathing shuddered to a stop, cold flooding through her body until she gasped. She couldn't do this, not again. She couldn't have his life on her conscience, couldn't cause him unimaginable pain. Aaron's screams still echoed through her dreams. She wanted to scramble away from him, run until she could no longer smell fear and blood.

A large hand clamped down on her shoulder. She looked over at Jack, his face serious for once, but his eyes were reassuring. There was a shirt balled up in his other hand. A sense of well-being passed through her body, warring with the panic. She took a second to pull the shirt over her head.

Finally, she took a deep breath and looked at the bleeding boy. The three deep gashes ran over his hip, probably a stray swipe from the bear, becoming shallower as they reached his stomach. It was all that saved him. If those gashes had been deeper around his stomach, he would have bled out in seconds, the contents of his abdomen lying next to him. If she could staunch the bleeding, seal off any arteries, he might have a chance

"I'm sorry, this will hurt. But you won't be dead," she apologized softly.

She put two hands over the gash that ran over his hip to his stomach and pulsed out a quick blast of heat. The boy's scream curdled her stomach, but she moved to the next gash and repeated the procedure. And again. She was as grey and shaky as the boy when she was done. He'd passed out, thank god, but his color didn't look good. She turned to see Lida was blue, and she was barely breathing.

Mira was yelling down the phone for a medical evac. Finally getting the answer she wanted, and thrust the phone back in her pocket.

"I'm taking the injured to the Vancouver compound. Lida is in stasis, but I'm not sure if I can keep her alive until they get here." She looked at Jack. "Give me a hand putting them in the SUV?" Jack nodded, picking up the boy at his feet like he was a doll. Azar raced to open the back, dragging their duffel bags out and dropping them in the dirt at her feet. Jack laid the boy gently into the cargo compartment. Mira was there, holding Lida, and sliding her into the back seat. The tiny woman lifting the much larger Ghul looked strange, but Mira was stronger than her diminutive stature portrayed.

They went over to the two other injured Weres. Mira placing a cooling hand on the woman's burn, and Azar pulled the dagger out of the man's shoulder. His eyes burned with hatred, and she was tempted to put the blade back in. Instead she sealed up his wounds and found a little bit of satisfaction in his girlish scream. Jack's eyes were also cool when he looked at the man, and he unceremoniously helped the man to truck. He whispered something in the man's ear, and the guy turned even whiter. He hurriedly hopped into the front seat of the SUV under his own steam. Mira sealed his hands in bindings of ice, along with the woman with the burns, just in case they got any ideas on the way to the airfield.

"I'm getting choppered out. I'll arrange transport for you, Danian and Jack, as well as the captives at 0600. Be at the airfield." With that, she was in the SUV and roaring down the road.

Azar stood next to Jack as the cloud of dust settled around them. She turned and saw what had once been the front yard of Jack's cabin. It was now a scorched, muddied ring, blood stains marring the ground. It looked like the battleground it was. The trees around the yard seemed largely untouched by her flames, and for that she was thankful. The last thing she wanted to do was inadvertently start a forest fire.

"Sorry about this," she murmured apologetically as she waved her hand at the mess in front of them.

He shrugged as he picked up the bags and moved toward the cabin door. "I'll bill the Djinn Council."

The sun had started to set, and the wind was cold. The dusk was eerily free of noise. The mountain breeze had picked up and was slicing against her bare legs.

"It probably wouldn't have been so bad if you'd helped," Azar said peevishly. He held the door open for her, and she stepped into a room of naked people. It was like Woodstock in there.

"I apologize, but like I said, I can't raise a hand in violence. They fully intended to eat you after they killed you, so I couldn't step in. It was within the circle of nature. If they'd had any other plan, I may have been able to help." He shrugged. "However, you seemed to have it under control." His smile was full of respect, and Azar felt herself blush. She noticed Ibsali was back to being a painting on the wall, and she breathed a sigh of relief.

She briefed Danian about Lida's condition and Mira's orders, and then set about finding clothes for everyone. She raided the small chest of drawers pushed up against the end of Jack's single bed. Azar got her own duffel bag from the porch and pulled on some sweats.

When they were all fairly dressed and huddled around the fireplace, Azar allowed herself to relax a little. She sat next to Danian and Jack at his little hardwood table, and Jack poured them all a stiff drink.

"Is it hard for you to keep them in this state?" she asked Danian. She didn't know much about mind control, but it sounded like hard work.

Danian shook his head. "No, I've implanted the control deep. It'll stay there until I, or another Jann, undoes it. But the effort of creating such deep control has worn me out," he said with a large yawn. "If you think you can handle things here, I'm going to go and have a quick power nap."

Azar nodded. "Sweet dreams."

He grinned as he walked away. In truth, the Jann scared her a little. The fact that the Jann could implant control so deep within a person that they would never rouse, well, that terrified her. Walking around like a zombie, never functioning on this plane again, it was a horrifying thought. Though, there would be worse fates than being stuck in her oasis with Bast.

She ran her hand through her hair and looked at

the Fae across the table. He was a fable, a myth, a man with such an unnatural visage that he was beautiful. Not in the same way that Bast was beautiful, or even the way Keenan was good looking. They were too conventional, which is a word she'd never thought she'd apply to Bast. No, Jack's beauty was that of nature; not the beauty of snow capped mountains or anything so ordinary. Jack's beauty was that of early morning fog, or the porous surface of a river rock. You couldn't quite put your finger on it, but you knew that it was perfect in its perceived imperfections, untouched by humanity.

"Jack, can I ask you a kind of personal question?"

Jack cocked his head at the wistful tone of her question. "Of course."

"How do you survive being alone? Century after century of solitude, it sounds unbearable to me. I'd rather remain the way they are, locked in their mental cell, then have to endure a millennium without companionship." Her voice was more adamant than she intended as she pointed at the huddled group of Were.

Jack didn't say anything for a long time, just staring into the flickering lights of the fire. She studied his face, with his slightly wild eyebrows, unforgiving slashes over his strange, moss colored eyes. Two little creases marred his forehead, the almost-human imperfections softening an otherwise inhuman face. His high cheekbones and the soft lines of his face should have made him look feminine but instead they made him look approachable. Almost human.

He finally focused back on her face, and Azar found it hard to draw her gaze away from those eyes. There was no menace or lust in his expression, no wariness or deception. The face that looked back at her was something pure, undiluted by the grim industrialism of the modern world.

"When I was younger, I had companions. Women who would come and live with me in the wilderness, and I'd watch them grow old and die. Even those of my own race. The Fae are long lived, but I am immortal. One of the few, true immortals. After a few millennium of heartbreak, I decided no more. I could not take the loneliness, the sadness that would always follow one of their deaths. So I made the earth my companion; its smallest creatures to its tallest structures. I found solace in nature's embrace." His smile was bittersweet. "I, like nature, can adapt to almost anything."

He saw her look of pity and smiled. "Don't worry, I haven't been living like a monk. I have enjoyed every kind of woman that nature has had to offer over my long years. Women with bodies like the juiciest of peaches and skin like the richest of cream." She had a feeling that only Jack could make being a player sound poetic.

He bounded to his feet and strode over to a record player in the corner. He chewed his lip as he flicked through the vinyl records, giving a little "aha" of triumph when he found what he wanted.

Soon, the smooth sound of Dean Martin's *Sway* curled around the room, and Azar smiled too. It was a song made for dancing.

"Will you be my companion and bring me happiness, even for just a night?" Jack asked as he sauntered back to her. The question sounded indecent but his tone held no guile. His face promised just a dance, even if his words didn't. His hand reached out to her, his eyes daring her to dance with him.

She loved a challenge, almost as much as she loved to dance. "Just a dance. No sampling of any peaches," she warned jokingly. He just smiled and held out his hand.

She took it and he pulled her straight into his chest, his large hands spanning across the small of her back. He gently began swaying to the music, his movements gradually getting faster, his footwork getting more complex. He led her around the room, his body swaying against hers to the rhythm of the big band. His eyes sparkled with mischief and heat.

He twirled her quickly and when she spun back into his arms, he dipped her back so low that her hair brushed the ground, her breasts straining upwards. He was a masterful dancer, and she wondered where he had learned to dance like this in the wildernesses of the world.

He danced to steps of his own, but they told their own story, like he was seducing her with music and magic.

His hands were strong and sure against her back as he pulled her back up and into his chest. She could feel every muscle of his body against hers as he held her close and just moved them slowly around the room. The touch of his hands and the sensual way he swayed to the music was making her uncomfortably hot. He spun her in his arms again, stepping forward to stop her mid rotation, so her back was pressed against his front, one hand on her hip, the other still holding her left hand firmly. He dipped his face into her neck as their bodies swayed in perfect sync, and she let out a little gasp as he spun her back to face him again.

She lost herself in the music, and in Jack. The

song blended into the next, and the next, Jack's rhythm changing to the beat of the song.

When all that was left was the crackle of the blank space at the end of the record, Azar finally came out of her trance and leapt away. Sweat dripped down her back and she didn't think it was from the exertion of dancing with Jack. Swallowing hard, she turned her back on him, gathering her wits. When she'd gotten her raging hormones under tentative control, she turned and smiled politely.

"Thank you for the dance." She kept her voice purposefully steady, her face schooled into a mask of polite nonchalance, as if she didn't know what they'd just done was akin to vertical foreplay. He just looked at her knowingly, a crooked smile on his face. She mumbled some excuse about feeding the Weres so she could turn away.

She walked steadily over to the kitchen and busied herself making sandwiches. She kept her back to him, and hummed lightly to herself as if her body wasn't in turmoil. She could understand why humans were beguiled by the Fae, and happily gave up their lives and loved ones to spend the rest of their days amongst creatures like Jack. She had almost been as entranced by Jack as the Weres were by Danian. If Jack had tried to kiss her, she wasn't sure she would have stopped him, and that made guilt burn like acid in her gut.

Jack had disappeared from the cabin by the time she had turned to hand a sandwich to each of the entranced Were creatures. It sounded strange, but if you put food in their hands, they would eat it, and if you put a glass in their hand, they would drink the contents. She got them all settled, and sat down to watch them in their artificial bliss.

She recognized Aaron's ex-girlfriend from her file and gave the girl the stink eye. She had caused all this drama, and hurt Aaron in the process. In Azar's book, that was a far more heinous crime than attacking Lida, or even conspiring against the Djinn. Aaron had been through so much, and she had kicked him while he was down. She found grim satisfaction knowing that she would get her come-uppance. The Djinn would question them all before they sent them back to their respective packs for punishment.

The night was so silent, and her prisoners so docile that she found herself bored. She pottered around, keeping busy as the night passed. She read one of the newer books in Jack's bookcase, too scared to touch the older ones in case she damaged them.

Jack had returned sometime in the wee hours of the morning, and had offered to watch the prisoners, as he didn't need sleep. She had politely declined. She knew that if by some freak of nature they broke the Jann trance and tried to stab her and Danian in their sleep, he would be powerless to prevent it. As long as they intended to eat them, of course. So she'd remained awake and kept a polite distance between herself and Jack, until Danian took over and she excused herself to get some sleep.

Azar crawled onto the bed and shut her eyes. She was almost instantly bombarded by images. She was in her oasis, and Bast had her in a hard embrace. He squeezed her so hard that she thought her metaphysical spine might break.

"I was so fucking worried. Word filtered in that there had been a Were attack and someone was critically injured, but they couldn't tell me who, and Killian was fucking unreachable." The words tumbled out in the space of a single breath.

Azar had never heard so many expletives pass over his lips. She rubbed his back reassuringly.

"I'm fine. It was Lida; they caught her off guard. Mira took her to the Vancouver compound." She looked around her oasis. It wasn't quite as concrete as usual. There was no wind, and everything seemed a little two dimensional. "I can't believe we can still come here now that you are in Stuttgart. I didn't realize your reception reached that far," she teased.

After the traumas of the day, being in his arms felt good. He let out a relieved breath and sat them down on the sand dune. She couldn't see the individual grains of sand like she normally could.

"We are connected; I could reach you anywhere. Just the quality of the Oasis is affected. I can teach you to control what you see in the Oasis if you like. Just think about your heart's desire, and the Oasis will respond. I am merely the projector, you control the film."

He kissed her like he needed her more than his next breath. Before she knew it, her clothes were gone and she was straddling Bast's hips. "I just need to see you," he growled.

His hands roamed every inch of her skin, assessing her. Branding her. He sat up and she wrapped her legs around his waist, her chest pressed against hers. He kissed her neck and collarbone, his arms wrapped around her back. She just closed her eyes and gave over to the sensation, giving them both what they wanted. He loosened his grip and leaned her back, his hot breath running down between her breasts. He kissed his way back up her body and lifted her hips up. She kissed his jaw, nuzzling her face into his neck.

Just before he pushed his way into her aching flesh, and her eyes closed involuntarily from the pure bliss, she could have sworn she saw Jack in her oasis.

CHAPTER 10

The trip to the airport the next morning was uncomfortable to say the least. They'd piled all the Were prisoners into the back of Jack's beat up old truck, and tried to avoid using the main roads where the humans would see. A truck bed full of barely dressed humans would raise a fair amount of suspicion. Luckily, it was early and still dark, the locals were still hiding from the cold night air in their soft warm beds.

Danian sat in the truck bed with the Weres and Azar rode in the cabin with Jack. One of the younger Were girls was sandwiched between them on the bench seat. Azar had studiously been avoiding eye contact since last night's events. But she'd learned something very valuable about Bast's gift. Apparently, he didn't automatically know what was in her oasis, unless he could actually see it for himself. Just because he created the oasis, didn't give him omnipotent knowledge of every rock, tree and leaf. Or person. She was pretty sure he'd have something to say about another man being there. She felt like an idiot.

Seeing Jack in her oasis, while she was making love to Bast meant nothing. The dance had just worked her up, and put Jack in the forefront of her mind. That was all. She nodded to herself, and put the matter to rest.

The airport was no more than a clearing of trees, and a huge army carrier helicopter landed in the space at exactly 0600, sending debris flying around. She looked at the aircraft skeptically, as a pilot jumped out and told them to load up all the Weres.

"Are you sure we are all going to fit?" she asked, and got an unimpressed look in return. Well, the idea of falling out of the sky made her hesitant, so he could think her stupid as much as he liked.

She and Danian started loading the Weres into the helicarrier one by one. They were actually very biddable in their fugue state. She'd even gotten kind of fond of some of the Weres during her babysitting duties. She'd named them, like she would puppies, and some of the names had stuck, even with Danian.

"Can you give Sparkles a bit of a boost?" Danian yelled down over the rotor noise. Sparkles was one of the diminutive Werebirds, and she was a tiny little thing, shorter than even Mira. Azar had given her the nickname Sparkles, because whatever her Oasis was, it made her pretty blue eyes sparkle with glee.

Last, but not least, was Princess Fifi, a 6'3 rough looking guy, who she thought might have been the Werebear. He looked mean, even in his blissed out state, scars riddling his body from years of fighting. Mean or not, he boarded the plane docilely, so she and Jack were left on the ground. Jack gave her a lift into the helicopter, and she squashed down the little thrill that went through her as his big hands curled around her waist.

He slid the door shut as he boarded behind her and took the seat next to hers. The seats lined either side of the helicopter, a small aisle in between. They were definitely at capacity; she was jammed between Princess Fifi and Jack. Her heart lurched as the chopper left the ground, and she counted down the minutes until they landed. Jack must have been able to feel her tension, because he put a comforting hand on her knee, and a wave of calm washed through her body, even as her heart sped at his touch. It must have been one of his gifts, because he had laid a calming hand on her when she was patching up the Were boy as well. She gave him a tight smile, and he removed his hand. It was going to be a long trip.

The pilot told her, through a headphone contraption, that they were going to fly to the compound in Vancouver, and then board a private plane to New York City. Apparently, someone had paid off a customs guy not to notice the twenty-seven comatose people on the plane with them.

They were in Vancouver quicker than she thought possible, and the transfer from chopper to plane went smoothly. Azar breathed a bit easier on the plush private plane. The seats were huge and leather, and she sat up the back next to Sparkles. Jack was right down the other end of the plane talking to Danian. She closed her eyes on the flight, and surprised herself by going to sleep.

She woke when they made a rough landing into JFK and she resisted the urge to kiss the tarmac when they alighted in the private hanger. She'd missed her city, no matter how beautiful the Canadian wilderness had been. She'd missed the smog, the constant buzz of noise and even the suffocating crush of people that lined the city streets.

A squad of Adel met them on the tarmac, and loaded the captive Weres into an armored bus. Danian went with them so he could remove them from their trances once they were secure. Although he said any Jann could remove it, he explained it was like trying to untie a knot that someone else had tied. It was just easier if he did it himself.

Another black SUV pulled up for her and Jack. Azar was surprised to see Joia behind the wheel. Jack still carried Ibsali somewhere on his person, but it was camouflaged to the naked eye.

Joia strode around the front of the hood with her normal purposeful stride. She thrust her hand out to Jack, and gave him a firm handshake.

"It is an honor to welcome you to New York City. The Council is convening at our headquarters here, as you requested, but it will take a couple of days for them all to arrive. An audience has been tentatively scheduled for three days time."

Jack nodded agreeably. Azar was fairly sure he did most things agreeably, from growing seedlings to hauling decapitated bodies. "Until then, I can take you to a hotel at the Council's expense or the

Director has offered you our most deluxe suite at the Adel compound. It's entirely up to you."

She had never heard Joia be this polite to anyone, not even Killian, who was her boss. The feisty Sila must be very aware of the fact that Jack held Ibsali to sweeten her usually sour demeanor this much.

Jack's response was lost to the breeze as she tossed her duffel in the back of the SUV. She hesitated, unsure before she walked back around to the passenger seat. She told herself she was sitting up front so Jack had room to spread out in the back, plus it was the proper place for her as a member of the Adel. It was not because she didn't want to be in the back seat next to Jack. *The Queen of Denial, everybody*, her inner voice taunted.

Jack must have chosen to stay at the compound, because they crawled along in the traffic towards the Adel HQ. She wasn't worried that they'd be staying in the same place. Quite frankly, her neurosis hadn't gone that far yet. The private chambers for the Councilors and their guests were on the floor below the Adel barracks. She was sure her clearance level didn't even allow her to stop at that floor in the elevator.

The trip was blissfully silent, and by the time they were driving down into the underground car park, she was unsuccessfully trying to stifle a yawn. She longed for her bed, in her crappy little dorm room. Thankfully, Joia dismissed her as soon as they got to the elevators, and Azar didn't protest. Jack squeezed her shoulder and gave her a warm smile.

Azar threw a guilty look between them. She didn't think Jack was going to break millennium long tradition of nonviolence to kill one reasonably insignificant Sila Adel. But she did think that it was brave of Joia to be alone with the man who could so easily place his hand on Ibsali. But Joia was fast, well trained, and had huge brass balls. She'd be fine.

She waved goodbye to Jack and shuffled out of the elevator. Her eyelids felt like lead, and it took her two failed tries before she could put her key into the lock on her door. Eventually, she got it in the hole and stumbled through the doorway, falling face first onto the bed after two steps. She kicked the door closed with her booted foot, and let the encompassing blackness take her.

SOMEONE WAS NIBBLING on her ear in the blackness of sleep.

"Not tonight, Bast. I'm exhausted. I don't want to play in the oasis," she grumbled and rolled over.

"How about we just snuggle and go back to sleep." A hand ran up her side and warm breath tickled her ear.

"We aren't in your oasis, *Jaaneman*."

It took a moment for Azar to process that statement, and then her eyes shot open. Bast's smiling face was leaning over her, right there in her tiny little dorm room. She wrapped her arms around his neck and pulled him down on top of her, squeezing him tight. He rolled his considerable weight off her.

"It's so good to see you too, in the flesh." His saucy grin made his eyes sparkle. His arm snaked possessively around her hip, and she nuzzled into his chest. "The Sila Councilor arrived to see your green friend and brought me in her entourage." There was something off about his tone, but Azar ignored it. There was time to sort out any problems later. Right now she just wanted to be in his arms. She snuggled down into the warmth of his body.

He kissed the top of her head and sighed happily. "Tell me everything."

Azar recounted the trip to Hearnes Creek, omitting the dance with Jack. Bast told her that Lida was still recovering in Vancouver, but he'd heard her prognosis was good.

She told him that Lida threatened to kill her as

soon as she got a chance, and his face closed down into a scarily cold mask. "I'm going to see Lila and straighten this out now." He went to move off the bed, but she smiled and held onto his arm. As much as she wanted to see Bast scare the smugness right out of Lila and her prissy half-sister, she wanted him with her more.

"It can wait, we have plenty of time."

Her happiness faltered when Bast's face shut down into its neutral mask. That was never good.

"We have to talk." Her heart stuttered in her chest at his words. He sat on the bed next to her, and wrapped her hand in his. "The Sila Councilor has requested me for her personal bodyguard for the next fifty years, in Stuttgart. I can't deny this request, and neither can the Adel."

Azar felt like she'd been hit in the gut with a baseball bat, and now she was seeing ACME stars. Everything was slow to process. Bast, in Europe, while she was here, in NYC. They wouldn't have their fifty years together. The only silver lining to her servitude was the man lying next to her, and now if felt as if it was being torn away.

On the heels of the dazed feeling however, was raw anger. It had to be Killian who suggested this. They'd all been drifting along fine until he showed up. Now, Bast was being shipped off to Europe to be that old Sila's personal boy toy? Azar didn't believe in coincidences like that.

"That son of a bitch!" She leapt off the bed, ignoring her crazed look in the mirror, and Bast's confused face.

She slammed out of her room, and down the hall to the elevator. She jammed the button for the elevator, but it wasn't coming fast enough to satisfy her rage. She opened the stairwell door and took the stairs two at a time to the lower floor, and the Control Room. She barely registered the people moving out of her way, or the fact that her hands had lit up like a Fourth of July bonfire. All she could think of was that she was going to spend the next fifty years alone, among strangers, people who looked down on her, or outright despised her like the Ghul. She would have no one left in her corner.

She slammed through the doors of the control room and her eyes shot straight to Killian sitting at the head of the conference table. People gasped around the room, and leapt to their feet but they were too slow. She threw a fireball at Killian's shocked face. He quickly lifted his hand, extinguishing the flame instantly. As soon as the flame made contact with Killian's hands however, the slave cuffs around her wrists constricted, and Azar screamed.

Blood spilled where the cuffs cut into her skin, and Killian was around the table instantly, concern on his face even though she'd just tried to take off his head with a fireball.

"You stupid little fool! What the hell is wrong with you? You can't try to kill your master, no matter how ineffective the method may have been. The Anadari Bracelets will remove your hands as punishment!"

Azar could barely hear him as she screamed, the cuff bracelets crushing the bones in her wrists. A discombobulated part of her mind thought that they should have a handbook for Anadari Bracelets, because that would have been good information to know before she'd tried to rage maim her brother.

"Make it stop!" she screamed.

Killian put both his hands around one bracelet and whispered something in the old tongue. Instantly, the bracelet relaxed its grip on her wrist, and blood rushed back to her hand.

Her wrist had huge gashes, and blood ran down her arm as she clutched it to her chest. He whispered to the other bracelet, and it loosened also. The pain was still unimaginable, her wrists felt like they'd been smashed by a sledge hammer and she dropped to the floor, moaning. The bones had definitely been crushed.

Killian picked her up like a child, his face stoic. Azar's pain-hazed gaze took in the room, which only held a few people thank goodness. But every one of those faces contained shocked horror at what just happened. She was unsure if it was witnessing the cruelty of the Anadari Bracelets, or the fact someone attacked the Director of the Adel and lived. Either way, she shut her eyes against their faces.

Bast was just outside the doors when they got out of the room.

"What the fuck happened?" His eyes went to her bleeding, twisted wrists.

"You tell me? She burst in the room and threw a fireball at my head!" Anger radiated from Killian. "Go back in there, and convince everyone that this incident is to stay in that room. Tell them it's a direct order, and I'll be back to confirm it once I've dealt with the slave." His voice was pure contempt. "The last thing we need is for this insubordination to get back to a member of the Council while I'm out of the room. I don't think even Saraf could prevent her head from rolling if they found out she tried to kill the Director of the Adel."

Bast barely nodded, casting a pained look at Azar, and then at Killian, before turning to walk into the Control Room. Saraf, the Councilor for the Ifrit, and her father, had saved her from a death sentence once. She'd been so enraged in her tantrum, she hadn't thought of it being considered treason. What an idiot.

Killian took her to one of the empty conference rooms and laid her on the table. His hands lit up, and he held her wrists again. The fire flowed into her wounds, knitting up the torn muscles and fractured bones. The stupidity of throwing a fireball at one of the strongest Ifrit warriors in history, sunk in. She wasn't prone to murderous rages, so maybe subconsciously she'd known that it wouldn't hurt him

"Are you going to explain what the hell that was?" He was looking at her wrists intently, checking how they'd healed. He bent them back and forth, rotating them and testing the muscles and tendons. It would be a shame to have to break them again.

"You're sending Bast away to Europe because he's a threat to your position. I'm going to be completely alone because you have some macho who's-dick-is-longer problem with Bast. The Ghul want me dead for some unknown reason, and the only person who has my back, the man that I love, will be halfway across the world with the same bitch Sila who coerced him back into the Adel in the first place. I bet this was her plan all along." Her eyes stung, but she was fairly sure it was from residual pain.

He gave her a disbelieving look. "So, let me get this straight. You almost got your hands amputated because you were chucking a teenageresque tantrum, due to someone, not me by the way, sending your boyfriend away? Newsflash Azar; this isn't a Shakespearean play. He signed a binding contract with the Adel, and by extension the Council. They can do with him as they wish. Hell, if that 'bitch Sila' as you so eloquently put it, wanted me as a bodyguard, I'd be obliged to comply. This isn't a grand scheme to separate you from your lover boy, at least not on my part." He stood and stared down at her disapprovingly. She felt like a bug.

"I am the Director of the Adel, not Bast, and I have been for the last hundred years. I'm not so insecure that I need to send away my competition. So you can lose the hard done by attitude, because quite frankly, you've had it good so far."

Her cheeks flushed red. What was her problem? Ever since she'd donned the Anadari Bracelets that marked her as a slave, she was no longer herself. She felt like an insect in a world filled with giants. She was so out of her depth, with none of her prized control that she'd worked so hard to gain in her previous life. The loss of the last familiar thing from her old life just hit her hard. Her face crumbled and tears lodged in her throat, but she kept it in. She'd embarrassed herself enough in front of Killian.

She pushed herself up off the table and into a sitting position, ignoring the shooting pain in her wrist. Killian was staring at her face, like he was trying to hold her tears in her eye ducts using Jedi mind tricks. In the end, he just threw his hands up in the air and gave her a frustrated look.

"Go cool off in your room while I try to undo the mess you've created." He stopped at the door. "Actually, get the hell out of here. I'm giving you the day off. Go visit a park, or a strip club or whatever it is that gets your panties unbunched. But whatever you do, lose the self-pity, because it will only get you killed around here."

With that he walked out of the conference room, and she was banished like a naughty child.

CHAPTER 11

Azar's car was still in the parking lot of her apartment building, so she had to catch a cab from the compound. When she slid into the back seat, she'd directed the driver to the first place that popped into her head. Now, standing outside of her old firehouse, she wondered what the hell she was thinking.

She'd been lost in her thoughts on the way over, everything swirling around in her mind, but she'd made one decision on the cab ride. She refused to spend the next fifty years brooding over what she had lost, trying desperately to hold onto the little bit of normalcy she had achieved. It would be pointless and painful. She needed to accept the things she couldn't change, otherwise she was going to do something stupid and end up dead. As bad as slavery was, having her wrists squished to the point of amputation was worse.

She took a deep breath and straightened her shoulders. She knew what she had to do, and she knew it would be painful, but it was the best thing for her sanity at this point.

After her 'accident' on the Staten Island Ferry, the fire house hadn't blinked when she said she'd like to change her position from full-time to relief fire-fighter, just until she was back on her feet, both mentally and physically.

This had been the Adel's idea of course. It had been agreed by the powers that be that having a presence in the FDNY was a good thing, but they weren't going to just let her continue on with her life the way it was. So they'd gradually eased her out of the position, under the guise of PTSD.

Now, when she walked through the roller doors of the fire house, the cheers of welcome warmed her soul. The guys were doing equipment checks, and they dropped what they were doing to come over and slap her on the back, some of the guys wrapping her in those big bear hugs she missed so much. Everyone talked and laughed at once, and she fielded their questions on her health and well-being as best she could. They were a great group of guys, as close to brothers as you could get in this job, and there was a lot of love and respect in the house.

Joe was the last one to come up and hug her tightly. Joe had been her best friend before every-thing went down, and she loved him and his family like her own.

Azar stepped back and looked at him cautiously. "Can we go somewhere to talk?" Concern lowered Joe's naturally bushy eyebrows, his face instantly serious. Joe was Italian; he had dark haired good looks and a good guy smile. He led her into one of the firehouse's closed cubicles.

"Are you okay?" he asked as she shut the door behind her.

"I'm fine. How is Linda? Has she had the baby yet?" Azar felt terrible that she didn't know. They were like family, and she'd just dropped off the face of the earth, not a word in over a month.

Joe's face broke into a grin. "Yeah, three weeks ago. A girl!" Joe already had three boys, and Linda had told her repeatedly how desperately she wanted a girl. She was glad she had finally gotten her wish. She would have to send an oversized teddy bear and flowers around to the house, or something. She missed Linda and the Marconi's.

She sucked in a large breath, and let it out as a sigh. "Joe, I've decided to take a trip, just get away. Go back to my roots, to my people, until I get my head on straight. I've got myself a training position over there, and it will give me a chance to really get to know my heritage." Let him think she was talking about going to Iran. "Since the accident, nothing has felt right. I just need some time to figure everything out, re-evaluate what I want in life."

There was a kernel of truth wrapped tightly in that swath of lies. She was so good at this now. Half-truths were beginning to come naturally to her.

Joe sat down on an office chair. He nodded once, but he looked sad. "We're going to miss you. We already miss you."

It broke her heart. She was going to miss them too. "It's only for a little while."

Lie.

She knew that she would never see any of them again. Joe would be an old man by the time her servitude was complete, and she would have barely aged a day. It was best to let go of them now. It was inevitable that she would have had to do this eventually, but she'd hoped to have another decade with them at least.

"I'll miss you too. But while I'm gone, I need a

favor." She pulled her car keys out of her pocket. "I want you to take care of my baby."

Her car was a beautiful Shelby, and Joe had coveted it since the first time he'd laid eyes on it. Now, his mouth dropped open in shock. "I'll sign the pink slip over to you, and then it's all yours until I get back. Drive her, love her, okay? I don't want her sitting around wasting away because you are too scared you'll wreck her. She was made to be driven. But be careful, you aren't a Formula One driver and she's getting old," she scolded semi-seriously. As a rule, she never let anyone drive her car, but she had no use for it now, and wouldn't for a long, long time.

Joe was clearly excited to be able to drive her baby, but there was a shadow across his face.

"Are you sure you're okay, Az? You're getting help, right? You aren't thinking of doing anything permanent? Because we love you, and if you need help, Linda knows people and we'll support you every step of the way."

She looked at him confused, and then it dawned on her. He thought she was giving him her car because she was going to end her life. They'd been taught that someone giving away their possessions was a sign of someone planning to commit suicide. It had been in the mandatory training. They'd plucked a lot of people off a lot of ledges over the years.

Tears welled in her eyes, and she wrapped her arms around her friend, letting his warmth envelope her one last time. "I'm fine, Joe. I'm not going to do anything desperate. But thank you so much for caring for me like that. I'm so..." She didn't know what to say, especially when she really was saying goodbye. She pulled back, and cleared her throat, blinking back the tears that threatened to fall down her cheeks. "I should go see Fuentes. I'll see you soon. Give my love to the family, yeah?"

He nodded and she gave a little wave as she walked down the long corridor to the back of the building where the Captain Fuentes' tiny office occupied a corner. The corridor held the pictures of firefighters from the house that had died on duty in the last hundred years. All of them looked proud and fearless in their dress uniforms. Azar was glad she wouldn't be here to see the faces of any of her friends in those simple black frames. It was a dangerous job, if you weren't an invulnerable fire being.

Fuentes was a stocky man, who had seen a lot, which had resulted in him going prematurely grey. Or maybe it was keeping up with his former Russian

Prima Ballerina wife that had sent him grey. When he looked up from his paperwork, he seemed genuinely happy to see her.

"Nazemi, come on in. Ready to return to full duty?" He indicated for her to sit on the chair in front of his desk. She cleared her throat uncomfortably.

"No, Sir. In fact, I've come here to resign. I've gotten a job offer at a training facility in Iran, and have decided to pursue it." The Captain looked as shocked as Joe had but she pressed on. "I just really want to thank you for all the support and opportunities you have given me in the past couple of years, Sir. It has meant the world to me to have the support of someone I respect so greatly." The Captain smiled warmly, but shook his head.

"Geez Nazemi, you don't have to lay it on quite so thick, I was already going to give you a good reference." He gave her a wink and chuckled, before his face turned more serious. "I support you with whatever you need to do, Azar. You know there are groups and professionals that the FDNY can put you in touch with, if this is about your abduction. But if you think a change in scenery is what you need, then I wish you the very best of luck." He gave her a cheeky grin, that hinted at the humor beyond his normally formal demeanor. "But remember, there is always a place for you within the walls of this firehouse if you get sick of the sand and the soaring temperatures."

Now it was her turn to laugh, and stood to shake the Captain's hand.

"I'll email you my formal resignation Sir, just wanted to let you known in person." The Captain nodded and that was that. She said goodbye, and sent her love to his wife, Natalya.

For the next two hours she mingled among her friends and colleagues, saying goodbye to her old life. She laughed and reminisced, and by the time she walked out of the roller doors, tears stung the back of her eyes. But she wasn't finished yet.

Azar called the one person she'd been trying to avoid for three months. Keenan.

THE ONYX FELT strange during the day. There were no screaming metal bands, or Goth teens dressed all in black with metal dripping from their bodies. In fact, in the daylight, The Onyx seemed almost dull.

She said hello to the Were security guards as she walked in, some giving her a friendly, but forceful, pat on the back. She felt bruised by the time she left their group and made it to the bar.

Oliver was stocking the bar with a petite woman, definitely human. Oliver looked up and grinned, lifting her day instantly.

"Hey babe," he drawled. He jumped the bar to hug her, and she held him tightly. She needed a really good cuddle today. He held her shoulders and looked down into her face. "I heard you went all cray-cray on the head of the Adel. I have to tell you Az, that's not a good way to stay alive and intact." His words were light but his tone was serious.

She nodded, not even questioning where he'd gotten his intel from. By the end of the day, she was pretty sure the whole paranormal community would know she'd tried to fry the head of the Adel, which would make her a laughingstock. If they didn't decide to behead her for treason.

Oliver asked the girl behind the bar to pour her a whiskey on the house, and the girl gave her a dirty look. Azar wondered if she would spit in her ice.

Azar raised an eyebrow at Oliver. "You really shouldn't sleep with people you are working with; trust me I know."

Oliver gave her a too innocent shrug. "Wasn't me. I'm waiting for you to wake up one morning and decide you can't live without me." She rolled her eyes but smiled.

Oliver handed her the whiskey, and directed her to a booth at the back. "Speaking of which, he's over there."

She sighed, straightening her shoulders, and walked over to booth where Keenan was sitting. Across from him was another woman, a Djinn, probably Sila if she didn't miss her guess. The woman turned, giving Azar a dirty look as she slid out of the booth. Apparently, it was a day for hating on Azar.

She took the Sila's place across from Keenan and smiled warmly. She'd forgotten how handsome he was, with his black Irish features, and those blue eyes. He was a heartbreaker.

"Who's the woman?" Azar asked, mainly curious, but if she was honest with herself, a little jealous.

"Aaliyah; she's Danian's partner. My other handler." There was warmth in his tone, and Azar's jealousy grew until she squashed it. She couldn't have her cake and eat it too. So she just nodded.

"Judging by the stink eye she gave me just now, I think there's other parts of you she'd like to handle."

Keenan choked a little on his drink. "I've sworn off women, especially the mythical, I-didn't-know-they-even-existed type," he said as he scowled down at his glass, as if it was the whiskey's fault he choked.

"Not even the beautiful Aaliyah?" *Not even me?* The subtext was there, but she refused to say it out loud. She was here to break up with him, good and proper. "It's probably a good thing. Nothing but disaster can come from going there."

He stared at her, a mirthless smile on his face. He didn't have to say the words; she knew the irony of the statement. Her warning him off the Djinn, when she had been the cause of his precarious position in their world in the first place.

"I know, I know. I'm sorry. I hate myself for you being in this situation. I think I have a stomach ulcer with your name on it. I just want you to be careful is all." He gave her a poker face and leaned back in the booth, looking as if he didn't have a care in the world.

"Why did you ask me to come here, Azar? Danian told me that he has been giving you status reports when you ask."

Azar had thanked her lucky stars every day that he'd drawn Danian as his handler. There were other Adel in the intelligence division that he could have had, one of the Ghul or the Shaitan, and his life would have been significantly more perilous, and probably a damn sight shorter.

"I just needed to reassure myself that you were okay. If anything happened to you, I wouldn't be able to live with myself. I know that this is difficult for you, these dual worlds and allegiances. I just want you to know that I haven't just dropped you in the proverbial shark tank and left you there to be torn to pieces. If you need my help, I'll give it to you the best I can."

But it all seemed so inadequate. She'd broken his heart and stolen his life, and no amount of promises could fix that. His eyes ran over her face, assessing her.

Finally, he shrugged. "I'm fine. My welfare is not your problem anymore, you made that pretty clear. But if it makes you feel better, after the initial shock of the whole thing, I've adapted. I like Danian and Aaliyah, and we've figured out a mutually beneficial way to get along. I'm not here pining over the one that got away." He gave her a hard look that reminded her of the Keenan she'd known before she'd seen him naked, but beneath that she could see the hurt that was hiding deep in his heart. "When you didn't return my calls, I figured you'd meant what you said when you left."

She'd never gotten any of his calls, being under-ground in the Adel compound meant no cell reception, but she wasn't going to tell him that. This was the best way. Let him think that she didn't care, even though right now her heart felt like someone was stabbing at it with hot pokers.

He finished his drink and stood, coming around to help her out of the booth. Her head knew that letting him go was the best idea, she was sure of that much.

When she was standing toe to toe with Keenan Reilly one last time, he leaned close until his whiskey infused breath brushed against her cheeks. "I'm not going to tell you that I wasn't angry and hurt, because I was. But you know what they say, time heals all wounds." He closed the distance and his lips touched hers, a gentle shadow of a kiss. "Well, time and anonymous rebound sex." He grinned, and stepped away. Her mouth dropped open, and her heart hammered against her chest. Apparently, some leopards never changed their spots. Or should she say some tomcats. Keenan Reilly had been the Casanova of the NYPD for as long as she'd been at the fire department.

Aaliyah must have decided her beau had spent

enough time with his former flame, and came over to stand at the booth.

"It's time to go, Reilly. We have work to do." She turned to Azar and gave her the once over. Azar had the feeling she'd been found unworthy. "Ifrit."

Keenan winked over his shoulder as he left, looking every bit as handsome and roguish as he had when she'd first met him. Swallowing hard, she ground her back teeth to stop herself from doing something stupid. This was for the best.

"Bye, Reilly." And it felt like a real goodbye. She had a life that wasn't a safe place for a mortal man with a short life span. She repeated this over and over in her head until her heart got the message.

Azar ducked her head into Donovan's back office but he wasn't in. While she was ignoring the obvious, she decided not to examine the sense of disappointment she felt when she didn't get to see the testy Shaitan.

Wandering back to the bar, she flopped heavily onto a stool. She'd finally cut all ties to the human world and all that was left was to get very, very drunk.

She smacked a hundred bucks on the bar. "Hey Oliver, I'm under strict orders to get my panties unbunched, so rack up the tequilas."

Oliver grinned and grabbed a bottle of Patrón and two shot glasses. "I'm done for the day, so I'll join you. It's unhealthy to do shots alone." He sat down on the stool next to her, and poured out two shots. She grabbed hers and held it in the air to toast.

"To unbunching panties," she toasted.

"To going commando so bunching never happens," he countered.

They clinked their shot glass and downed the first shot, and the second shot in rapid succession.

"Bast is being shuttled off to Europe for the next fifty years," she said, grabbing the bottle of Patrón and pouring another shot.

"Ah, so that's why you went full nutbar at Big Bro. I'm really sorry Az, you know I have your back if you ever need me. I love your crazy ass." He gave her a one arm hug from the bar stool next to her. "And it's quite an ass." He leaned over and kissed her cheek hard. "Hey, now the old guy is gone, does it mean I'm in with a chance?" He teased hopefully.

Azar punched him in the arm. "Only when you're dreaming, Pussy Cat!" And sometimes when she was dreaming too. She smiled at him. Her old friends may be gone, but she had a full range of new ones. They were different, but equally as special. Oliver would always have her back, the whole pack would. "But I love you too."

"That calls for another toast," he poured another two shots. "To love and pussy... cats," he purred and she seconded the toast, laughing.

The rest of the night was a bit of a blur. At some point, the club had opened, and then there was dancing, and belly shots off some college kid with great abs and a love of tight leather. At one point, she took her panties off, soaked them in tequila and lit them on fire. She kissed Oliver, and the college kid, and then Oliver again. And Oliver a lot more. Then they danced until she couldn't feel her feet anymore.

It started to get hazy after that, but she would never forget Jerry hoisting her over his shoulder in a fireman's carry and dragging her drunken ass back to Donovan's office.

She must have dozed off, because then Bast was there, carrying her out to his car. She snuggled into his side as he drove her home.

"Bast?"

"Yes, *Jaanaman?*"

"I completed my mission. I no longer have any panties to bunch."

"I saw that, Baby. The whole club saw that," he laughed. "I should have known better than to leave you with the cat. He is a bad influence and the way he looks at you…"

Azar briefly thought she might be terribly embarrassed by that in the morning, then passed out.

CHAPTER 12

She didn't know why someone was banging on her door like a drumming monkey on amphetamines, but they were going to die a painful death as soon as she could move without wanting to throw up.

"What the hell is wrong with you?" she croaked loudly, then instantly regretted it as pain speared through her skull. She felt like she had a mouth full of cotton balls and her eyes were stuck together with Krazy Glue. Her door opened and closed, and she struggled to raise her head to see who it was. There was a half-eaten hot dog on her night stand, and just looking at it made her want to puke.

"Well, I see you took my advice. I always

wondered what a hangover felt like, seeing how it is such a bemoaned fact of human life. Looking at you now, I'm glad it will only ever be a hypothetical question. You look like shit." Killian's voice sounded smugly amused, and if she could have summoned the energy to throw something heavy at his smirking face, she would have done it in an instant, slave cuffs be damned. Unfortunately, all she could do was groan and bury her face in the pillow.

"What do you want? Did the Council decide to chop off my head? Because right now, that'd probably be a mercy," she mumbled into her pillow. She really didn't need anyone to witness her half-human humiliation.

Killian cleared his throat uncomfortably. "I've been thinking about what you said yesterday, about being alone now that Bast has been transferred to the Sila Councilors political seat in Stuttgart. So, I've come to invite you to a family dinner. Offsite. Father will be there of course, and my mother. Also a couple of our siblings, and perhaps their mothers. Whoever is in the country really." More throat clearing. "We usually get together once every couple of years, or whenever Father commands it. But I thought introducing you to a couple of us at a time might be a better plan. I left my twin sister Keeley in charge of the arrangements. You'll like her, she has a certain spunk about her too."

Azar managed to sit up in bed, prying her eyes open. Her gaze ran thoughtfully over Killian. He actually seemed like he cared. Apparently he wasn't the cold heartless asshole that everyone had warned her about.

"I'd like that," she mumbled, because her mouth was still drier than her desert homeland.

Even though the thought of meeting so much family, and spending time with her father, filled her stomach with leaden butterflies, she found that she genuinely meant her statement. Killian gave her a little smile, then his face was back to its neutral mask of her commanding officer.

"I've done as much damage control as I can after yesterday's little outburst. The news couldn't be contained, after all even the Djinn have cell phones. I convinced the higher ups that it was a family dispute, rather than a slave attacking the head of the Adel. It's lucky for you that our race has such a history of violent domestic squabbles, otherwise tonight's dinner would be a wake rather than an introduction." The corners of his mouth turned up slightly at his own joke. "I'll collect you at five. Wear a dress. Our elders are still quite traditional in their views."

With that, he slipped back out the door.

Azar squinted at the clock. It was three in the afternoon already. After she dragged her sorry body out of bed, she noticed a huge bruise on her left shin. She didn't know exactly what happened last night in those pesky blank spots, but she felt as if she'd climbed Everest.

Hoisting herself into an upright position, she grabbed her robe and toiletries kit. She was going to stand under the shower until she either pickled in her own skin or came out feeling half alive.

BAST WAS STRETCHED out on her bed when she stumbled back into her room, wrinkled but feeling better. He spread out his arms and she curled up in them with her cheek on his chest. This was what she would miss the most. Her stomach clenched and her heart ached.

"Thanks for coming to get me last night." Her words were muffled by his chest. He kissed the top of her forehead.

"You're welcome. I think Jerry was one step away from putting you in the dumpster, pack status be damned. I'm fairly sure Oliver is actually in the dumpster right now." He let out a soft chuckle and squeezed her tight. "To say you were both shit-faced would be an understatement. You two together are a force of nature. You're lucky I'm a secure man, and don't mind sharing you with that big, furry asshole."

Azar liked the vibration of his chest against her cheek as he spoke. It was like a deep rumble that reverberated through her body. She tried not to read too much into what Bast said. She knew he meant sharing her, as a friend. He didn't mean sharing her, together. Naked. She had a brief flash of Oliver's lips against hers, tasting of tequila and bad decisions. The idea of Bast and Oliver together was enough to melt her brain. Another memory flash of Oliver dancing on the bar without a shirt on, his abs rippling in the strobe lights much to her delight, and the delight of the female patrons. She also remembered Jerry punching him in the thigh, and catching him as he fell off the bar. He didn't seem happy. Bast was right; Oliver was probably snuggled around a garbage bag of dirty paper towels and empty beer bottles at this very moment. The thought made her smile. It had been a wild night, but no matter how bad she knew she should feel logically, she didn't have a single regret.

Bast's eyes stared down at her, seeing into her soul. Or at least that's what it felt like.

"I'm having dinner with my family tonight," she blurted out. Nervous fear crawled along her skin and made her sweat at the thought. She'd had friends that she'd considered family over the years, like Joe and Linda, but she hadn't had blood relations since she was five. These were people who would probably outlive her, and they would either love her or hate her until the day she died. That was a lot of pressure.

"Mmm, I know. I ran into Killian in the hall this morning and he asked if I thought it would be something you'd like. I don't know who was more uncomfortable, him or me. But I thought it couldn't hurt and told him so. I also bought you a present."

He shifted her off his chest, and she reluctantly settled on the pillow. He leaned over the side of the bed, and put a large flat box on the comforter at her feet.

"I remember the state of your wardrobe before you were conscripted. I shudder to think what it is like now. Besides, I want everyone tonight to understand that you are special, and I want you to feel special too."

Azar sat up and undid the bow. God, she loved this man. He knew what she needed before she did. Once cognitive thought had returned to her alcohol muddled mind in the shower, she'd been fretting about what to wear tonight.

She undid the bow and pulled the lid off the box. Hidden in the folds of tissue paper was a black satin dress, with tiny pink roses patterned across the smooth fabric. She pulled it out and held it up.

The bodice of the dress had a sweetheart neckline, but had black lace panel across the chest and long black lace sleeves. It had a half circle skirt and she knew it would sit about her knees. It was a stunningly beautiful dress, and Azar felt her eyes mist. She couldn't believe she was going to cry over a dress.

"It's beautiful," she murmured. She leaned over and kissed him; a soft gentle kiss that gave life to feelings she had yet to put into words. "Thank you."

Bast smiled. "It is merely an ornament. You are the one that is beautiful." He gave her a sultry look. "You know, you haven't given me a proper homecoming yet." The heat in his voice would have melted butter, and it had a similar effect on her insides.

Before she knew it, her robe was on the floor and she was under Bast.

"Is the ability to get a woman naked and under you in five seconds a secret Jann ability?" She joked as he kissed his way across her body.

"Uh-uh, it's a Bast original." His breath was hot against her skin, and a pulse of heat ran through her body. He nipped at her hip bone, along the gentle curve of her belly to the other hip. He was teasing her, and she could barely contain her moan.

"I think you should show me what other original moves you have. But you better make it fast because Killian will be here to pick me up in an hour. It would be awkward if he interrupted anything."

Boy, was that an understatement. She would curl up in a ball and die of embarrassment if that happened.

Bast looked up at her from where he was resting his chin on her abdomen, a devilish grin across his face, his body nestled between her thighs. She knew that grin and it made her heart rate soar.

He nipped the skin of her inner thigh, then the inside of her knee and Azar held her breath as he got to apex of her thighs. Her thought processes shut down as his mouth claimed her core and her body bucked towards the warmth of his clever tongue. He pinned her in place with one hand on her thigh, and his tongue swirled and dipped until she thought she was going to peel out of her skin. The man had skills. Like crazy, good skills.

One final gentle glide of his tongue had her spinning over the edge, and she tangled her hands in his hair roughly as she moaned his name. He slid up her body and kissed her hard on the lips, his tongue exploring her mouth with as much skill as it explored other places. She wrapped her legs around his body and held him tight against her. The muscles of his back flexed as he levered up on his elbows to look down at her face.

"Mmm, I love the taste of you," he growled against her lips. "I'm going to do that again when you get home tonight, but for now..." He flipped them over so fast she got a head rush. She was straddling his hips and he was looking up at her body with such open need that her core clenched in anticipation.

She eased herself down on his cock torturously slowly, until he was whimpering with need. He gave her a pained look, grabbed her hips and slammed her down, making her moan loudly as he filled her. He sat up, wrapping his arms around her body and pulling her close, his cock burying itself deeper inside her. He caught her eye, and watched her intently as she started to move, his hands on her hips helping her keep the rhythm. Her head fell back as the pleasure made her limbs feel fluid, and Bast wrapped his hands in her hair, tilting her head back so he could look in her eyes.

"I want to watch your face as you come."

A sheen of sweat broke out across her skin as she raked her nails down his shoulders, fighting to make the pleasure last a little longer. Bast's own deep moans echoed hers and they moved in symphony. She struggled to maintain eye contact as her orgasm built, and then her body was spasming around his, her eyes closed as the pleasure swept over her.

Bast was still hard inside her, and he picked up his pace, his moans becoming guttural as he brought her to the brink again, thrusting hard into her bone-less body until he threw his own head back in release.

When her muscles stopped twitching, she rolled onto the bed next to him. She caught her breath and snuggled in beside him, loving the warmth of his body.

"Do you think that will ever stop being so epic?" she croaked out. Her throat was dry and scratchy. Yeesh, she hoped her neighbors didn't complain.

"I don't think so. I'm willing to go again if you want to test the theory," he joked.

Azar felt limp. She didn't think she could go again, even if she did have time.

"I love you, you know that right?" she whispered into his chest.

"I know. I haven't loved anyone the way I love you in a long time," he stroked her hair, which was now a tangle of knots. Whoops. But Azar sensed a story there.

"You know, the sex is amazing, but I know very little about you. You seem to know everything there is to know about me. So I want to know, who was the last person you loved the way you love me?"

"Probably my wife."

Azar bolted upright in bed. "Your what?" she screeched.

Bast laughed and pulled her back down beside him. "Relax. It was a lifetime ago. Literally. She's been gone a long time." She snuggled herself back into his side.

"You better start explaining," she grumbled. She couldn't believe that she'd been seeing him for months and he never thought to mention that he'd been married once, no matter how long ago it had been.

"We got married when we were twenty, against the wishes of the Jann elders. They frown on marriages before you have done your servitude. They think, rightly I might add, that a person of twenty is merely a babe in the supernatural world. But we were in love, and in a significant amount of lust, and we had the folly of youth on our side. We got married in secret, and we lived contentedly until we turned twenty-five and had to undertake our servitude. I got placed with the Adel, and she got a worse assignment. She was very beautiful," he swallowed hard, "and got sent to live with an old Werewolf king in Russia." His face grew hard.

"The Wolf King was obsessed with her; he loved and hated her beauty, hated that she wouldn't be his forever. If one of the other wolves even spoke to her, he'd have them skinned alive in their animal form. She spent years isolated, being beaten. The Council will permit a lot of mistreatment, but Erikkah was one of the Jann's favorite daughters. When they found out about her mistreatment, they started the process of removing her from his mastership. When he heard, he took off with her, giving up his kingdom to one of the many younger wolves that were always challenging him. The Adel couldn't track him down. By the time they found them, it was too late. He'd torn her apart when he'd felt threatened. They brought her body back in a tiny box."

Azar shuddered at the thought of the terror and pain Bast's wife must have felt every day, and her heart broke for him too. It explained some of the darkness that always shadowed his eyes.

"I didn't really want to go on after that. I stayed with the Adel and worked until I forgot the pain, long after my servitude finished. Eventually enough time passed that I didn't feel the all-consuming rage anymore. Instead, I started to see that the Council, the Adel, even our whole society was wrong. The fact that Erikkah had to live with that monster for ten years before they lifted a finger to help, just showed me what a flawed and cruel system governs our society. So I left the Adel. You know the rest."

Even after a innumerable years, she could hear the pain in his voice, and see the hurt in his eyes. He bared his scars for her to see, and now she finally understood why he was so willing to give up his freedom for her. It was an echo of a past trauma, a chance to make amends for the wife he couldn't protect.

She ran her hand in small, soothing circles on his chest, allowing him to wrestle his demons back into their mental prison. She kissed a scar that puckered on his shoulder, an old war wound from a battle long gone, and wished she could kiss away the pain of his emotional scars. But that wasn't possible; all she could do was show him love and allow him to heal. They lay together for a while, wrapped in a comfortable silence.

AZAR BARELY HAD time to have one more quick shower, sprinting to the communal bathrooms and back. By the time she had eased on her beautiful dress with the utmost care, then swiped on some lip gloss, there was a knock at the door. She slid her feet into the matching pair of peep toe shoes that Bast had produced from under the bed again. Azar had actually checked to see if there were any more surprises squirrelled away under there.

She tottered over to her door now. It took her a bit to get her land-legs in anything higher than combat boots.

Killian was standing at her door, a beautifully tailored black dinner jacket and charcoal chinos gracing his huge frame.

"Good evening, Azar. You look nice." He gave her a genuine smile.

Azar mumbled a thank you and reached around

the door to get her clutch. "Okay, I'm ready," she said hesitantly.

"Have her home by nine," Bast called from his place on her bed, and she rolled her eyes.

Killian frowned as he offered her his arm, which she took gratefully. She was much more adept at walking around in boots than high heels. They walked in companionable silence to the elevators, riding down to the private parking garage.

They stopped in front of a Lamborghini Aventador, and her jaw fell to the floor. Holy shit. It was a sleek matte black, so low that it barely reached her chest. If there was a car that meant business, it was this one. It just screamed money, sex and power. She looked around the private parking garage and realized there wasn't a Toyota in the place. Every park was filled with some kind of luxury car. She raised her eyebrows at Killian over the roof of the Lamborghini.

"The Djinn; keeping luxury car makers in business since 1901?"

Killian laughed and slid into the driver's seat. Azar slid into the plush leather passenger seat with reverence. It was a beauty to behold, inside and out. Deep orange highlights ran through the interior. The leather upholstery was buttery soft. It was a luxurious coffin. Who would be able to resist bringing this baby up to its twelve cylinder potential on an open highway? But what a way to go! It purred to life, and Azar let out a little squeak of excitement.

As Killian guided the machine out of the garage, it slipped into the night and roared powerfully down the street. The thrum of the engine reverberated through her chest like a rock concert. She became vaguely aware of Killian talking to her over the noise of the engine.

"We are having dinner at Father's place on Central Park West. It's not his primary residence, of course. His palace is in his seat of power in Eastern Europe. But most of the Councilors have residences in most regions."

"Who is the Councilor for North America?" Azar asked out of interest. She'd meant to look it up, but never found the time.

"The Ghul."

Azar screwed up her nose. Great. She was going to have to move once her servitude was over. Last thing she wanted was to be under the rule of the Ghul.

Killian informed her that the Sila controlled Western Europe, the Shaitan controlled Africa, the Marid the Asia-Pacific countries and the Jann controlled South America. Azar appreciated that he gave her the information with cool professionalism and not as if she were stupid because she didn't know this already, when every five year old Djinn child knew this information and more.

It put her teeth on edge when people told her things really slowly, as if she were stupid rather than uninformed. She'd already known that the Council divided up the world into territories. In theory, the territories were just to make it easier for all Djinn to have access to one of the Council members, and the rulings were supposed to be enforced worldwide. In practice, however, the laws and rulings were enforced differently in every territory. It's why the Adel who chose to stay on after their servitude considered themselves members of every race, and of none. They enforced the letter of the law, no matter where they were.

The car continued to purr through traffic, like a puma on the scent of its prey, until they idled opposite Central Park. Killian slid the Lamborghini effortlessly to the curb in front of a beautiful nineteenth century townhouse.

As Killian moved around the car to open her door, Azar had the distinct feeling that she was Cinderella, and she'd just arrived at the ball. It was hard for the orphan who lived on the streets to reconcile herself with this level of outrageous luxury. Standing on the footpath in front of the doorway, her mouth hung open in pure awe.

"This place has to be at least four stories," she exclaimed breathlessly.

"Six actually, if you count the wine cellar and rooftop solar. Are you ready?" He dismissed its grandeur as if it were nothing.

No, she wasn't ready. She actually had the sudden urge to flee. These people weren't her people, with their flash foreign cars, Central Park adjacent monolith townhouses and countless fortunes. What could she possibly have in common with any of them, other than the blood in her veins? She didn't do designer, or Fabergé or lighting your cigarettes with hundred dollar bills. She was second-hand furniture, Walmart tank tops and pizza from the box.

A cold sweat broke out on her body. This had been a bad idea. No family was better than a family who justifiably thought you were trash.

She turned to Killian to tell him that she was going to catch a cab home, that she wasn't feeling well. But one look at the compassion on his face had her stiffening her spine. He put his hands on her shoulders, as if he knew she was about to bolt.

"Relax. All this is just a byproduct of how long we live. We aren't like that; well most of us anyway. I'm sure that they will find you as charming as I do. But you will never know if you leave now." He gave her a mock stern look. "So suck it up, Princess, because it's time for a long overdue introduction to your family." He put an arm around her shoulders and propelled her towards the ornate front door.

Azar sucked in a deep breath and exhaled slowly. She chanted to herself that it was going to be fine. She'd survived a crazed Ifrit wielding the sword of inevitable death, so this was going to be a cake walk. Killian banged the heavy brass knocker shaped like a lion's head.

Saraf, her father, opened the front door. He looked at her and smiled broadly, stepping out onto the stoop to wrap her in a warm hug. A hug!

Azar stood stiffly, partly from shock and partly due to a lack of experience allowing people in to her personal space.

"Azar, I'm so glad you could come," Saraf boomed as he thumped Killian on the back lovingly. "I was so happy when Killian suggested a family dinner. I've been keeping my distance. I didn't want to overwhelm you. You'd been through so much." Sadness drifted across his face, but it was quickly chased away by warmth again. "But when Killian told me about the little incident of the other day, we knew it was time." He gave her a look of concern, and slight disapproval, as if she and Killian had been fighting over the last cookie and gotten into a scrape, rather than her turning homicidal on his ass and almost getting her hands amputated. She snorted internally, it was all a matter of perspective.

Saraf ushered them into an old cage elevator, and went up a single floor. It rattled and squeaked precariously, and she was glad when it shuddered to a stop.

She let both men exit the elevator first, giving herself a few seconds to take in the room beyond them. The doors had opened into an enormous open plan kitchen and dining room. The eight or nine people milling about the floor hardly reduced its sense of spaciousness.

She stepped out of the elevator hesitantly, and Killian returned to her side in a show of support.

Saraf cleared his throat "I'd like to introduce Azar," he said casually.

Then they were coming at her in waves of joyous noise and bodies. Manicured hands patted her arms, and voices struggled to be heard over the top of one another. She inadvertently sidled a bit closer to Killian.

Noticing her discomfort, he put a hand out to stop them. "Okay people, one at a time. She's here all night. No need to scare the life out of her." There were a few embarrassed smiles, but everyone seemed to take a deep breath and move away at once. The whole thing made her heart pound loudly in her ears.

The woman in front of Azar just rolled her eyes at Killian, as if he wasn't the head of the Adel, just a pain in her butt. She knew immediately that she had to be Killian's sister, Keeley. If the sibling attitude hadn't given it away, her appearance would have. Although Azar could see similarities between herself and Killian, Keeley was nearly identical to him, from the shape of their facial features, to the color of their eyes. She was essentially a softer, more rounded version of Killian.

"Hi, I'm Keeley," she confirmed. "It's wonderful to finally meet you. We've been waiting over a century for this moment." She reached out and grabbed both of Azar's hands, holding them tightly, her face painfully sincere. A little bit of tension left Azar's shoulders, and she murmured a similar platitude.

Now that the initial impact was over, Killian excused himself to say hello to his mother. Not letting go of her hand, Keeley led her into the kitchen. Everyone seemed to be leaning around the kitchen island, each holding a drink, studiously trying to act casual. A tumbler of Scotch was passed to her by a guy who looked nothing like Azar at all. He had fair skin, and dirty blonde hair. He did have her eyes though. Actually, they all had similar shaped eyes and brows. It was the only real family trait shared by all, otherwise they seemed to vary in shape, size and color. She thanked the guy, er her brother, and he smiled. Actually, they all had the same smile too.

"You're welcome. I'm Caspar, and the saucy brunette over there is my wife." He pointed to a woman in a beautiful white lace dress who was talking to Killian and an older woman, who Azar assumed was Killian and Keeley's mother. Caspar elbowed the guy next to him. "This is my brother, well yours too of course, but my full brother, Cy."

The man next to Caspar didn't look much like his brother at all. He had caramel colored hair and a solemn look, but his eyes were warm. He murmured a hello, and gave her a half smile. She had a feeling that the gesture constituted quite an animated

GRACE MCGINTY

expression for the man. Azar took a thankful sip of whiskey.

Keeley excused herself to check on dinner. She gave the men a stern look as she left and they both grinned back at her.

"You guys must have been trouble when you were younger." They had mischief written all over them.

"You have no idea. We have another brother, Darius. Our mother says, that between the three of us, we aged her three hundred years. That's her in the kitchen with Keeley." He pointed to a little round woman with the same blonde hair as Caspar, who looked in her late forties. "She loves to cook. Keeley has barely been able to get into the kitchen all after-noon." There was such familial love in his tone that it made Azar's heart ache with longing for the mother she barely knew.

The evening passed in that way, people drifted over to her to introduce themselves and spend a little time getting to know Azar. What Azar didn't plan on was the huge download of information. For instance, she now knew that both Caspar and Killian's mothers lived in the townhouse together, and had co-parented their children, although neither of them had been in any sort of romantic relation-

216

ship with Saraf for at least three hundred years. She knew that Cy and his brother Darius were both members of the Adel in South America and Cy was currently on leave. She knew that Caspar and his wife Renelle had put off having children for a hundred years, and that it was a talking point amongst the Djinn society, who believe that procreation is the primary duty of Djinn couples.

She learned that she was Saraf's youngest child. Killian's mother, Siobhan, told her that Azar's disappearance had really affected Saraf. Apparently, he'd searched for decades to find her, until the trail went truly cold. Azar hadn't known what to say to that, or what to think about the sympathetic look on Siobhan's face.

When they sat down to eat, Azar sat between Malee and Cy. Azar could tell immediately that Malee was the most like herself. She was also half-blood, and her mother had died over two centuries ago. Malee looked perfectly elegant in a flowing white blouse, and a tight pair of jeans. She laughed freely and took no crap from the guys; she'd punched Caspar when he'd joked about her having a raunchy tryst with someone from his company.

Caspar hadn't joined his brothers in the Adel, instead sitting on the Ifrit Business Cooperative, a corporation that handled the business affairs for the Ifrit race. Malee, she had gathered from the others, was a crusader for the rights of mix-breed Djinn, and was fighting to have the laws regarding inter-marrying with humans or other supes, and even within the races, changed. Breeding between the races was still forbidden, due to the somewhat grue-some results of such unions. Azar had been shocked that it was illegal, but she guessed it explained some of the looks she got from the other Adel in the compound. She'd thought it had been all directed at her, but apparently some of it was because she and Bast were doing the nasty.

The fact that it would essentially be forbidden for her and Bast to have children was something she'd have to mull over later.

At another time or place, Azar would have grilled Malee over the rights of less than half-blood offspring, Freya specifically. But as it was, she was sitting around the table with the who's who of Djinn society and it just didn't seem like a wise topic to start.

When Keeley placed a platter of sliced roast beef on the table, the guys fell on it like wolves. Azar laughed as they pushed and snatched. There was a dainty clearing of a throat at the other end of the table.

Caspar and Cy's mother, Fiona, was giving the boys a very stern look. "I did not raise you like savages. Pass the platter to Azar, as she is the guest of honor." She gave Azar a motherly smile. "I can only guarantee that this will work once, dear. Next dinner party I'm afraid it's every person for themselves at meal time." She gave a frustrated sigh, and Azar could tell she'd tried to instil manners into these loveable barbarians for decades before giving up.

She accepted the plate from Cy, three pairs of hungry eyes watching her. She served herself a slab of beef, and Malee grabbed a piece while it was close, before handing it back to Cy. Bowls and dishes hustled around the table, until everyone's plates were piled high. Conversation was a pleasant hum around the room.

Cy stuffed a whole potato in his mouth and then turned to her. "So, I heard you tried to murder Killian yesterday," he said conversationally.

Azar's fork stopped halfway to her mouth, and the rest of the conversation around the table shuddered to a halt. Azar felt Cy jump as Keeley kicked him under the table. "What? I did!" Caspar shook his head and Killian pinched the top of his nose. Azar looked down at her place.

"Would you believe it was a bad case of PMS?" she asked sheepishly.

Cy laughed and nodded sagely. "I would definitely believe that. Women are crazy, and Ifrit women are the worst." He got daggers from every woman around the table then. Completely unfazed, he stuffed another chunk of beef into his mouth.

Malee patted her arm. "Don't worry about him. He spends too much time surrounded by brawn, and no brains. Their idea of conversation is limited to boobs and farts." There was a murmur of agreement amongst the women and the conversation returned to normal.

Azar was onto the last bites of her dinner when her phone rang. Oliver's name glowed on the screen. She excused herself to answer.

"Hey Oliver, what's up?"

"I need you at Bast's apartment ASAP!" His tone was frantic, almost pained, and he let out an inhuman noise.

"Shit, Oliver are you alright? What's happening?"

"It's Donovan. The Shaitan came for Freya." Another anguished sound came through the line. "They are going crazy in there. The pain is radiating out of the apartment. I can't get hold of Bast. Hurry!" The line went dead.

Azar stared at her phone in shock. Then she looked at the dinner party, and everyone was watching her. Fuck, what was she going to say? Sorry guys, I have to leave because two Shaitan are fighting and torturing everyone in a fifty yard radius over a kid I've been keeping hidden from the Djinn Council? Yeah, probably not.

She stuffed her phone back in her clutch. "I have to go." She'd have to try Bast on the way over.

Killian stood. "Is everything okay?" Cy stood too. Crap.

"Everything is fine." Killian raised a single brow. Stupid lie. They all heard. "Alright, it's not okay, but it's nothing you want to know about. I just have to go." She headed toward the elevator. "Thank you for dinner, Keeley. It was nice to meet you all. Sorry to leave so abruptly." There were some worried farewells, and Killian beat her to the elevator.

"I shall drive you where you need to go." His voice was firm.

"You can't. It's not an issue for the leader of the Adel," she argued as the elevator descended floors.

"I'm coming with you. In an unofficial capacity if I must. But I am coming, so there is no use arguing.

Now get in the car." Her Anadari bracelets had her opening the door before she even processed the words and she shot him an evil look. There definitely should be a rule about siblings having control over these things.

She slid in the car and it roared away from the curb. She directed him to Bast's place near Coney Island.

"Are you going to tell me what's wrong, or do I have to compel you to do that too?" It didn't help that he had his Director's voice on.

"Fine, but you aren't going to like it. It's borderline illegal." He just gave her a bemused look, as if he expected nothing less.

So she told him about Donovan, and Freya's abilities, about keeping her a secret due to the Shaitan's "purification" regime. She left out the part about sending the girl to live with the Sterling Forest Pack. That was unnecessary information. She told him about the Shaitan assassin, and the fact that they were having a fight in Bast's apartment building.

Killian shook his head, but there was a small upward tilt to his lips. "I knew the moment you walked into that conference room, all full of swagger, that you were going to be trouble. Malee is going to love you," he laughed as he pulled the car into a spot down an alley. He threw his jacket over the back of the car seat. A savage grin curved his face. "I haven't been in the field in such a long time."

Azar had a feeling she might see Killian's famed skills before the night was out. She was man enough to acknowledge that the possibility scared her more than it should.

CHAPTER 13

The wave of nauseating fear hit Azar as soon as she stepped into the foyer of Bast's apartment building. Wave after wave of terror inducing anger poured down through the solid concrete floors. She heard a whimper from the corner of the foyer and found Oliver huddled in on himself. It took every ounce of her self-control and training not to huddle right there next to him. She sprinted over, visually checking him for any injury.

"Oliver, are you okay?" She knelt on the floor in front of him, and caught his shaking shoulders. He gave a barely imperceptible nod.

"This is as close as I can get. The humans all left in droves. Even with my natural resistance, the fear is crawling beneath my skin like bugs." He scratched at the skin on his arm, and Azar noticed it was getting a little furry. Oliver needed to leave, right now, before he shifted in public. Although all the humans had left, it wasn't a risk she wanted to take. She helped him to his feet and led him towards the doors.

"Go back to The Onyx, get Jerry over here. Donovan might need a quick getaway." She cast a furtive glance in Killian's direction. Oliver nodded hazily and staggered out the front door.

Killian was standing in an empty elevator, one arm holding the sliding doors open. She straightened her shoulders and stepped in. She punched the number for Bast's floor, and the level of soul crushing tension rose with the floor number on the LCD panel. The elevator music was a stark contrast to the suffocating terror. It felt like a really bad horror movie; the music would stop, and she'd step out into the hallway and an ax-wielding madman would chop off her head, much to the gruesome horror of the teenage cinema audience.

By the time she got to Bast's floor, she could hardly keep from retching up her dinner. Aside from a slight tension in his jaw, you wouldn't know there was a psychological war being waged a few feet away by the expression on Killian's face. He looked like he was here for a dinner party. She could hear the shouting now, in the old tongue but it made little sense to her.

She could pick out a few words, like murder, die, pain, and it wasn't reassuring her that the situation was going to be easily resolved. Luckily she had the director of the Adel as back up; she just hoped that Donovan wouldn't see it as some kind of betrayal.

Azar aimed a hard kick at the bottom of Bast's apartment door and silently apologized. Actually, it was the least she could do. Where the hell was Bast when she needed him?

The door slammed open and two sets of dead black eyes turned towards her. Both of them looked shocked by the appearance of Killian, more so than herself, and Azar didn't take it to heart. Killian already had an impressive fireball of blue flame in his hand.

She quickly took in the scene. A tall dark Shaitan that she didn't recognize held Freya by the chin, stretching the little girl's face up so he could place a bright bronze dagger to the taut skin of her throat. The maternal part of Azar wanted to leap to the aid of the girl, to just turn feral on the man until he was forced to release the child. But the recently trained

Adel part of her brain assessed the situation, and decided not to make any rash moves. A little slip of the blade on the quarter-blood girl, and she'd be as dead as any human. Donovan was storming back and forth; pure wrath swirled around him like a thick fog.

"It's okay Donovan, ratchet it down. This assassin," she spat the word out with all the contempt she could muster, "knows this is over. He isn't going to risk killing a child, in cold blood, in front of the Director of the Adel." She said the last bit slowly, in case the assassin had been living under a rock and didn't know who threateningly held a fireball in his direction at that particular moment.

Donovan consciously tried to tamp it down, but she could tell it was difficult; the fear for his daughter's life would be demanding that he kill the threat in front of him, consequences be damned. Azar watched him struggle, but the tension lessened. It was still there, but she no longer wanted to peel her skin off to escape it.

"Drop the knife," Killian stated. It wasn't a request, it was an order. The guy looked torn between his obedience to the leader of the Adel, and fear of his race. And probably the fact that he was now outnumbered three to one. Eventually, he dropped the ornate knife to the floor and shoved Freya away. She wasted no time in flashing across the room into Donovan's arms. The little girl's face was soaked with tears, the front of her pale pink shirt damp. A small cut on her neck showed how firmly the assassin had been holding the knife against her throat. The sight of that droplet of blood made Azar growl low in her throat. He would pay for that.

Killian strode over to the assassin, who was now kneeling on the floor. She didn't know how Killian did it, but she watched on approvingly as he looped the guy's hands in cuffs of fire. The fire stayed a quarter inch from his skin, as long as the assassin didn't move his wrists too violently, he would be safe from third degree burns. She was going to have to learn that technique.

Azar went over to Donovan who was stroking Freya's hair, whispering soothing noises. Donovan met her eyes over the head of the little girl, who was nuzzled so far into the crook of her father's neck that Azar thought they might need a surgeon to extract her.

"You brought the fucking Adel Director. Are you fucking insane?" His voice was chillingly cold. Yup, this was going to be an awkward conversation.

"I was having dinner with him when Oliver called. He ordered me to let him come along basically. What did you want me to do? Ignore a direct order?" As if that were even possible. She changed the subject. "What the hell did you think you were doing? You vacated an entire city block. What if it hadn't been me and Killian, but a squadron of Adel who had no vested interest in either you or Freya?" Her voice was a stern whisper. She snuck a look at Killian, who was calling for prisoner transport. He finished his call and strode over.

"Donovan." He nodded curtly, and Donovan begrudgingly returned the courtesy. "The girl is going to have to come to the compound."

"No!" Both Donovan and Azar yelled at once. Freya's arms went tighter around Donovan's neck. Azar refused to let the little girl be locked in a cell for just existing.

"The girl has done nothing wrong under our laws. But her very existence presents some problems, as you well know, or you wouldn't be hiding her. The Shaitan will just send someone else to resolve the issue, and you both know it. She'll be safer back at the compound, where it is impossible for assassins to gain access to her."

"Unless they are already on the payroll," Donovan growled.

Killian gave him a hard glare. It was a possibility; Azar knew personally that just because you were a member of the Adel, didn't mean you weren't an assassin for your race. Lida was case in point. And Freya made a far easier target than Azar, so she had to agree with Donovan on this one.

Killian must have sensed her objection, because he raised a hand to stop it. "I will personally guarantee her safety until we can get this cleared up. We will put the issue before the Council as soon as possible. They will decide on the best course of action." Killian's protection was the equivalent of a squad of Special Forces bodyguards inside of Fort Knox.

"And if the Council agree with the Shaitan, that the problem is better off being resolved," that was the most hypocritical word for murder she'd ever heard, "rather than becoming a Djinn wide issue, what then?" Azar taunted.

Killian's mouth thinned into a hard line. "Then no matter how hard you hide her, she will be found. This is the only course of action, Donovan. Let it go, before they find a reason to charge you with treason, and the girl no longer has a protector."

Donovan's eyes shot to hers, and they shared a knowing look. He knew that if anything happened to him, Azar would fight tooth and nail to keep the girl safe. So would Bast. The girl would not be without a protector.

Donovan finally nodded his assent. "But she stays with Azar, at all times." He fixed her with a hard look. "Don't let her out of your sight." The 'or else' was implied.

Donovan turned away, whispering something into the girl's ear as he gathered up some of her things. Freya didn't let go of his neck, but she had loosened her grip. He picked up a stuffed, spotted cat and Freya squeezed it tight beneath her arm. It kind of looked like a jungle cat.

Azar fought back a smile and raised her eyebrows. "A gift?" She raised an eyebrow at Donovan but addressed the question to Freya. The little girl let out a tiny smile and absently rubbed the toy's ear between her fingers.

"Oliver gave it to me. Sometimes, he turns into a cat just like this but way bigger, and lets me ride him like a pony!" Excitement bubbled in her voice, memories of jaguar rides around the apartment obviously trumping the remnants of fear. Kids were so resilient.

Donovan put her down and told her to go and get her toothbrush and a few toys to take with her. It was endearingly domesticated.

"He's meant to be protecting her," Donovan half-heartedly grumbled. No one could begrudge Freya a single moment of happiness. Plus they both knew that if someone had come to harm her during these 'pony rides', Oliver would have been ten times more dangerous in his Jaguar form.

They turned and looked at the assassin trying to lie perfectly still on the floor, avoiding the flames binding his wrists. A few red welts on his wrists showed that he wasn't trying hard enough.

"Oliver had only been gone five minutes when that piece of filth came through the door. I guess I owe the cat a thank you." He swallowed hard. "You too."

Azar just grabbed his hand and squeezed it tightly. Touchy-feely moments of thanks were never her forte. She never knew what to say, so her policy was to just say nothing.

Adel prisoner transport turned up just as Freya emerged from her room, a bulging Barbie backpack in her hand. She took in all the soldiers, weapons strapped to their sides, and hid behind her father again.

Killian was saying something to the Adel in charge, who was nodding obediently.

The assassin was mumbling something over and over but the guards were paying him no attention as they dragged him towards the door. He looked back at Freya. "I couldn't do it! I couldn't hurt her." His face was a mask of confusion and pain as they finally dragged him out into the hall and into the waiting lift. The guy was probably losing it; she would be too in his shoes. The Shaitan accepted failure about as well as they as they accepted half-bloods.

Freya struggled to put the overstuffed backpack on her back. "Of course he couldn't hurt me; he loves me." She said it with such pure conviction that Azar just stared, unsure what to say. She looked at Donovan and he looked just as confused. From where she was standing when they'd walked in, it looked like the Shaitan planned to hurt Freya. The Shaitan weren't known for their remorse. Maybe the girl's mind was compensating for the trauma.

Freya smiled up at her, and it was like the sun coming out during a tornado. "I made him love me."

Azar's mouth dropped open as what the girl was trying to say clicked into place. She rocked back on her heels and stared. If Freya could channel positive emotions, bend people to her will using love as a weapon, such a revelation would unbalance the Shaitan's power. It could unbalance the very fabric of Djinn society. There were three benevolent societies, and three malevolent societies. For one race to flip sides, to evolve out of the niche that it had so carefully been put into a millennium before, well it could be catastrophic. Or it could be a wonder, but whatever it was, it was change, and neither the Shaitan, or the Council itself, embraced change well. No, it was best that Freya's abilities remained a secret, for the girl's well-being. The shock on Donovan's face was almost comical.

Azar threw a quick look over her shoulder at Killian, but he was still talking to the Adel in charge. "That's really good sweetie, I'm very proud, and so is your Dad. But I don't think you should tell anyone else about this, okay?" Freya shrugged and nodded.

Killian announced it was time to go, and Donovan bent down to hug Freya. She kissed his cheek noisily and slipped her hand into Azar's.

"The Council are assembling in two days time, and I imagine Freya's situation will be heard then. I will call you when I have more details," Killian said, but he didn't make any empty promises about how he thought the whole situation would play out. Donovan's eyes found hers, and the worry and fear in them was so unlike the Donovan she knew that it made her heart hurt.

She nodded to the worried father, a reassurance and a promise. She would do her best for the girl, even if it killed her.

CHAPTER 14

"Strike!" Azar yelled, her voice echoing off the walls. Freya ran around her, her arms stretched out, pretending to be an airplane and Azar laughed. "Hey kid, this is water jug ten pin bowling, not football. There's no showboating here." She ruffled Freya's dark hair until it stuck up at odd angles.

They were playing a makeshift game of ten pin bowling in the gymnasium, using empty water bottles from the coolers in the cafeteria, and a one pound medicine ball. What had started out as an easy way to get Freya out of Azar's dorm room had caught on, and soon it was a huge competition. There were teams now, and she finally grasped how competitive the Djinn really were. They'd worked out some kind of scoring handicap that took into account the weight of the medicine ball and the distance they stood from the pin. The rules had quickly compounded but everyone seemed to be having fun.

Freya was smiling and cheering as Bast stepped up to the line. He was on their team, and the guy could seriously bowl. She leaned back against the bleachers, and took in the smiling faces of everyone around her.

When they'd arrived at the compound with Freya, she had expected bedlam, or at least antipathy. But Killian had given a very dire warning about how the girl's safety was paramount, and the values on which their society was founded. He was very clear that any blatant flouting of those values regarding Freya, or any child, would be dealt with severely and summarily.

Azar wasn't sure that he could legally kill someone on the spot for assassinating a child, who was for the most part human, but his bluff worked because Freya had been accepted as some kind of compound mascot. The cooks in the cafeteria gave her extra dinner rolls and handfuls of after dinner mints. Scary Adel members brought her puzzles and toys to play with. Even the Sila doted on her. The

Sila! They were the natural enemy of the Shaitan, but they braided Freya's hair, bought her pretty wool dresses and told her how to count cards at casinos. All within the last two days!

It was like stepping into the twilight zone, and as far as Azar could see, it wasn't because she was using her abilities on the entire compound. But maybe, instead of the underlying threatening feeling you usually got with Shaitan, the switch to positive feelings had her leaking out happiness. Or maybe she was just a great kid who people couldn't help but like.

The Djinn population had been steadily decreasing for centuries, so each child was now treasured. Plus, no one knew who Freya was, or her parentage. They only knew there had been a threat on her life and she was in the compound for her protection. Luckily, there had been no other Shaitan Adel in the compound at the time. She didn't know if that was a coincidence, or due to Killian's influence, but Azar was thankful for small mercies. They were still waiting for the Council to convene, but that could be in hours or days.

Killian had told Donovan within two days, but the Council members kept their own hours and didn't care about the timeline of the common plebeian.

"Azar!" Freya tugged on her sleeve. "It's your turn. We are down ten points, you need to strike!" She crossed her arms as she said strike and Azar smiled. She still had the stuffed jaguar under her arm, and she never went anywhere without it or Azar. Damn, the kid was cute. It made her a little, well, clucky. Not that she would ever mention that fact to a single soul.

She shadowed the girl everywhere. In the last day and a half, there hadn't been a single moment that the girl had been further than four feet from her side, and always within eyesight. Although everyone had been kind to Freya, Azar didn't let her guard down for a minute. When she couldn't have her eyes on Freya, Bast took over guard dog duties. He was the only other person she or Freya could trust, and that included Killian. Her brother would do what he was told, no matter how badly it grated against his conscience.

She stepped up to the designated line and grabbed the heaviest medicine ball from the pile stacked beside it. She'd swung her arm back to deliver it down the lane when the gym door opened and Malee walked in. Her roll went wild and she only knocked down the two water bottles on the left. There was an audible groan from Bast, but Freya patted her back and smiled.

"It's okay, at least you tried," she said sagely. She was eight going on thirty-eight.

Malee walked over to her, grinning sheepishly.

"Malee, what brings you here?" Azar found herself genuinely happy to see her half-sister. She remembered Freya next to her. "This is my BFF, Freya." She wrapped an arm around Freya's shoulders. Freya politely said hello, her old world manners impeccable. Malee squatted down in front of the child.

"Hi Freya," she said brightly. "Did you help invent water cooler bowling? It looks like half the compound is here."

Malee wasn't wrong. When someone had suggested a round robin competition, dozens of people turned out. Due to the Council convening, all their personal security was currently residing in the compound as well, just sitting around twiddling their thumbs. Most of them had jumped on the chance for some healthy competition.

Malee listened intently as Freya told her how they'd just lost the game, and were now out of the competition and her sister nodded sympathetically.

Bast called Freya over to help referee the next game and Freya waved goodbye. Such was the competitive spirit of the Djinn, that they needed referees for bowling matches.

"Cute kid," Malee said a little wistfully and Azar smiled at the echoing of her earlier thoughts. "Let's sit and talk?" she suggested.

They climbed the stairs to the highest part of the bleachers. "So Saraf mentioned in passing to Killian, who mentioned it subtly to Keeley, who told me outright, that it might be judicious for me to be here today to support you and Freya." She gave a little half grin. "Such is the dissemination of information in this family. Saraf has to be impartial, and Killian has to follow the rules, but as long as neither of them approached me directly, everyone is staying on the right side of the law."

She was extremely thankful that Saraf shirked his responsibilities and arranged it so Malee could be here. She would do a much better job of protecting Freya's rights than Azar could. Advocating for the rights of half-bloods was Malee's passion.

"This is the first time that the rights of a Djinn with less than half-blood has ever been discussed by the Council, so I'm not surprised that they are keeping it very in-house and not doing a public hearing. They don't like to admit that there are far more mixed bloods than they like to acknowledge." She lowered her voice. "If the hearing goes how I think it will, I know some people who can take Freya, an underground society. They'll make sure she is protected, both against our people and the humans." Malee's face was burning with intensity and somehow it made her even more beautiful. Despite her hushed tones, several gazes were turned towards them.

"We've got that figured out already, but thank you. Your help would be very much appreciated for the trial, though." Azar put a hand over her sister's. "Seriously, thank you. I owe you one." Malee just smiled and rubbed Azar's arm.

"What is family for? Besides, this is my passion, and if they hadn't kept it so shrouded in secrecy, I would have offered earlier."

Azar had been tempted to call Malee herself, but had decided against dragging any more of her family into this mess. But now that she was here, she couldn't be happier. Malee's arrival also meant that today was D-Day, and the interminable wait was finally over.

Malee nudged her, and she finally noticed the deafening silence that had fallen over the gym. Her gaze frantically searched for Freya, but she was safely tucked beside Bast. She followed the direction of everyone's gaze and realized that Killian and Jack, the mythical Green Man, were standing in the door. Malee's mouth was hanging open as she took in the formidable figure Jack made. He was in a grey suit today, and it made the ethereal green glow of his skin even more pronounced.

She lifted a hand and waved, and Jack smiled, striding across the gym with Killian in tow, as if he hadn't just stepped into a room of Adel on high alert. He climbed the stairs easily and sat down next to her. Killian squeezed Malee's shoulder and sat on her other side.

"Azar." He said her name like it was a lifeline. "You are possibly the only Djinn that has anything resembling common sense in this Danu-forsaken city." Jack's tone was downright huffy. Azar noticed they still had an audience, and cleared her throat. Killian turned to the crowd.

"Everyone out!" he boomed in his most authoritative voice and the room instantly cleared. Azar stood to move, her Anadari bracelets making her obey the obvious command. "Sorry, Azar, not you," he ordered apologetically. Bast stood at the base of the bleachers, Freya's little hand in his own. Killian sighed. "Nor you Bast. Come on up, and you may as well bring the child too." Bast picked up Freya and swung her onto his back, piggy backing her up the stairs three at time.

Azar decided to get all the introductions out of the way in one go.

"Jack, this is Malee, my half-sister, Bast my, uh, boyfriend." She cleared her throat. She didn't know why it still seemed so strange to say that. "And the short one is Freya. Guys, this is Jack, also known as the Green Man, the Heart of the World." Apparently that last part was his official title. Talk about a high pressure position.

Jack shook Bast's hand, and then bowed deeply before kissing the back of Malee's hand. Malee blushed so red, Azar was slightly worried she'd stopped breathing. But she eventually coughed a little and murmured a polite response.

When he got to Freya, who had climbed off of Bast's back for a better look at the Fae man, Jack got down on one knee and kissed her hand, much the same as he did with Malee. Freya giggled and Jack cocked his head to the side.

"It is a pleasure to meet you, Freya the Short. You are someone very special. You will be a beautiful butterfly that has emerged from an ancient chrysalis.

Never forget." His tone was solemn, and the others looked on in bemusement. They thought Jack was talking about her small stature, but Azar knew better. Freya nodded once, equally as solemn. She seemed to know better too.

Azar tried to contort her face from shock into bemusement like everyone else. She hadn't told anyone of Freya's benevolent abilities; her ability to project love and happiness. She hadn't even told Bast. She didn't know how Jack knew, but she was certain he did. As if he sensed her shock, Jack gave her a considering look as he stood.

The moment over, Freya asked to go and climb the ropes in the now empty gym. Malee offered to watch her, and when she saw Azar's hesitation, she too got down on one knee in front of Freya and held both of the little girl's hands in her own and recited something in the old tongue. Killian responded also in the old tongue.

When Azar and Freya just looked on in confusion, Malee translated for the group.

"It was the pledge of fealty in the old language. I said 'I pledge my honor to Freya of the Shaitan, never to raise a hand in malice nor to allow any malice to land on her shoulders whilst she is in my shadow. If harm befalls her, my life shall be forfeit as her own, so that I may follow her into the earth and protect her from the Devil'." She shrugged. "Well, that's the rough translation. Killian responded that he had heard my pledge and will fulfil my forfeit if the time comes." Apparently, it was an afternoon for shocking revelations and Azar just sat there gaping like a fish.

Freya's tiny singsong voice piped up. "So you pinky swear?"

Malee laughed, and took the little girl's upheld pinky. "I pinky swear."

Freya turned to Azar and nodded, running down the stairs.

Killian's booming laugh echoed around the room. "She got a pledge of fealty, and all she needed was a pinky swear. The wisdom of youth is under-appreciated in my opinion. Let's just hope she doesn't fall off the ropes and break her neck, because I really don't want to honor kill my sister today."

Azar grimaced. "Maybe not the ropes? How about you play on the swiss ball instead?" She yelled down at the pair racing across the shiny gymnasium floor. Malee just waved her away and helped the little girl up the first rope.

Azar shook her head. "So Jack, you look nice.

Going to church or something?" she joked and Jack scoffed.

"I wish. No, I just had a meeting with your Council of Wise Elders, though there wasn't much wisdom in that room." He glanced at Killian. "Present company excluded, of course. I offered to find all the Great Weapons for them, and just hand them back to the Djinn for safe keeping. They turned me down." He muttered something in some dead language. "I gave them a dire warning and an easy solution without cost, and they say thanks but no thanks."

Killian looked pained. Azar wasn't sure if it was because Jack was spilling classified secrets to a slave, or if the Council decision was really as stupid as Jack made it out to be.

"The Council sometimes cannot see past their own history and traditions," Bast said solemnly, and Killian nodded sadly in agreement. Up until that point, Bast had sat quietly, taking Jack's measure.

Jack sighed heavily, as if the weight of the world rested on his shoulders. Which it was, in a very literal way. "It is often the way in the governing of supernaturals. It is easy to get so bogged down in the quagmire of convention, that they lose the ability to evolve and just become another dead race. Look at the Airathis." When everyone looked at him blankly, he shrugged. "Maybe that was a bit before the Djinn started to write down histories. Long story short, they were so caught up in superstition and tradition, their numbers dwindled until the last were killed out in a volcanic eruption in what is now Italy. But that is beside the point. My job is to keep the balance, but how am I meant to do so when those I am meant to be protecting fight me with short sighted obstinacy?" Yep, he was definitely huffy. "But you are important Azar, so you need to know. You need to help me. You are the balance." His eyes were fervent.

She was the what? But before she could ask he recited what he told the Council.

According to Jack, strong magic was reverberating around the world, echoing in the depths of the largest rainforests to the highest peak of Kilimanjaro. It was old magic, magic that could only be created by one of the ruling families of the Seelie or Unseelie court. As in the entire ruling family. That was like the atomic bomb of magic. And the purpose of this all-pervading magic?

To raise the Great Weapons from their earthly tombs. Literally raising them to the surface of the ground. One day soon, the remaining Great Weapons could be just lying on top of the sidewalk for anyone to find, be they human, paranormal or Fae. The thought made Azar feel sick. Their greatest weaknesses in the hands of a potential enemies, or a complete innocent's, like the guy from Hearnes Creek.

But that wasn't the worst part of it. The part that truly filled her with dread, was the why? Why would one of the Fae ruling families expend that much energy to raise the Great Weapons? Somehow, Azar didn't think it was to give the weapons back, like Jack had offered to do. Jack said that now that the magic had brought the weapons closer to the surface, he could feel the reverberations of the weapons if he was in close enough proximity. Kind of like a homing beacon.

"So you're telling me that the Council refused your offer, knowing that there was a potential threat out there, and that you could find the weapons faster than anyone within the Djinn?" Bast snorted with disgust. "I'd like to say I am surprised. Pride and suspicion over the protection of our people every time."

Azar's gaze darted around the room, as if one of the Council members would appear and try Bast for treason. Killian was giving Bast a hard look, but he seemed sympathetic to Bast's viewpoint.

Azar chewed her lip thoughtfully. "So, just to clarify, you think that one of the Fae courts means to obtain the Great Weapons and what? Start a war? Hang them on the wall as decoration?" Jack shrugged his massive shoulders.

"I do not know for sure. Maybe their reasons are purely innocent, but as you Americans say, I wouldn't bet the farm on it." Silence settled over the group as the news sunk in. A possible war with the Fae did not bode well for the Djinn. Their numbers were too small, and they were already under attack by a militant subgroup of Weres.

Jack's words about her being 'the balance' worried at the back of her mind like a thorn. It didn't seem like a throwaway comment, and Azar wanted to understand exactly what he meant. Something in the words rang true.

"Can we just backtrack for a minute? What do you mean I'm the balance?" Jack cocked his head to the side, a considering look on his face.

A door slammed shut, interrupting the moment. Azar let out the breath she didn't realize she'd been holding and turned towards the gym doors. A Shaitan that she knew by face, but not by name, was standing there in a slick black suit that told her he was one of the Shaitan Councilor's personal guard.

"The Council want to see the girl."

Azar stood, and Malee held tightly onto Freya's hand down on the gym mats. She realized both Bast and Killian had stood behind her when the guard turned towards them. "The Council stated you would not be required, Director. In fact, the girl is to come alone."

"Over my dead body," Azar said, her adrenaline leaping, prepared for a fight. "I stand as her temporary guardian; she doesn't go anywhere without me. Nowhere." She growled the last bit, but the Shaitan guard seemed unimpressed.

"The Council requested only the girl."

"The Council can kiss my ass. You can take the both of us, or I can kick your ass right now. But between you and me, that suit won't look so pretty when I burn a two foot hole in it." The guard stared at her, then at Bast and Killian behind her, and sighed.

"Whatever, you crazy bitch. If the Council wants you out, they can kick you out themselves." He smoothed the jacket of his suit. "Besides, I just bought this suit."

Azar flew down the stairs, taking them five at a time. It was a miracle she didn't fall and break her neck.

Malee still had hold of Freya's hand, and she led her towards the doors. The guard finally noticed her and visibly grimaced.

"What the hell are you doing here?" Malee just stared him in the eye. The Guard swore. "I guess you are coming too? Christos is not going to be happy."

He turned and marched out of the room, and Azar grabbed Freya's hand, throwing a quick look over her shoulder at the three men remaining in the gym. The look of concern on Bast's normally neutral face had her worried. Jack was still looking at her quizzically, as if staring at a puzzle piece that didn't quite fit.

CHAPTER 15

The further they walked down the hallways toward the conference rooms, the tighter Freya's death grip on her hand became. Azar squeezed her shoulder reassuringly and murmured something she hoped was comforting. The Adel they passed in the halls on the way to the elevators threw them worried looks, although no one knew the real reason Freya was in the compound.

The elevator doors slid closed behind them and she couldn't help but draw comparisons between herself and Freya. Less than four months ago, it was Azar in this elevator surrounded by Adel, her future equally as uncertain. She had been the one standing there, shaking like a leaf, praying the lift would break and she'd be stuck in there forever. Azar bent forward and picked the girl up, wrapping her in her arms. Freya clung to her neck, her little body trembling. She hushed her, whispering vaguely reassuring promises and trying to calm the girl's racing heart.

When the silver doors slid open again, she carried Freya to the conference room. The guard ushered them in, and she recognized the faces around the table. Every Councilor was here, including her father, who gave her a small smile.

The Councilor for the Shaitan had a mean sneer on his face. "You seem to have brought too many people, Peter. Do I need to send you back to Kindergarten with the infants of our race?"

The guard, Peter, bowed his head low. "At this point, your Honor, that would be a pleasure. They refused to allow the girl to come alone. This is a new season Armani suit." He shrugged as if that explained everything, and by the understanding way the Shaitan Councilor was nodding, apparently it did.

"You are dismissed. Shut the door behind you." Peter bowed again to the room of Councilors, and left. The Shaitan Councilor, Christos, turned back to their little group. "So the weak-blooded Shaitan gets two half-blood Ifrit protectors. It sounds almost like the punchline to a joke I once heard." He was staring at Malee with amused malice, like a cat that enjoyed torturing a mouse to death with inane banter. Malee just rolled her eyes.

"I wasn't aware you knew any jokes, Christos. I just assumed that the only thing you found funny was pulling the wings off bugs and watching them flail around." Her face was pleasant, regardless of the acid in her words. There was a twitch in Christos' face. It could have been an angry tick in his jaw, or a smothered smile, who knew? But from the familiarity between the two of them, Azar assumed this wasn't the first time they had matched wits.

"You are quite correct. I do find that amusing," he replied, completely deadpan.

"If you two have finished flirting, can we get this underway? We all have places to be." The Sila Councilor's voice didn't seem even remotely amused, and Christos threw her an irritated look. *Hmm*, Azar thought, *perhaps he was amused*. If there was ever an infatuation doomed to end in disaster, it was this one.

Azar looked around the room. Everyone looked far less formal in the close surroundings, without the peanut gallery that came with a public hearing. It was not nearly as intimidating.

"Azar, you can put the child down, no harm can come to her in this room," her father said in a calm voice. She shot one more look at the faces around them and lowered the girl down, sitting her in one of the office chairs that surround a large hardwood table. Its top gleamed without interruption, and the workmanship was some of the most beautiful she had ever seen. It looked like it had been made from a single slice of an ancient tree, the massive rings gleaming through the polished top. The edges had been smoothed, and expertly chiseled into a beautiful flowing curve. The office chairs around it almost seemed sacrilegious. It deserved equally beautiful high backed chairs, not executive swivel chairs from Ikea.

There was one glaring absence from the room. No Donovan.

"I assume you are looking for Mr. Rixton? I'm afraid he got a little tied up in Hoboken." The cruel twist to Christos' smile marred his otherwise handsome face. Well, his face would be handsome if you didn't look at his eyes. The cruelty in them negated any outward beauty. Azar had no doubt that the Shaitan Councilor had ensured that Donovan couldn't be here to defend his child, or himself. A lead balloon of dread settled in her stomach.

She forced herself to look Christos in the eye, which was no easy feat. His expression made her skin crawl and her heart hammer with fear. But she held herself steady, and stared. "Then I guess it is fortunate I am here to advocate on their behalf, isn't it?" She sat down next to Freya.

Malee sat on the girl's other side. "Me too."

She noticed her father's eyes shining with contained mirth. She didn't think the Shaitan Councilor got a lot of lip regularly.

Christos stared at Malee. "Indeed. Well, let's get this ridiculousness under way, shall we? I move that the child represents a danger to the stability of our system, and should be summarily disposed of, and a precedent set that any other 'Djinn'," he snorted derisively, "of less than half purity be disposed of in a similar manner, as seen fit by their race."

There was an uproar around the room, voices booming over the top of one another, including hers and Malee's, yelling the loudest.

"Such wholesale slaughter could not be approved by the Council, especially when the subject at hand is a child," someone shouted, she thought it might have been the Marid Councilor.

The Ghul yelled as well. "You are being short-sighted. In five hundred years we will no longer exist, as our bloodlines would be bred out until we're basically human."

It went back and forth like this until the Jann Councilor stood up and banged the conference table once, the noise reverberating around the room.

"If we could show some decorum! From what I recall, we do not murder the innocent, it is one of our key covenants. So unless someone suggests we rewrite a millennium old document to include the summary execution of children, can we stop being juvenile and come to a conclusion like educated adults." He sat back down. "Besides, you are making the child cry."

Every eye swiveled to Freya, and she was indeed sobbing. A wave of guilt swept through Azar. In her indignation, she hadn't given thought to how scary all that yelling would have been for the child. She pulled the girl onto her lap and stroked her hair, hugging her tight.

"The Councilor for the Jann is correct. We cannot approve the Shaitan's drastic solution," Saraf said considerately. "But the members for the Ghul and Sila are also correct. The child poses quite a predicament. Child, do you even possess the slave mark? A little birthmark on your body that looks like this?" He drew the six pointed emblem of the Djinn on a piece of paper and slid it over to Freya. The little girl bravely dragged her face away from where she'd tucked it in Azar's neck and looked at the drawing. She shook her head.

"I did not think so. She cannot be controlled by the Anadari bracelets without the slave mark, and therefore cannot be compelled to fulfil the one hundred years of servitude required by our laws. Indeed, it is unknown if she will even live to be a hundred, or how much of her human nature prevails over that of her Djinn heritage. Therefore, I regret to say that she has no place in Djinn society and cannot be protected under our laws."

If they treated her as if she were human, the Shaitan could send someone to finish her off and the most they would get is a slap on the wrist. The Djinn did not place much value on the lives of humans, and her father was basically demoting Freya to that status.

Seeing the beginnings of her argument, Saraf raised his hand. "That being said, she, and others like her, are still the flesh of our flesh, and while they will not get the full support of the Djinn laws, I believe a law should be passed that protects them against any purification fanatics." He fixed the Shaitan Councilor with a hard stare, "Any misdeed against them will be treated as harshly as if it was done against a full-blooded Djinn. Perhaps, just to make it a little more binding, any misdeed against those of less than half-blood purity, will be treated as if the misdeed was done to a member of the Council." And that meant a very public execution, if what Azar remembered from the law texts was still relevant.

She sat back in the office chair, speechless. Saraf had essentially cast Freya out, never to be a part of her own people, but gave her an ironclad protection from the Djinn. Whilst it wasn't the best possible outcome, it was the best that they could have hoped for. Now it just needed to be passed by the rest of the Council members.

A vote was put to the Councilors, and all except Christos of the Shaitan and the Ghul Councilor passed the proclamation.

The Jann Councilor shuffled some papers in front of him, and cleared his throat. "Excellent. It has been quite a full day. I am ready to retire to my chambers." He turned to Freya. "You have been most brave today. I am sure that someone has made provisions for you?" Azar nodded confirmation over Freya's head. "Although you can never be a part of our world, and gain the privileges and pleasures that come from being raised amongst our people, you are in the unique position, standing on a precipice between our races. Sometimes you may feel like an outsider, as if you do not belong anywhere, but remember that you are free in a way we are not. You are unbound."

The Unbound.

The title for Freya and those like her reverberated around the room, settling into the history books quietly, in a way that would not be noticeable for decades. When Djinn historians tried to trace the etymology of the title for the less-than-half-bloods, it would lead back to this moment, and to Freya's trial. But at that moment, the Council was unaware that they had changed the face of their history forever, and annexed a subculture of people who were formerly nameless outcasts in the world.

AFTER THE TRAUMA of the conference room full of Councilors, the actual transfer of Freya to the Sterling Forest Pack went smoothly. Although it was no longer totally necessary for Freya to go into hiding, her status amongst the Djinn now abundantly clear, Donovan decided it was still the safest course of action for the girl, at least until the mandate was read out at the next general meeting, when it officially became law.

That was when Donovan finally arrived at the compound, looking as if he had been put through a meat mincer and with murder in his eyes. Donovan wouldn't tell her the specifics of what happened to him, only that he'd been held against his will by some of the Shaitan Councilor's personal guard until after the Council had ruled on Freya's life. His face was covered in bruises, and he held himself stiffly. He'd been beaten, and quite badly if the way he limped was any indication, but his expression was pure malice. She was torn between insisting she patched him up, and running for the damn hills.

When Azar had filled him in on everything that had happened, she wasn't sure what shocked him more, the fact that any harm brought upon the Unbound, the label had really stuck with her, would be treated as if the harm had been brought upon a Council member, or the fact that Melee had pledged her fealty to the girl. Apparently, inter-species fealty pledges never happened. Not in a couple of hundred years, anyway.

Donovan was going to take Freya to a diner on Route 87, where Oliver would collect her and see that she got settled in to her new home amongst the pack.

As Azar waved to the girl from the foyer of the compound's main entrance, she found herself over-whelmed with maternal panic. What if the Weres treated her like a freak, made her life miserable? What if she made the Weres miserable? What if the Shaitan tracked her down before the mandate had passed at the general meeting, which was scheduled after the trial of the W.A.D members?

But most of all, Azar felt incredibly sad to be saying goodbye to Freya. She knew she would see her again soon, but the girl had been her constant shadow for days, and she'd become used to having her right there. Now Freya was gone, she felt like she was missing something.

Bast, who had come to say goodbye too, wrapped an arm around Azar's shoulders. "Are you okay?" he asked softly.

Azar nodded. She couldn't really tell him she was feeling downright maternal for the first time in her long life. As if there was something she had been missing all these years, some hidden joy that she didn't realize she'd lacked until it was gone. That would completely freak him out.

Plus there was the whole interracial dating thing;

she could just imagine what people would say if they had a child. Hell, she didn't even know what the kind of child they would have. She had heard whispers of misbegotten children, half formed, or crazed, that were born from the union between different species, but she didn't know if that was just urban legend or based on fact. She vowed to herself that she would look into the matter before she made any decisions or voiced any of her desires to Bast. She'd just enjoy the time she had left with him, before he headed back to Stuttgart with the Sila Councilor.

The trial of the Weres who had killed the two Djinn kids was set for the next day. Apparently, the Councilors were all very eager to get back to their own territories. The loss of Freya, and soon Bast, made her feel incredibly lonely all over again. Though this time she was determined not to flip out and try and kill someone. She would take her fate with grace and poise. She snorted internally. She never took anything with poise in her life.

They met Malee on the way back in the bowels of the Compound. She was rugged up in a pea green wool coat, and her tight jeans were tucked into combat boots. The effect of the outfit should have made her look juvenile, or at least grungy, but instead she looked self-assured, and graceful. She had handled the Shaitan Councilor without batting so much as an eyelid. Azar had sensed a history there, and her curiosity got the better of her; she just had to ask what the story was. Malee waved her hands and a little color ran into her cheeks.

"Christos and I battle more frequently than either of us would like. We cannot stand each other; I cannot abide everything he stands for, and he sees me as a nuisance, protecting people from his barbaric laws. If I wasn't my father's daughter, he would probably have had me offed decades ago." She waved her hand dismissively. "I live to be a thorn in his side, the arrogant asshole."

Azar didn't know if holding such a view about a Councilor was considered traitorous, but she was inclined to agree. Christos was indeed a scary, scary arrogant asshole. Bast laughed loudly, and several people turned to look.

She wasn't so sure that Malee's main emotion towards Christos was hate, although she didn't doubt that a part of her did hate everything he stood for. But if anyone knew that there was a fine line between love and hate, it was Azar. It made her a little sad for her half-sister. If her relationship with Bast was frowned upon, then any kind of romance between a half-blood Ifrit and the Councilor for the

Shaitan was a one-way train to Apocalyptic Disasterville. She just hoped that Malee knew what she was doing.

Everyone hugged and said goodbye, and she watched Malee until she turned the corner and left. A warm smile lit Bast's face.

"I've got a surprise for you," he whispered in her ear. A small shiver of anticipation ran down her spine. She really enjoyed Bast's idea of a surprise. He led her to his room, which was pretty much an exact replica of hers in layout, except he'd moved all his plants from his office in Coney Island to this room when he'd taken up his servitude for her.

Now, as they entered the room, she let out a small gasp of surprise. The room was filled with flowering rose bushes and candles, rose petals covered every surface. In the middle of the bed sat a tray, with a bottle of wine, a bowl of strawberries, a dish of whipped cream, and a crystal bowl of Hershey kisses. On the TV in front of him, the menu screen for *Dirty Dancing* waited to be played.

"Chocolate, wine, strawberries, whipped cream and Patrick Swayze. If there was ever a textbook seduction scene, this would be it." Her voice was low and sultry.

"It's hard to import romance into the compound;

this was the best I could do." He wrapped his arms around her. "And tonight isn't about seduction, tonight is just about you and me, being together, and letting me pamper you."

She raised her eyebrows. She definitely didn't believe the part about no funny business. When they were together, it was like throwing a match into a tinderbox. They would combust, whether they wanted it or not. But she appreciated the thought.

He led her to the bed and pressed play, nestling her against a huge mound of pillows, her head resting on his shoulder. He fed her strawberries as the opening credits started, and the unique sound of Frankie Valli and the Four Seasons, *Big Girls Don't Cry* filled the room. He handed her a glass of red wine, and she swirled it around in her mouth, the smooth flavor telling her that it was a great vintage. She let herself melt into Bast's arms, and just be.

This was what it would have been like if she were raised within Djinn society. She would have already done her servitude, and Bast would have done his, and they wouldn't be in the compound but in Azar's little apartment. Or maybe they'd have a house of their own, filled with plants that hated Azar, and a big fireplace where they'd make s'mores every weekend and watch black and white movies. They'd have dinner parties with her family, maybe even Mira and her father Moselle. They'd have a dog and a cat to sit in front of the fireplace, but no kids because it was forbidden.

On the flip-side, there would be no Pack or Oliver, as she would not have been in a position to recognize and track down the Rogue Ifrit. There would have been no reason to go to The Onyx, so she wouldn't have met Donovan or Freya. Maybe they'd be living in a world ruled by the Balraka.

She let out a heavy sigh. For all the complexities that ruled her life now, fate had given her a good life, filled with love, a new family and more friends than she knew what to do with. Sure, she may have had all those things if her father had found her when she was a child, and a whole lot less suffering in her early years, but she wouldn't be the person she was today, and she was proud of that person.

She let out a sigh, and closed her eyes. She just wanted to rest in the arms of the man she loved for a while, without having to evaluate her life choices for once. Her lids started to feel heavy and she let them droop. She fell into the blissful sleep of the loved.

What felt like minutes later, Bast was shaking her awake.

"You are going to miss my favorite part," he whispered loudly.

"You have a favorite part of *Dirty Dancing*? Is there something you want to tell me? No judgment. If I was a guy, Patrick Swayze topless would make me doubt my sexuality too," she mumbled groggily, yawning widely. He just shushed her.

On screen, Johnny was saying that famous line, and pulling Baby up to do an impossibly perfect dance that they hadn't really been practicing because they'd been bumping uglies for a week. But hey, Azar appreciated the sentiment as much as the next estrogen laden woman.

"I can't believe you woke me up for this," she grumbled. Bast hugged her close and laughed.

"Well, your snoring was ruining a perfectly romantic moment." He ducked his head to miss the cushion aimed at his face, and grabbed her around the waist, hauling her into his arms. His hand slid up to cup her face, and he kissed her temples, her eyelids, the tip of her nose and then nibbled at her lips until she opened them, allowing him to suck her lower lip into his mouth. She gave a satisfied moan, and shifted to straddle him. His smile was pure trouble and she couldn't keep the answering grin off her face.

No seduction? She hadn't believed it for a second.

CHAPTER 16

Azar ducked her head to hide another yawn. She hadn't realized how tedious trials were when you weren't the one in the firing line. She sat high in the stands of the Ifrit section of the hearing room, listening to the charges being read out to the fifteenth, or sixteenth, member of Weres Against Djinn. It didn't help that they'd decided to accuse and sentence each member separately, listing their crimes before releasing them to the punishment of their individual packs, clans, flocks and so on. It was so tedious that even the Council members were taking turns presiding over the trials.

Saraf's voice droned on. "The Djinn find you guilty of one count conspiracy to harm, one count of grievous bodily harm, one count of manslaughter, four counts of assault..." The Were on the stand was Princess Fifi, though apparently his name was really Oswald McNamara, and he was a Werebear. Apparently, they were solitary and the Adel had had a hard time rustling up two other Werebears to mete out his punishment. She swung her eyes to the Werebear contingent sitting in the visitors seating. They didn't seem impressed to be there either, and Azar would happily bet that as soon as they picked up old Ozzy from the Adel cells, they'd take him out to the car park, punch him in the head a couple of times for inconveniencing them, and then they'd all go their separate ways. They didn't really care about right or wrong, or maintaining a system of justice within their species, unlike the Werewolves, who had already solemnly swore that punishment will be swift and brutal. They had been very careful not to mention the word execution, however.

"Do you swear to punish Oswald McNamara to the full extent of your governing laws?" Saraf asked the visiting Werebears. "Keep in mind that breaking an oath to a race as long lived as ours can be a very detrimental action." Apparently, Saraf didn't think they were taking this seriously either.

"We swear to punish him to the full extent of

Werebear law," the one with the shaggy lumberjack beard replied. It was a nicely worded response to a politely worded threat. Azar knew that the Werebear law was little more than a warning to not reveal themselves to human society, and to stay the hell out of each other's territory. There was no system to punish wrongdoers. They were all about spur of the moment, vigilante justice. The subtext seemed to be a giant F.U. to the Djinn, all the while appearing agreeable to the court. Azar appreciated the balls it took to do that, but she was pretty sure she'd be the only one. The Djinn had a superiority complex within the supernatural community. They enjoyed their position as the apex predators.

Azar couldn't see Saraf's face, but if it mirrored the rest of the Council members, it was less than happy. Unfortunately, these were the provisions that they'd agreed upon with the other leaders of the Were community, and they couldn't change the punishment for just one Werebear. So Saraf let it go and moved on.

"So be it. The Djinn will not forget the Werebears' helpfulness in this situation." F.U. right back.

Oswald was led to the other Werebears, and he sat between them. They gave him a truly scathing look, and then set about ignoring his existence completely.

The Councilor for the Ghul was the next presiding judge, jury and executioner. "The Council for the Djinn would like to call Rebecca White of the Sterling Forest Pack."

This was Aaron's ex-girlfriend and the leader of W.A.D, although no one had confessed as much during interrogations. They'd all stated that they were a democratically run group of nature enthusiasts, blah blah blah, just out for a run in the Canadian wilderness and that they were attacked by Lida. Their stories were almost all exactly the same, word for word, and short of torturing them, not one of the prisoners would consider recanting their story.

The Adel had wanted to call Aaron as a witness, but Anton had forbidden it as his Alpha. Apparently, he was well within his rights to decline, because no one had pressed the matter.

Rebecca White padded up to the dais barefoot, graceful in the way of predators and the paranormal. All the Weres in the room were eerily silent. They might not have admitted out loud that she was their leader, but their silence in that moment was telling.

The Councilor for the Ghul's voice boomed through the silence. "Rebecca White, you are accused and found guilty by this Council, of conspiracy to commit genocide, conspiracy to cause harm to the Djinn, manslaughter, attempted murder, grievous bodily harm, four counts of assault, and inciting violence against the Djinn. These charges carry a penalty of execution, however, your Alpha has negotiated with the Council to exact punishment through the traditions of your pack. Please, do not think us fooled. We know that you are the leader of this hate group and with the arrogance of youth, you thought that you could exact revenge against an entire race for the ill treatment of one of your own. Your misguided crusade could have led to war between our peoples, which would have led to mass casualties on both sides. It is due to the peaceful intentions of those older and wiser than you that such a war did not come to pass." His gaze swung to Anton, who was sitting in the visitors seats below the Ifrit section. "Do you swear to punish Rebecca White to the full extent of Werewolf Pack law?"

Anton inclined his head solemnly. "We do. Rebecca has forgotten the covenants that have kept the Pack safe and flourishing for centuries. A wolf that antagonizes the farmer by killing his flock does not survive to the next full moon. Rebecca will be punished for this crime in the way of the Pack."

Rebecca's eyes were wild as she swung an incredulous look at Anton. Obviously she thought he would support her stance. Her eyes turned stormy with anger. "You are a weakling! You would let them push us around as if we are nothing but dirt on their shoes. You are not my Pack Master!" She spat the words at him like venom.

Anton shook his head unhappily. "I accept your challenge for Pack Master. When we get back to our dens, we will duel for leadership."

Rebecca's face went white, and her gaze grew even wilder. Azar could almost taste her regret over the outburst. Rebecca opened her mouth to say something, but smoke filled the room, accompanied by a loud bang and a flash.

Azar's first thought was that a flash/bang grenade had been thrown into the room. She vaulted over the railing and onto the floor in front of her father's Council seat. The Adel had all moved to protect the Council members, and the Were were all on their feet, their bodies poised for attack. But no attackers came out of the smoke.

When it began to clear, there were two men standing on either side of Rebecca White on the dais, dressed in what appeared to be eighteenth century courtier wear. One was wearing sapphire blue velvet short pants, tucked into tall black boots, with a frothy white shirt under a ridiculously ornate frock coat. The second man was almost his twin, except his clothes were emerald green instead of sapphire blue. It looked like they'd just appeared from the Renaissance Faire. It was so unusual that Azar could only stand there and gape, letting her fireball fade down to the size of an orange.

Rebecca looked at the men standing around her before scuttling backwards toward Anton and the other Weres. *Better the devil you know*, Azar thought.

The men held their hands above their shoulders, confident smirks twisting their faces. "Let us not be hasty," the blue one said in a cultured voice, his accent almost British but a bit off. "We are merely messengers."

Jack strode to the dais from the shadows at the back of the room. "What are you doing here, Drustan?" There was palpable anger in his voice, and it made Azar edge closer to him. The Councilors were covered, but if these two were here to take Jack captive, then the Djinn were in serious trouble. If they could use Jack to find the Great Weapons, for whatever nefarious reasons, it didn't bode well for the Djinn.

The man in blue, who must have been Drustan,

looked shocked to see Jack striding towards him, but the expression was quickly chased away by scorn.

"Brother, I did not expect to see you in the halls of the Djinn. The last the Courts heard, you were hiding away in the wilds of some forest. How have you come to be in the middle of the concrete jungle?" Although the words seemed innocuous, each one was dripping with disdain.

Christos, the Shaitan Councilor, let his voice and malice echo around the room. "I think the more pertinent question here is who the hell are you?"

Cold shivers crawled up and down her spine, and they slowly intensified until they felt like bugs crawling through her body, just under the skin. Azar knew that the little display was barely a taste of Christos' power. She forced herself to edge slightly closer to Jack while everyone's attention was on the Shaitan Councilor. She was only a few feet away when the two men in the middle bowed low at Christos, and then to each of the other Councilors in turn.

"Pardon our poor manners. I am Drustan, royal messenger of the Unseelie Court. This is my compatriot Brennus, royal messenger of the Seelie Court. We come with a combined message from our respective Royal Courts for the Council of the

Djinn." He turned towards the Weres in the room, who had huddled into a defensive mass. "It is convenient that the animals are here too, for you were our next errand. Brennus, if you will?"

Jack's back was stiff, and his muscles were held so taut that she could see them trembling under his light cotton shirt. Drustan threw him another sneer over his shoulder.

The other man spoke, unrolling an old school parchment-style proclamation. His voice was so deep and melodic, that Azar got side-tracked listening to the rumble and pitch of his voice rather than the words. Jack pinched her on the arm and she snapped out of it.

"... of the Royal Houses, do request that the Djinn of all continents submit to Fae rule hencewith. Failure to do so will result in a declaration of war from the combined might of the Fae. The Royal

Houses of the Seelie and Unseelie Fae have benevolently given the Council of the Djinn up to seven days to agree to subjugation under the combined rule of The Houses. The status of the full-blooded members of the Djinn will be granted the same rank as the full-blooded members of our own nobility. Half-bloods will be given permanent servitude, and will become the trusted servants of said nobility."

The silence was so still, a pin dropping would have sounded like a cymbal crash. Everyone sat in silence, and Azar realized that the majority, including the Councilors, were entranced by Brennus' voice. The silence stretched on until Azar couldn't stand it any longer.

She cleared her throat. "I don't speak for everyone here, but I can personally say kiss my ass." Drustan grimaced and turned away from her, as if she was something distasteful. But her outburst seemed to have snapped everyone out of their trance, because suddenly there was a wave of angry curses being hurled at the two Fae men.

Brennus raised his hand and yelled, "SILENCE!" The room went instantly quiet. "Furthermore, the Seelie and Unseelie Courts hereby declare that all Were creatures will return to their rightful standing of servitude to the Fae, in their ancient role as the Fae's servants, laborers, pets and concubines." People must have realized they were being entranced earlier, as fewer succumbed to the spell of Brennus' voice the second time.

Anton stood, his back straight and regal, his alpha powers swirling thick on the air. "Never."

Drustan looked down from the elevated dais to the Weres. "You were given a warning as a courtesy, Wolf. You stand no chance against the Fae. You were created to be our playthings, and it is the role to which you will return. This is fact. I suggest you start coming to terms with it, because we can be benevolent masters, or we can break you all individually."

With that, he screwed his up his nose and looked back at the Councilors. "The position offered to those of you with full-blood is a generous one. Your lives will continue in the same pattern as usual, however you will be governed by the Fae, and not by your Council. You will find the Fae rule is a generous one." His voice rose, and grew hard. "However, if you war with us, you will get no generosity and when you have lost, you will find yourself subjugated with the half-bloods and the Weres. Your can choose the severity of your subservience, but have no doubt that the end results will be the same. You will be ruled."

He turned to Jack as the voices of the Djinn started to bounce off the walls in terror and outrage. "Brother, you should return to your homeland and your people. The Court has missed you. It is best that you aren't seen to be aligned with these creatures when the clock strikes their final hour."

The look on Jack's face was unmasked hatred. There was definitely old and bad blood between these two. "I am not your brother, Drustan. Your people are not mine. I am a lion and you are but a house cat. I stand with the Djinn in this matter."

"Then you can watch them fall around you," he replied with barely concealed malice and with another flash and thunder clap, they were gone.

CHAPTER 17

The explosion of noise after the Fae poofed out of existence was deafening. The hysteria was palpable. The Djinn had spent a millennium reassuring themselves that they were the big fish in the pool, only to realize that the pool was infested with sharks and they were just as much prey as the rest of the supernatural world. Apparently having the rug pulled from underneath you was a noisy business.

The Councilors were hustled away by their respective security teams, and Azar briefly caught a glimpse of Bast escorting the Sila Councilor out of the room.

Azar leaned into Jack's side. "Well, I didn't see that coming."

He gave her a smile that had no humor in it. "I did. Let us go and find out if your Council will see reason now."

He put a hand on the small of her back and guided her through the mass of Weres and Djinn who had spilled down to the main floor. She caught Anton's eyes in the middle of the writhing mass and stopped, put one hand over her heart and bowed her head. Anton nodded back. He had understood. Azar would fight for them if she could. She was Pack, and she took her place seriously.

Jack hustled her along, and the crowd stared at them and moved away, as if he were about to bite. Despite the fact that he'd been moving around amongst them for days, and had just openly pledged his allegiance with the Djinn. People needed an active focal point for their fear, and he was conveniently located. It raised Azar's ire and she death glared back at every person who looked at him like he was a disease. Despite her anger, she saw that Jack looked as serene as usual.

"Don't worry, their anger doesn't bother me. You should try being green in the Dark Ages. Before that, I could convince them that I was Jack of the Green, here to make their crops grow and make sure their cows didn't fall over dead, but come the Dark Ages people wanted to stone me to death."

Azar raised her eyebrows. "Are you trying to tell me that it isn't easy being green?" She worked very hard to keep her face straight, and apparently Jack wasn't familiar with Kermit the Frog, because he just nodded stoically.

They finally left behind the crazy crowd, and headed to the emergency stairs. She was pretty sure that the Council members would convene to the conference room where they'd heard Freya's case yesterday. They would be in full war council mode. Or maybe they were deciding to sell out the half-bloods and the Weres. She wouldn't put it past them.

They climbed the old stone stairs, which looked like they belonged in a medieval castle rather than a subterranean compound in the middle of NYC. There was a large contingent of bodyguards blocking the door to the conference room, and when they saw Jack, they converged into one tight wall.

"This floor is closed. You will have to turn around and go back where you came from." A large burly guy, who actually looked like he was meant to be security, or a gorilla at the zoo, growled at her and Jack. The underlying menace didn't faze Jack in the least.

"I wish to speak to the Council. I believe they will be as eager to speak with me as I am with them." He sounded completely reasonable, like there wasn't a dozen highly trained killers crowding the hallway, just looking for a reason to maim something. Azar guessed that being immortal, and actually unkillable, would give a person that kind of self-assurance.

Azar thought that so many bodyguards in one hallway seemed like overkill, especially due to the fact that the Fae had just popped into the room, even when it was full of guards. She was pretty sure a dozen guards would still be inadequate protection if they decided to pop in with a more malicious intent.

But she didn't think the guards would react kindly to her musings, so she held her tongue and tried to be as inconspicuous as possible behind Jack's broad shoulders.

One of the guards went into the room to convey Jack's request, and Azar couldn't see Bast or Killian in the remaining crowd of guards. They were probably already in the conference room with the Council Members. It was reassuring that there were at least two calm voices of reason in the room.

The guard re-emerged and waved Jack forward towards the door. When Azar tried to enter the door behind him, the Gorilla Guard thrust out a beefy arm and blocked her way.

"The Fae only," he growled. Azar wondered if had any other pitch than a grizzly rumble. Maybe it was his natural voice, the result of one too many punches to the voice box.

Jack reached back and grabbed her hand. "She comes with me." His voice was so authoritative, the guards could do nothing but comply.

After seeing Brennus' little voice trick earlier, she wondered if it was a trait that all Fae could do with their voice. She'd remember to ask, but not now surrounded by trigger happy bodyguards itching to shoot holes in something. They let her pass unmolested and she strode into the packed conference room.

Although it was quite a large room, it was filled to the brim with Adel bodyguards, the Council members, as well as the commanding officers of the Adel. Everyone turned towards Jack as he walked in, and she saw Killian sitting at the conference table, Bast at his back. Both their eyes were looking between her and Jack, and that's when she realized she was still holding Jack's hand. She snatched it away, and then mentally slapped herself for looking so guilty about an innocent gesture. Her face burned red with embarrassment, and she prayed that someone would speak and shift the focus off her.

Killian was looking between her and Jack appraisingly, and Bast's brow was knitted as he stared at the Fae man. She wished she could have gone to him, wrapped her arms around his neck and kissed him. She would have told him that she loved him and she barely even knew Jack. Sure she lusted after him a little bit, but she loved Bast in a place that was buried deep in her soul.

She'd carefully omit the crazy attraction she had to Jack, that felt like she was one half of a magnet being pulled inexorably toward the other.

The Jann Councilor finally spoke. "Please, sit." He motioned Jack to the only available chair.

Jack pulled the chair out and offered it to her. She gave him a warm smile but shook her head. He took the seat, his long legs stretching under the table.

"I've come to re-offer my services in finding the Great Weapons." The weight of so many measuring stares would have crushed a less powerful man.

Christos broke first. "You have to see our predicament here, Green Man. We are trying to understand your altruistic motives. Altruism isn't something we encounter much in this modern era.

Except perhaps in the case of your Ifrit protector there, who seems to want to throw herself in the path of every possible misdeed she can find." He was mocking her, but she'd take it as a compliment.

Apparently, Jack was going to interpret it as a compliment too. "Indeed, she is quite a special person. But please do not misunderstand my intentions. My motives are extremely self-serving. My job, or perhaps purpose would be a more accurate word, is to keep the balance amongst all living things on this planet. I have decided that to keep the balance in this situation, the Great Weapons must be returned to Djinn hands. After that, the rest is up to you. It is not my place to interfere with squabbles over power."

The Sila Councilor scoffed. "Do you mean to tell me that you have no vested interest in your own people? That you have no care if the Fae rise or fall?"

"They are not my people."

"Are you not Fae, Green Man?"

"I am more than Fae, and less. I am Tuatha Dé Danann. I am the direct descendant of the goddess Danu. I am irrevocably tied to the fate of this planet. I am the Earth and the Earth is me. The Tuatha Dé Danann share many of the same characteristics as the Fae, and in times gone by, we passed so many centuries in their Royal Courts that we became tied to the Fae in the minds of the supernatural community. But in actual fact, we are quite different. Tuatha Dé Danann are the personification of the goddess Danu. What you now call the Fae are the People of Danu; her followers, if you will. So to answer you question, I am not Fae."

Azar tried to wrap her head around the whole concept. She was not up to date on her Celtic theology.

Christos apparently didn't have any such trouble. "Let us rephrase our question then. Are you sure you have no vested interest in the survival of, as you put it, your followers?" His tone was still mocking, but she was beginning to think that cruelly sarcastic was just Christos' default

"You cannot beat the Fae armies." He said it as if he had witnessed the future and already knew the outcome, without a shred of doubt. There were protests from around the table but Jack just raised his hand. "That isn't a reflection on your fierceness in battle, it is merely a fact. The Fae have not been living out amongst the humans. They have stuck to their mounds in the Emerald Isle, and bred armies and trained them to be the most elite warriors to walk the Earth. They outnumber you significantly and they have more magic than the Djinn possess, even those who you deem pure bloods. And you all possess a fatal flaw. One cut from a Great Weapon, and you cease to exist. The magic in the weapons is old and lost to the Fae, and I believe they wish to regather them to recreate their enchantment."

He stood and strode around the room, and she resisted the urge to follow him. His face was serious, she knew that he was about to drop an even bigger bombshell. She tensed her jaw.

"It is a fact so old that it isn't even written in your histories, that long before there were humans or the Were, before even some of the Fae races, the Djinn were indeed once the slaves of the Seelie Fae."

There was a dull roar of denials around the room, as if they thought that the loudness of their protests could change what they heard. Jack turned and grabbed Azar's wrist, his hands wrapped around the Anadari Bracelets. "It is true. Even these cuffs are Fae workmanship. They were used to keep you all permanently enslaved. The fact that you still use them to this day, even founding your entire societal system around their use, has baffled me for millennia. You were the slaves of the Seelie Court, until one of their Kings took a Sila as a lover, fell in love and she convinced him to release the Djinn from their eternal slavery. He was a good king, a kind king and it was eventually what got him assassinated." His voice grew hard. "There is no place in the Royal Courts for softness."

The room was so still that it was as if the crowd was holding its collective breath.

It was Saraf who broke the silence "Be that as it may, how will the Fae defeat us here in the Americas, if they cannot set one foot outside of Europe?" Saraf made a good point, although they must have found a way around it, because there were two standing in the hearing room less than thirty minutes ago. Three if you count Jack, which apparently he didn't.

Jack actually smiled. "The thing about the Fae is that you have to trust them to do exactly as they say, and any inferences you may garner from their words will be on your own head. In this case, the law states they aren't to tread a foot out of Europe, so they learned to levitate."

"Are you serious? They just learned to levitate?" Azar thought she whispered, but everyone turned to look at her. She forgot there was no such thing as whispering amongst the supernatural ears of the Djinn. Well, at least not in such close quarters.

"Through breeding programs, they have promoted the ability to levitate within their bloodlines." The thought of them using their people like broodmares made Azar feel a little ill. "Indeed, Brennus and Drustan stood a mere fraction of an inch off the floor in your court room, but it was enough that they didn't break the ancient mandates of the Fae."

Azar wasn't sure why the idea that they could float seemed so outrageous to her. She could sprout wings and encase herself in fire. The Jann could actually become incorporeal, turning into smoke and air. The Sila could blast you with a lightning bolt from a mile away, and the Shaitan could crush your will to live with a hard look and a soft word. The Marid could draw all the water from your body, and the Ghul could draw out all the blood. They were a species of physical impossibilities. It was juvenile to believe that we were the only ones blessed with such talents.

The Marid Councilor finally spoke. "Tell us what you need to find these weapons before they get into the hands of our enemies. We will not concede to the Fae. Enslaving even a small portion of our population will only lead to enslavement of us all. It may not be for a century, or a millennium, but it will happen eventually. I will not stand by and let us go down in our histories as the Council that allowed us to be enslaved again."

Jack inclined his head, a small smile of satisfaction and relief brightening his face. "I need Azar."

Killian's eyebrows dipped low as he frowned at Jack. "What do you need her for?" He sounded like an overprotective father.

"Indeed, what use would you have for a half-blood Ifrit? She isn't overly powerful, and has no special skills that I can see," Christos appraised her body slowly, like a man studies a woman, not like a ruler assessing an asset. "There are Adel members who are more powerful, better equipped to help you on your wild treasure hunt. There are even Adel more beautiful than this half-breed, if that is where your need lies." He made it sound sleazy and insulting simultaneously. Azar flipped him the bird. He laughed mirthlessly. "You know I could have you imprisoned for your lifetime for such an insult to a Council member?"

Saraf cleared his throat. "Not if it was completely justified, Christos. You can be an insufferable asshole at times. But please answer the question Jack, why do you need my daughter?" Great, apparently her father was going to try the overprotective father act as well.

Jack paused, weighing his answer thoughtfully. "I believe Azar is important in the coming war. She will need to be with me while we search for the Great Weapons. Call it a gut feeling. I am open to any other Djinn you would like to add to the search party, but Azar is non-negotiable." He shrugged, like that should have been enough explanation in itself. Azar didn't think that explained a damn thing, but she wanted to go with Jack to search, so she wasn't going to argue. Exercising restraint twice in one afternoon. It must have been a new record.

Saraf and Killian both looked as if they were going to argue, but the Sila Councilor cut them off. "So be it. We will relinquish her servitude over to you for the time it takes to recover all of the Great Weapons. Don't argue, Saraf. This is what must be done to protect our people, and your needs are not greater than the safety of our society."

Saraf nodded his head in acquiescence, but he didn't look happy about it.

Killian had other plans. "Fine, but Bast goes too. We need someone who has authority on this mission and he is fourth in charge at this compound. We cannot spare Mira or Joia if there is a battle coming."

Azar could have kissed him and strangled him. Not being alone on the road with Jack, faced with constant temptation, was a good thing. Having Bast there, creating this awkward lust-triangle, was not such a good thing.

But Azar need not have worried. Once they'd added Bast, the negotiations began between the Councilors about who would go with them. Saraf argued for Cy, Azar's half-brother, because he was the most highly decorated field soldier available in the vicinity at the moment, and his combat skills would be needed in case of attack. The other Councilors argued that having two of his children, and the boyfriend of one, on the mission sounded too much like a conspiracy. Perhaps Saraf wanted all the weapons for himself? Saraf argued that it was safest for the Ifrit because Drakhul, the Great Weapon that targeted the Ifrit, was locked up nice and tight in the vaults below the compound. Getting cut by any of the other Great Weapons would not hurt the Ifrit. Back and forth they went for an hour, trying to get the balance between the benevolent and malevolent Djinn, between the different races, the different skills that would be necessary, etc.

On and on they went but eventually they settled on Azar, Bast, Cy and a Sila warrior named Vivian. The Sila Councilor argued that seeing how Ibsali was right down there in the vaults with Drakhul, then they should have a representative. The Sila were not naturally warriors, being more famed for their diplomacy, but apparently this Vivian could hold her own against Cy, and that was a glowing endorsement.

That seemed to appease the Council and ensured that the balance of benevolent and malevolent Djinn was maintained. Bast was given temporary control of Azar's servitude, meaning he could boss her about and she would be compelled to follow it. Apparently this was more palatable than handing it over to Jack himself. Bast gave her an impish grin, but she trusted him not to abuse the privilege.

The team being settled, they returned to planning for war and the team was dismissed to prepare for their mission, to be commenced ASAP. Bast and Jack went to the stores to get weapons and supplies that they thought they might need, and Killian and Azar went to the gym to collect Vivian. On the way down to the gym on the floor below, Killian called Cy. From what Azar could tell from one side of the conversation, Cy didn't understand why Azar was included in the team either. But he was a good soldier, and he accepted the mission without argument, ETA fifteen minutes.

When they pushed through the doors of the gym,

Azar knew immediately which of the training Djinn was Vivian. She was taller than Azar by a couple of inches, and every inch of her body was hard muscle as she punched the workout bag with punishing force. The muscles flexed under her skin, and Azar would have been surprised if she had even 1% body fat. She was quick and strong, and Azar could easily see why they thought she would be an asset on the trip.

Killian introduced them, and she reached out to shake Azar's hand. She had a confident handshake, and it endeared her to Azar immediately. She accepted the mission without complaint, asked intelligent questions about the Fae, the weapons, possible destinations and unlike Cy, didn't even question Azar's presence in the team. She just left to pack and Azar watched her go with a brand new girl crush going on.

"Wow," she whispered as Vivian strode from the gym with a self-possessed swagger.

"Indeed," Killian chuckled. "Come on, we better go get you kitted out properly so you don't die." And with that cheery thought they headed to the stores.

CHAPTER 18

The mosquitoes were the size of quarters, and she had blisters the size of pennies on her feet. The humidity was cloying, and there was a permanent layer of moisture on her skin. Jack's super-wonderful-internal-magic-sensor had led them deep into the Amazon in Brazil, near the border of Bolivia. She was sitting on her pack, lost in her own thoughts. The complete isolation of the jungle tended to make a person introspective.

They'd flown into Porto Velho almost four days ago, and driven a beat-up old Land Rover to Lábrea. From there, they'd ridden in a fairly unseaworthy boat down the river, and trekked through some inhospitable terrain, always trusting that Jack knew where they were going, and that Cy knew how to get them back. Apparently, it wasn't Cy's first adventure into uncharted wilderness, and Azar had sent up a small thank you that her father had pushed for his inclusion in the expedition.

Azar had actually enjoyed getting to know Cy better. Without his brother Caspar there to do all the talking for him, he'd actually opened up about himself and the family. Well, her family too. He told her funny anecdotes about his brothers, and family dinners where there were stand up fights across the table. He told her about his life in the Adel, and that he'd chosen to stay in the Adel after his compulsory servitude because both Darius and Killian were highly decorated members. She learned that Darius was his oldest full brother, and that there was only fifty years between Darius and twins, Keely and Killian. Azar had known that both Killian and Cy's mothers lived together and co-parented the children, but she didn't realize how much closer it had made those two branches of the family. Cy talked about them as if he loved them all.

Cy had given her so much information about her new found family that she probably could have written the family history by now. He told her all about the siblings she had never met. Ashtoreth, who lived in their father's seat of power in Mardin,

Turkey and was some kind of Council official. Yasmin and Roxx were full brother and sister and lived somewhere in Eastern Europe. Yasmin was an internationally renowned jeweler, though obviously no one knew she was Ifrit, and Roxx was the black sheep of the family. He was one of the best thieves in the world, and before that a pirate. He had stolen everything from diamonds the size of a fist to well-known abstract artworks that magically appear in railway station lockers. Cy shook his head and smiled as he talked of Roxx, his tone somewhere between exasperation and amusement.

Then there was Talia; the third youngest. She was a teacher and ran a boarding school with her mother, where Djinn families from all over Europe sent their offspring to be taught.

Cy told her about the time that their father had arrived to the New York townhouse with a human woman and a baby Malee. The mother had died of complications weeks later, and Cy's mother Fiona and Killian's mother Siobhan, had raised Malee together, almost two hundred years after Caspar had grown up and left home to do his servitude. He'd laughed when he told her that both Siobhan and Fiona had torn strips off Saraf for impregnating a human woman, knowing she would probably not survive the birth, even though Saraf had been the Councilor for the Ifrit at that stage. They'd argued for weeks, until Saraf had broken down and said that he'd had to do it for the survival of their race, how the numbers of infants born every year had dropped to double digits. He'd had to see if procreating with a human woman would result in Djinn offspring. Apparently all the Councilors and high up officials had agreed that it was the only course of action. It was almost two decades before they let Saraf back across the threshold of his own house, and he was only allowed to see Malee if the girl requested it.

Cy had shaken his head during that story. "They were furious when they found out he'd done it again with your mother. But when your mother ran, and he couldn't find you for decades, it almost broke him. He knew that your mother wouldn't live long after your birth, because all of the experiments the Council had conducted showed that the mothers only lived for an average of two years after the birth of the child. A couple of years after your birth, I saw him huddled in the library of the townhouse, crying into my mom's arms. He was convinced that you were probably alone and scared somewhere or dead on the street. Mom didn't lecture him so much after that. She knew he cared about the consequences of his actions."

Azar had fallen into her own thoughts for hours after that little tale, until they'd made camp for the night. Then she huddled close to Bast's body and tried to push down the memories of her childhood. Memories of begging for food, of the evil men who would come into the orphanage and look her over with eager eyes. So many bad memories that she wished she could forget, but that time had only dimmed.

Back in the present, she shook herself out of her reverie in time to see Vivian swipe at Cy with a knife. They were sparring, although how they found the energy to do such a thing after a ten mile trek through the jungle was beyond her. Vivian was good, and Azar could see why everyone had been content that she be included in the group. She handled a weapon with ease, and countered Cy's offensive moves with prowess. Azar didn't think Cy was really exerting himself, he was just sparring to focus his mind and keep his skills from rusting. He was maintaining his body the way a person would maintain a gun. They flowed around each other as if they were doing a well-choreographed dance, bodies crouched low, crab walking in circles.

Bast came to sit next to her, his back up against a tree after he'd hung the hammock. They'd decided on hammock camping to avoid the possible poisonous fauna that littered the ground of the Amazon. There were plenty of trees to utilize as well. Bast wrapped his arm around her shoulders and settled in to watch the sparring.

Cy and Vivian continued to circle, taking warning swipes at their opponent periodically. Suddenly, Vivian attacked, getting her arm within Cy's block. Cy had to drop his own knife, but he grabbed Vivian's hand and pressed a pressure point, forcing her to drop her knife too. Vivian's leg kicked out and swept around the back of Cy's, and the larger man went down with a thud onto his back. His own foot whipped out at Vivian's before she could dance away, and they both ended up on the ground. Cy wrapped his body around Vivian's leg, pushing gently against her knee with his body, until Azar thought it would pop. But Vivian tapped out and conceded, and Cy let go with a grin on his face.

"Can you feel the sexual tension in the air?" Bast whispered in her ear.

Azar wasn't sure that it was that way at all. Cy was completely appropriate and professional. He treated Vivian as he would any other soldier, with no deference to her gender. Although Cy wasn't going hard during the sparring, it had nothing to do with Vivian's gender, and everything to do with conserving his energy. He wanted to keep his mind and reflexes strong, not exhaust himself. Vivian in turn didn't seem to notice how handsome Cy was. She treated him like a higher ranking officer, followed orders, and didn't ask for any special treatment. If there was sexual tension there, Azar was missing it completely.

Maybe it was because she was too busy trying to dodge her own sexual tension. She had studiously avoided being alone with Jack. Not because she thought she'd jump his bones if she spent two minutes alone with him, but because the tension was there and Bast was too perceptive. It wasn't a conversation she wanted to have.

The man in question emerged from the forest to sit next to them. He'd been 'communing with the Earth' and he made it sound as if he and the planet actually conversed. She wondered if they participated in small talk. She'd imagined how that conversation would go in her head.

Jack would ask how the Earth was feeling, and she'd reply that she was feeling a little warm and was putting on some water weight, and she thought she threw her axis out last millennium and it still hasn't straightened.

Jack would complain about carbon levels and extinction rates. They'd joke about starting an ice age and beginning again, before getting down to business. For some reason, the idea amused her to no end. Apparently, Jungle Fever was a real thing and she was succumbing quickly.

"The Earth says that it is due west, where the trees form a circle and the earth dances with energy."

Azar screwed up her nose. Apparently with age came the ability to answer questions without actually answering a question. It was something Jack himself was good at. The 'Earth' had been giving them vague directions for days, and they were running out of time.

The Fae had given them a week to roll over or declare full scale war, with no prisoners, only slaves. She didn't think they'd abide by the humans Geneva Convention either.

Jack put his hand atop hers. "Azar, could I please speak to you in private?" She pushed down the surge of giddiness, and murmured her agreement as she stood. She paused to place a reassuring kiss on Bast's cheek.

Bast gave Jack a hard look that would have made anyone who wasn't a demi-god quake.

"Come, I'd like to have this conversation in the circle I have already made," the demi-god in question said as he led her out of the clearing that was their camp, and through the forest.

She heard more than saw the monkeys and birds scattering away from them in the trees overhead. She'd learned very quickly that the jungle was never quiet. It was a symphony of sound so pleasant, that it almost made up for the bird-eating spiders. The jungle had a primitive beauty that cannot be explained to people who had never been there. Sure, you could rattle off the animals and the fauna you saw, try to describe the musical calls of the different birds, or the earthy smell that permeated the under-growth, but you wouldn't be doing it justice. The magic of the jungle was in its rawness, the fact that so many things can't be explained. Perhaps no one had ever walked the trails they had walked. Most of the time she could guarantee they hadn't, as Cy had spent a lot of time cutting a path through the dense undergrowth when they'd strayed off the tracks. The idea that you were the first person to ever see this patch of forest was a heady experience.

They came up to another small clearing. Calling

it a clearing was probably being generous; it was more a six foot space between two giant trees. Lavender Irises bloomed in a large circle between the trees, and Azar knew that they didn't bloom that way naturally. Jack stepped delicately over the plants, careful not to bruise so much as a petal as he knelt in the middle of the circle. He motioned for her to join him. She too stepped over as if the flowers were made of spun glass. She didn't know much about the Fae, but she'd read enough Faery tales to know you didn't go stomping on a Faery circle if you valued your skin.

A sense of peace washed over her body in a wave as she crossed the invisible line. Jack waved her to kneel in front of him, closer than Azar would have liked, but if she was to avoid smashing into the flowers with her boots, she'd have to be mere inches away from his body.

He held out his hands, palms up, and she hesitantly laid her hands in his. He made a humming noise, his head cocked to the side as he was prone to do, like an owl studying something out of the ordinary near its nest.

"I did not believe it when The Earth suggested it. I believed it could not be true. It explained so much, but still I did not believe it true. But this is evidence I cannot ignore." His tone was nearing zealous.

Azar tried to draw back her hands but Jack held on tight. A little bit of fear crept into the recesses of her mind. She hadn't been paying attention to the direction they were walking, trusting Jack, and his assertion that he could do no harm. There were plenty of things that were torturous without being physically harmful. She took a deep breath and willed her mind to calm. Jack had done nothing untoward, other than being excitedly cryptic.

"That's great Jack, but either you tell me what you are talking about, or let go of my hands," she said with forced passivity.

Jack blinked a couple of times and looked sheepish. "I'm sorry Azar, I just got caught up in the moment. It's just been so very long..." He cleared his throat. "No, I'm getting ahead of myself here. Let's go back to the beginning. When Ibsali first came to me, I actually had no intention of giving the Great Weapons back to the Djinn. I thought they were a power too great, too tempting for your kind to have in their keeping, because there will always be one who seeks more power than they have and will use them for ill. I'd captured your friends, and incapacitated them, ready to tell you all to get on your way.

You would never know I had Ibsali in my possession." He grinned wide, showing a row of perfect square teeth that shone like polished white seashells.

"Then you burst from the forest, all naivety and sassy comebacks, and the Earth murmured beneath me. I turned your fireball into a carnation, and the Earth screamed at me that you were the balance. I had no idea what it meant, but I trusted the Mother, so I took you back to my cabin and gave the Djinn back Ibsali. I stayed close to you, hoping I could find what it was that made you special." He smiled as his thumb ran over her pulse point in an action that managed to be both soothing and erotic. "Indeed, you held a unique position in the supernatural community of New York; you are Djinn, Human and a member of a Were Pack, an honor I don't think has been bestowed on a Djinn in nearly a thousand years. But it didn't add up. I couldn't converse with the Earth in your concrete jungle; all I knew for certain was that you were important, so I did what I could to help your situation.

"Everything played out as you know, and we ended up here, in the lungs of the Earth. Since we have arrived, she has repeated to me that you are the balance. She's basically yelled it at me, and let me tell you, that is not a pleasant experience. Finally, she talked to me in that gentle way of mothers when a child isn't listening." Jack paused, and Azar held her breath. "And she told me that you are the balance because you are Tuatha Dé Danann."

The idea was so preposterous that Azar scoffed impolitely. "Dude, you need to stop licking the tree frogs around here. I am not even a little bit Fae. Or Tuatha Dé Danann. I'm pretty certain that I am half Djinn, half human. Saraf is 100% Ifrit. There isn't anything but fire demon in that one." She explained it slowly, but he was looking at her patiently, as if he was waiting for her to make the inevitable link. Well, he would be waiting awhile, because this made no logical sense whatsoever. He waited, and waited. Azar shrugged and tried not to squirm.

Finally he sighed. "It is my belief that your mother possessed a drop of Tuatha Dé Danann blood. Just like the Djinn, the Tuatha have been guilty of preying on human women as well. If you think about it, it explains everything. Why your father could not resist your mother, even though he had promised not to sire any more half-blood children. Why you can step inside a Faery circle unharmed. Why I seem to be irrevocably drawn to you in a way that I haven't been drawn to anyone in a millennium. I thought it was simple lust for a beautiful woman, but it isn't. Your blood calls to mine." His eyes got fervent and his face implored her to understand. "Feeling your vibrations inside the sacred circle, so close to the Earth, I can feel the Tuatha in your blood. You are special. I can almost taste which of my brethren is your sire, but it eludes me. It has been a long time since I've been in the presence of the Tuatha. Sadly, most have joined the Mother." He sounded so alone.

Azar petted his arm awkwardly. She wasn't convinced. If her mother possessed this drop of divine Faery blood, why did she die after giving birth? Wouldn't the blood make her hardier? Plus, she was sitting in this circle too, and she didn't feel a goddamn thing except awkward. Apart from the wash of harmony at crossing into the Faery circle, kneeling inside the ring of irises and sitting on the dirt in their campground felt exactly the same to her. Her disbelief must have been written all over her face because Jack took both of her hands and clasped them in his oversized ones.

"I can prove it to you. If you did not possess some Tuatha Dé Danann in your heritage, you could not commune with the Earth, the Mother." He lowered both of their hands to the ground, and pressed them flat against the moist ground until her palms lay flat on the surface, his resting on top of her own. "Brace yourself."

Azar sucked in a breath, and when she let it out, everything was the same but different. They were still in the Faery circle, but the air was thick, almost tangible and golden as if it was the very last light of a summer's day. And so very warm. It was a strange sensation because the Djinn didn't feel the hot and cold except in an academic sense. But the warmth in the air inside the circle embraced her like a liquid. The noise of the jungle stopped, and she could hear the sound of her heart beating faster and faster. Jack's skin shone in the golden light, giving color to his icy paleness. He shone so bright, it hurt her eyes and she had to look away.

When she turned her face, her eyes fell on a woman. It had to be the Mother. She was a woman without features, an every-woman, and her shape shone golden from the inside. It was like staring at the sun, and she felt the tears streaming down her cheeks.

The woman had no discernible features, just light, but Azar knew she was smiling, because a feeling of giddy pride settled in Azar's chest, the instinctual part of her brain understanding that this Woman's happiness meant everything. The figure reached out to pull her in an embrace, and Azar's body went willingly.

As soon as she touched the Mother, she spoke to her. She didn't really speak, but rather showed her images and feelings. An image of a mother hugging a child, of a flower in time lapse budding to life, a set of scales but the stand was a metal statue of Azar. She showed Azar an image of Jack and the Mother touching hands, a look of pure adulation on Jack's face. A feeling of love and warmth. A memory of a man chasing a woman through a forest, and the man was strong and shining like Jack, but he wore furs over his shoulder. The woman had pale skin and long black hair, and she was running but her face smiled brightly back at her lover, her hair whipping around her face in the breeze. A feeling of regret and loss.

The next image was of a forest of dead wolves, then quickly flashed to burning buildings, the charred remains of people stuck behind glass doors. The fear and horror after that image was so strong that Azar almost choked on it.

A sense of purpose and urgency overcame her. In the next image, she sat on the Dais in the hearing room at the compound, and in one hand she held a puppy, in the other a crown, two very different daggers strapped to her forearms.

The woman leaned her shining face forward and pressed a kiss to her forehead, and Azar felt like she was drowning in bliss.

She fell forward, and Jack caught her against his body. He held her as her breath regained its normal rhythm, and her heart thudded at a slower pace in her chest. Azar didn't know what to say. Her whole belief system had just been rocked.

"That was…" her mind struggled to come up with a word.

"That was the Mother, the Earth. That was Danu."

CHAPTER 19

Azar sat cross legged on the ground, trying to tame her thoughts. Conversing with the Earth was possibly the most interesting thing that ever happened to her. Considering she sprouted wings and flew around on fire, that was really saying something.

"So, what did she say to you? If that isn't a too personal question, of course." Jack was still holding her hand. Azar hesitated, but Jack would be the only person who could understand what she saw, because some of that stuff was trippy. She knew some of it was obvious, like some kind of premonition, but some of it made no sense.

"Uh, I'm not sure. It's kind of like one of those picture riddles. I know she was happy to meet me, then a flower blooming, which I think meant she had watched me grow. She showed me a memory of you two holding hands, and she told me she loved you. The rest is pretty open to interpretation, I think. She was trying to tell me what I should do, or show me the future or something, but it's all very cryptic."

She wanted out of this circle. He was glowing slightly, making his face mesmerizing and she found it hard to drag her eyes away from him.

She needed to talk to Bast. He would ground her, help her make sense of all this shit. She counted backwards from ten and calmed her heart rate. Maybe she would explain it to the rest of the group. She trusted most of them implicitly. Well except for Vivian, who she hardly knew. Cy she'd only just met, but family loyalty meant a lot to him. She'd take a leap of faith and trust everyone. Five heads were better than one in piecing everything together. She stood and stepped delicately back over the Faery circle.

She stumbled back through the forest, and realized she had no idea where she was going. Jack came up behind her silently and held her hand, taking the lead. The trip back to the campsite was all a bit of a blur, but she could see Bast pacing around the edges, obviously agitated. He jumped on them as soon as they walked into the clearing.

"You've been gone for hours. I was worried!"

"We were worried," Cy corrected, his tone equally as stern and disapproving. Vivian sat by the fire, sharpening her throwing knives, obviously staying right out of the conversation.

"I'm sorry, but I can explain." She motioned them to sit on the fallen log that had been rolled over to act as a bench. "You better prepare yourself, because shit is about to get weird."

Azar explained as sanely as she could what had happened in the last two hours. All its bombshells and mysteries, laid before the group, with some clarification from Jack. By the end, even Vivian had edged closer and was listening with rapt attention, her knives forgotten. Explaining the experience of talking to the Earth was more difficult than she imagined. It also sounded far crazier.

At one point Cy checked her for symptoms of poisoning, or jungle fever, and seemed even more confused when there were none. Azar tried to put as much detail as she could remember into recounting her visions; the sounds, feelings, smells and sights.

"Ah, it has to be Dagda. Yes, the more I look at you, the more I can see it," Jack murmured.

"I find that hard to believe, seeing how he graced the earth, what, four or five thousand years ago? I think the family resemblance might have filtered out by now," Bast commented sarcastically. Azar could appreciate the skepticism.

"I meant in her energy, Bast. Dagda was one of the oldest, and most powerful of the Tuatha Dé Danann. It makes sense. The story of Dagda's folly was once a cautionary tale for the Tuatha Dé Danann. Let me tell you." He cleared his throat. "Now how do these stories start for the humans. Ah yes, once upon a time..."

DAGDA WAS SAID to be one of the first of the Tuatha Dé Danann, the biological son of Danu herself. He head an unearthly beauty, and he was worshiped as a Sun God by the human race barely out of their caves. One day, he fell in love with one of the human women, well as much as a deity could love a human. He fell in love with the emotion of love.

They made a child, and Dagda left, because Gods can have very short attention spans, even for love. The mother returned to her little squalid village.

The baby boy was born, and he was beautiful. The most beautiful child that had ever been born in that *village. His name was Daeg, and he grew up surrounded by the adulation of his fellow villagers, but his temperament was so even, there wasn't even any envy amongst his peers. Eventually his mother died, and he married the most beautiful girl in the village, who seemed like rough hessian next to his opulent silk, but Daeg loved her dearly. They had two beautiful daughters, and these girls inspired sonnets and poems from traveling mistrals. But eventually, Daeg's wife died, and the villagers noticed that Daeg himself was as youthful and beautiful as the day they'd met. Of course, we know it was the immortal blood running through his veins, but the villagers were primitive, and believed that Daeg was cursed.*

One year, the rains did not fall, and they had a devastating drought. They believed that Daeg's presence meant that their crops did not grow, that their gods had cursed them for tolerating Daeg to live. So they took one of his daughters, now beautiful in her womanhood, and staked her alive in a field. They set her on fire and prayed to their gods to bring back the rains. Daeg was nearly inconsolable. He raged and killed nearly the entire village before fleeing with his remaining daughter.

They traveled across Europe into foreign lands, and Daeg knew that he could only ever live in peace in the Faery kingdoms. His daughter was aging slowly, so he wed her to a rich king of one of the northern countries, and her beauty and kindness was so renowned that it became one of the most powerful kingdoms in all of Europe. Daeg returned to Ireland, to the Siths, and joined the Seelie Court. But while they accepted and revered his presence, he was always an outsider, as he was Tuatha Dé Danann, not Fae. So they placed him on a very lonesome pedestal until he died a few millennia later of loneliness and a broken heart.

AZAR FELT an overwhelming sadness at Jack's story. Her heart bled for Daeg, ostracized for an accident of birth. She felt pity for the daughter, whose life was taken, merely for being beautiful. When Azar had been on the run from the Djinn Council, she'd hated and feared the Djinn, because she knew that they had the capacity to be cruel and ruthless. But Jack's story showed her that everything that breathed had the capacity for cruelty, to kill what they didn't understand, or merely to survive. The humans were no better than the Djinn, and the Fae were no worse. Glorious purpose was in the eye of the victor.

She realized that everyone in the circle was watching her closely, waiting to hear her reaction. She mumbled an excuse and headed to her hammock tent. She needed to absorb the story down to her roots. She had to reassess who she was, to redefine her place in the world. She had to process the messages of Danu, because she knew the Goddess had her own agenda, and Azar refused to act until she understood what it was. She was already a puppet on a string for one powerful entity, she wasn't going to blindly hook up another tether.

She lay on her back in the tent for hours, going over and over the images from the Faery circle, and the story of Dagda and Daeg. She picked them apart piece by piece and put them back together until her mind shuddered to a stop and her eyes closed. But even asleep, the images wouldn't leave her.

It wasn't until Bast cuddled into her back and wrapped an arm around her torso, that Azar let go of her problems and fell into a dreamless sleep.

WHEN THEY'D FIRST SET off into the jungle, Azar had been amazed at the process of taking down a camp-site. It was like a well-choreographed dance, where everyone had known the steps and she bumbled along behind trying not to trip anyone over. A couple of days in, and she felt so confident in the routine that she was happy to do it in silence, going from one task to another until the campsite was stowed away in packs, and the only evidence that they'd been there at all was compressed leaf litter.

As they slid their packs on, Vivian finally broke the comfortable silence.

"Am I the only one who is worried that Azar's visions yesterday could have been a premonition? Like some kind of warning? Shouldn't we send someone back to town, warn the Adel about possible attacks?"

Actually, Azar had come to the same conclusion, but she didn't know how she was going to word it to Killian.

She was pretty sure that she got a premonition from an Irish nature Deity/Mother Earth was going to suffice. It might get her thrown in a padded cell. And if she told them the whole thing, with the puppy and throne and crown and shit? Yeah, she was definitely going to the padded room.

However, Bast was nodding in agreement. "I think we should split up. Azar and I will go back into town and try and get in touch with the Council. You guys should go ahead with Jack and retrieve the Great Weapon."

For a minute, Azar thought Jack would protest her absence, but since she'd gotten the message first hand from Danu, he didn't seem as preoccupied with having her attached to his hip at all times. Cy gave the idea some thought and agreed, so Bast shucked his pack and sat down to brief Cy. It took at least an hour of them going over every possible scenario and the subsequent course of action to be taken in the event of each. For instance, if Beta team that consisted of Cy, Vivian and Jack, weren't back in Lábrea within fourteen days, Bast would call for the Adel, and ask for a contingent of tracking wolves to pick up their trail from this campsite. If Alpha team, her and Bast, had to leave Lábrea before the fourteen days were up, they should leave word at the postal service etc. Eventually, they'd planned for every possible outcome, and everyone shouldered their packs again.

When Azar asked Jack if she could talk to the Earth without him, he merely shook his head. "It is one of the few boons I have, being the Green Man. To converse with the Earth can take centuries of meditation and practiced rituals to do without my assistance. Though, I'll be happy to teach you the rituals once we have retrieved all the Great Weapons. You are, after all, Tuatha Dé Danann. It may come more naturally to you than the Fae practitioners."

She couldn't help but feel a little disappointed. The feeling of absolute love and acceptance that she got during those few minutes with Danu were heady, and perhaps a little addictive. Plus, it would have been good to go back to Danu and repeat the visions, when she wasn't being blindsided by her ancestry. She gave Jack's hand a little squeeze and tried not to pout.

She kissed Cy on the cheek and gave Vivian a wave, as they set off on their paths, in opposite directions. It was a two day hike back to the river boat, and they had to hope that the locals would be there to give them a ride back to the Lábrea.

Azar could only feel relief that she was getting out of the jungle; she was not much of an intrepid explorer, or even a camper. She'd take driving the Shelby down a wide open road over bug bites and sleeping in trees any day.

It was also a relief to be away from Jack, and their metaphysical connection. It was like the drop of Faery blood in her system pulled towards him every time she was in his presence, and it required constant vigilance not to physically touch him every two seconds. It was like she was three different entities trapped in one body; the human who was a hard working American, the flighty Ifrit who still shied away from its own kind, and the newly found Fae, who'd been screaming out for the touch of its own kind for a century and now that it had found one, it wouldn't be denied. Although she didn't want to admit it to herself, and she would never, ever say it out loud, if Bast hadn't been along on this expedition, she had no doubt she would have succumbed to that formerly unknown piece of herself, and crawled into Jack's tent on the very first night.

THE SIGHT of the boatman's little thatch hut made Azar want to weep with joy. The two day hike out of the jungle went quicker; they were able to keep a faster pace and rested less, so they were out of the jungle in record time. When they came to the clearing that housed the pontoon dock and boatman's hut, the sun was just kissing the horizon on the second day. It wasn't the Tahj Mahal by any means; it was made of thick wrist sized branches lashed together then lathered with mud from the river and a simple thatch roof. As they peeked through the door, they noticed that the boatman wasn't there. They'd paid him to come back every two days to check if they were there, as they had no idea how long they would be in the jungle.

She lay down thankfully on a hammock that had been strung between two support posts and breathed a sigh of relief to be off her feet. Bast plopped down onto a rough-hewn stool at the small table. There was a little gas stove, and some canned goods in a locked food safe. Not that there was any threat of thieves down here, except the furry kind. They would be eating like kings tonight!

"If I never go hiking ever again, I'll die a very happy woman," Azar moaned. Her body ached from the fast pace, and the little fat that had coated her body was now gone. She was all definition and muscle. "And I stink," she added. Her first shower back from this trip was going to be the best of her life. Sweat and grime coated her body, and she was a dirty shade of brown.

Bast slowly raised himself from the stool, and moseyed over to the hammock. He leaned down and kissed her gently on the lips.

He made a small "mmm" noise in the back of his throat. "You're right. You do stink." He laughed as she punched him in the shoulder. "Is there room in that hammock for two?" She scooted over and they began the precarious process of both getting into the hammock with neither of them ending up on the floor. She snuggled into his chest, enjoying the moment of closeness even though it was unbearably hot.

She might stink, but he smelled exactly like he always had; the sweet smell of the desert air and something undeniably masculine. She hated him a little right then, but not enough to move her head from the steady thump-thump of his heartbeat.

"If I've deduced the days correctly, the boatman should be back sometime tomorrow afternoon, that should put us in Lábrea by about three. I can think of a very good way to pass the time," Bast purred into her hair as his fingertips ran lightly over her ribcage.

She rolled her eyes. "You just told me I stink! Your pick up lines need some serious work."

"I just won't breathe too deeply." She couldn't see his face, but she could feel his smile against her hair. "Besides, maybe I find that stale corn chip smell an aphrodisiac." Now he was openly laughing.

She rocked her body all of a sudden, gave a large shove and pushed him out of the hammock. Bast's chuckle bounced off the walls of the hut, and soon Azar was laughing just as hard, her ribs hurting in her already aching body. Bast reached up and tugged on her arm, tipping Azar out on top of him. Her arms and legs flailed about and she gave a little "oof" as she hit the hard muscles of his torso. The dirt of the floor beneath her palms was packed hard from years of use, and swept clean. She leaned in and kissed him, her cheeks hurting from smiling.

"You know I love you, right?" she said when she could draw air back into her lungs.

"I know." His smile shone with happiness. "I love you too." He kissed her nose. "Now I should make dinner for my *Jaanaman*. How do you feel about tomato soup and biscuits, hot off the stove?" She rolled off him to let him up and he bounded to his feet, then reached down to help her off the floor.

The forest seemed quiet for once. Azar cocked her head to the side, listening intently. Too quiet even. She shot a look to Bast, and noticed he was listening too, all mirth wiped from his face.

"Something's wrong," he whispered.

She nodded in agreement, reaching into her boot holster for her knife. She crept over to her pack and pulled out the gun that was secured in one of the pockets. Bast did the same, before peeking out of the doorway, eyes scanning the surrounding forest. Crouching, he eased out the door, and Azar followed him on his flank, her eyes searching the forest to her left. She saw a flash of movement among the trunks.

"We've got someone on the left," she whispered.

She kept her voice low. "And on the right. I think we're surrounded."

She lifted the gun, pointing it at the tree line, though the falling darkness obscured the shapes. She put her back against Bast's, their movements defensive. "I think we should take our chances with the piranhas. Ease towards the water." His voice was so low, it barely caught on the breeze.

As they stepped towards the water, the hidden assailants attacked. They came out of the trees with preternatural swiftness, and a tall blonde man in leather armor was in front of her before she could shout a warning. She moved the gun and pulled the trigger, and the man went down. Not a man, a Fae.

"It's the Fae!" she shouted at Bast, though she assumed he had already figured it out. The first guy was still writhing on the ground when a second assailant appeared, this one a woman. She aimed and shot, but the female warrior moved with such incredible agility that she was barely a blur. She was back in front of Azar before she could pull the trigger a second time.

Azar jabbed out with the knife in her other hand, catching the warrior under the ribs. The cold steel reacted with the Fae and she screamed, falling to the ground next to her now dead compatriot. Azar had no time to even spare them a glance, as three more came upon her, long swords swinging out in front of them.

"Give us the Great Weapon, and we'll make your death swift," the middle one said in a heavily accented voice. Azar snarled at the man, and fired her gun. They all dodged the bullet, and advanced faster. Azar dropped the gun. It wasn't going to be helpful without the element of surprise. As soon as the gun landed at her feet, she threw a fire disc at the approaching soldiers. They weren't expecting it, and it caught all three, the smell of burning flesh unnatural in the jungle. The fire wouldn't stop burning until it consumed them, but Azar had no time to worry about that as another five came out of the undergrowth. They were screwed.

Azar's gaze shot around to find an escape, but they were coming up the sides of them now, and she felt panic claw at her insides. They were trapped.

"You have to step away. I'm going to change forms."

She felt the solidness of Bast's body move away from her, and she felt incredibly vulnerable for a second. The five Fae warriors were almost in hitting distance now. Azar heard Bast grunt in pain, and knew he had been hit, but couldn't turn from her attackers.

Azar felt the fire consume her just as the first of the five attacked. His eyes widened with shock as he fell to his knees, an arrow in his back. The other four looked around, and four more arrows found their marks in eyeballs, necks and chests. Azar whirled around, and saw her attackers dropping like flies as more Fae poured from the woods and fought with the attacking Fae.

Confusion permeated the clearing, and not just her own. Azar used that confusion to spare a glance at Bast. He was on the ground with a dagger in his shoulder, but it didn't look life threatening, so she stood over Bast's body, protecting it from the new Fae, who she had no idea if they were friend or foe. She completed the change to Ifrit, and she was a beautifully terrifying sight. The flame streaked wings spread out from her body like a fiery backdrop, every inch of her body alight.

The skirmish was quickly over, the new Fae force easily outnumbering the group that attacked her and Bast. As the last of the originals fell, the new Fae laid their weapons at their feet, and bowed. If she was confused before, she felt like she was going crazy now. A tall blonde man, beautifully lean and muscled, his face too feminine for what she'd consider appealing, stepped forward and he had the undeniable presence of a leader.

"My Goddess, we mean you no harm, but you must remove the dagger from your compatriot with great haste or I fear the effects of the dagger will be too advanced." Azar's face screwed up in confusion, but she looked down at Bast, finally noting the intricate design on the dagger poking out of his shoulder. It was old and it was a design she had studied over and over for the last few weeks. It was Posidagi, the Great Weapon that was lethal to the Jann. Panic hit Azar like a freight train, her flame going out instantly as she fell to her knees next to Bast.

"No, no, no," she chanted as she pulled out the dagger and threw it away from Bast. "Baby, can you hear me?" Tears were blurring her vision, her hands going over the wound in his shoulder, where the skin around the wound was blackening quickly with necrosis. "You are going to be okay." The tears streamed down her cheeks now, and Bast's moans of pain were getting louder as the necrosis ate its way through his body. Bast raised a hand and cupped her face, his thumb wiping away her tears.

The pretty Fae man was at her side, looking down at Bast. "You must switch forms. If you are but air and smoke, the necrosis cannot spread. It is your only chance. Change!" he said urgently, and Bast's body began to fade from view.

She had never seen his transition from physical to air and smoke before, Bast had always assumed his human form when he was with her. Jann were known as the whirlwinds of the desert, air and smoke in their other form. Bast's body become semi-transparent when his eyes closed and his breath shuddered.

Her slave cuffs fell from her wrists. It was too late.

The only way the anadari cuffs could be removed is if her master died. As Bast's body disappeared from view, she fell back onto the ground and sobbed, trying to put the slave cuffs back on her wrists. She was too late.

Bast was dead.

CHAPTER 20

Strong arms reached down and lifted her off the hard packed mud of the river bank and carried her towards the hut. Fae soldiers were dispersing back into the jungle and six more surrounded the makeshift building. Azar saw all this through red rimmed eyes.

The wind had picked up, and leaf litter blew along the ground like tumbleweeds. The hair of the blonde captain tickled her face but she couldn't summon the will to brush it away. She couldn't summon the will to be anything but thoroughly devastated, even though she knew she should at least be wary of the newcomers. But she couldn't rouse enough emotion to even protest being carried like a child. All she could do was think of Bast, and the black death that ate through his body.

As she thought his name, the wind picked up again, and she thought she could smell his unique scent upon the breeze. She knew her heart was breaking. She memorized that scent, locked it away in her mind as something to be cherished for the next hundred years. The Fae man who carried her deposited her gently on the stool, and two more guards came through to stand on the inside of the doors. She was either in a well-guarded safe-haven or a well-guarded prison.

The thought snapped her out of her grief slightly. Bast would be appalled with her if she just fell to pieces. She sat up straighter and eyed the leader, who squatted opposite her.

He looked like someone who had been leading an army for years; his face was ageless, perfectly free from creases and wrinkles, but he had several small scars littered around his face. He was definitely formidable, every nuance of his posture ready for battle at a moment's notice, like a tiger that only appeared to be lazing. He was definitely Fae however, his ears were slightly pointed, his body loose limbed muscle. But it was the eyes that moved him from an ornately beautiful human to something supernatural; they were large in his thin face, and the irises filled them up, no whites could be seen at all, much like Jack's.

A particularly strong gust of wind knocked over a wooden cup on the table, and Azar unconsciously righted it. Slowly, the obvious filtered down into her grief stricken haze. There shouldn't be a breeze inside the hut. There shouldn't be a wind that strong inside the jungle at all. Her heart raced at the possibility.

"Bast?" she barely whispered it, her heart too fragile to hope for too much.

As if I'd ever leave you, Jaanaman. Bast's voice ricocheted around her head, the feeling new and not particularly comfortable, but the most welcome sound she had ever heard.

"You son of a bitch! I thought you were dead forever!" Her voice cracked at the end, and her rage was tinged with relief.

You don't have to speak out loud to talk to me. If you do that back in civilization, the human police will take you to a nice place with padded walls and very thick doors. He was gently joking with her, trying to bring her out of her unnecessary grief. She didn't know if she wanted to laugh or cry more. *I think we should find out who these people are first. They certainly came to our aid, but what they are doing in the wilds of the Amazon is suspicious to say the least. This isn't exactly a huge tourist hot spot for the supernatural communities.*

Azar took a moment to breathe, to regain her equilibrium. Her adrenaline was pumping through her body still, making her edgy and tense. The blonde man remained perfectly still in his crouch, his gaze taking in the nuances of her face as she spoke to Bast with her mind. She cleared her throat as the tightness in her chest eased.

"I'm sorry about that, I thought the worst." She didn't have to explain her tears to the man, but now she knew that Bast was alive, sort of, she felt awkward under the blonde man's stare. "But thank you. For the rescue, I mean. I'm Azar."

The man bowed his head, "I am Lorcan, the Black Prince of the Fae." Azar didn't know anything about the Fae social structure, and she kicked herself for not grilling Jack about it more.

She bowed her head in what she assumed was a reasonably respectful manner, but the Prince held up a hand and shook his head.

"Please, you need not bow to me. And if you will it, please call me Lorcan." Azar shrugged. She'd get the nuances of Fae etiquette another day. Lorcan's speech was heavily accented and far more archaic than Jack's.

Ask him what he's doing in the jungle, Bast prodded impatiently.

I'm getting there, don't rush me, she grumbled back.

"As I said, Lorcan, thank you for your well timed rescue. But what I would really like to know is what you are doing in the jungles of the Amazon. I thought you guys were tethered to the soils of Europe, so you can understand my confusion when I see you standing before me, in the Amazon. With your feet firmly on the ground."

"We were tracking your party, of course. This jungle is about as far from the Emerald Isle as a Fae can get. Many of us find it... distinctly uncomfortable. We are looking for the Green Man, the Heart of the World." Azar eyed him suspiciously. "I believe you'd like these returned as well." Lorcan indicated with his head, and one of the guards stepped forward and placed the dagger Posidagi and her slave cuffs on the table in front of her, before resuming his post. "I have urgent news for Jack, and we have tracked him from the woods of Canada to here. It has taken more time and resources than I would have liked." The last he said almost to himself.

"When we found the Faery circle, we knew we were right behind you, but then your party split in two. My second in command and half my squadron followed one trail, and I followed yours." She couldn't tell if he was annoyed that he'd picked the wrong path or not.

Ask him what he needed to tell Jack.

If you think I'm going to be your mouthpiece for the next fifty years, you are sadly mistaken. But she asked anyway.

Lorcan regarded her shrewdly. "You are my goddess, so I guess the news purports just as much to yourself as to Jack."

Azar almost choked on her own saliva. "Excuse me?"

"You are of the Tuatha Dé Danann, are you not? When we found the Faery circle, we knew that two of the Tuatha had been within the circle. We have one who can scent the signatures in the remaining essence." Lorcan seemed to hesitate. "When we got close enough, he assured me that you were the one with the Tuatha Dé Danann blood."

See, she gloated to Bast, *I even smell special. To think, all you could smell was corn chips.* The sound of his chuckle inside her mind warmed her to her very soul. The idea of a life without Bast had created a fissure in her heart, and she wasn't sure it was completely mended yet.

On the outside of her mind-meld with Bast, she was motioning Lorcan to continue. She wasn't really prepared for the man's smile though. It lit up the darkened room like a supernova and Azar forgot how to breathe. He let out a small matching chuckle.

"Your face when you are talking with your lover, it is quite comical. Your eyebrows are like small dancing worms." He chuckled again, wiggling his eyebrows so they danced on his forehead. "Sorry, there hasn't been much comedy in my life of late." He cleared his throat and attempted to regain his stoicism. "As I was saying, the news applies equally to you as to the Green Man. Do you know much of our society?"

Azar politely shook her head.

"Well, for several millennia we have been separated into two major courts, the Seelie Court and Unseelie Court. All manner of creatures come under the banner of the Seelie and Unseelie, but at the top of both food chains were the Fae. And the Fae worshiped Danu and her children, as was appropriate, believing them to be Gods amongst us. They fought off the previous inhabitants of the land, bound us to the soil of Europe and split us into two courts, of light and dark. I believe that they did so out of the best interest of the Earth, for when we first arrived, we were ravenous on the blood lust of victory." His face grew pensive, the look in his eyes that faraway look of an academic. This guy was a double threat. If he could use his brain as well as he used his sword, the Djinn were in trouble. "We killed or took as slaves every indigenous race we encountered, including the Djinn. We would have conquered everything in our path as we did Europe and the Middle East if the Tuatha Dé Danann had not physically restrained us. But that is for a philosopher and theologian to debate."

He stood from his crouch and paced around the room. She took in the other faces of the Fae in the room, and found that they all varied in expression, some looked bored with Lorcan's explanation, some were looking at her like she was Elvis Presley in their local Starbucks. But their bodies were all held at high alert.

"However, when Daeg, the son of Dagda, found his refuge in the Seelie Court, the result was, uh what is it you modern people say, that some of the shine wore off? Being in the presence of a god for so many centuries, the Seelie Court soon came to see him as just another Fae, one that was flawed at that.

He sympathized with the plights of the Djinn and the Weres, crusading for their release from slavery, which was a view that was unheard of amongst the Fae. Soon they stopped worshiping the gods, believing that they were no better than the Fae, who ruled and governed all the other supernatural creatures of Europe.

"When Daeg was slain in a skirmish between the Seelie and Unseelie armies over some disagreement lost to the winds of time, they began to believe that perhaps their gods possessed feet of clay. Perhaps they weren't all powerful, but were as petty and jealous as the Fae themselves. So quietly, they began to sow the seeds of dissent. For the first time in millennium, most in the Seelie and Unseelie Courts were of a single mind. The Tuatha Dé Danann were the shackles that weighed down the Fae, that must be eradicated so that the Fae could rise up in their place as New Gods. According to their plan, the Courts would rule not only the Seelie and Unseelie creatures, but the Djinn and the Weres and eventually the human race. They would be gods that would walk amongst us, or so they believed." His eyes grew hard and his face was a mask of disdain. It was a disturbing expression on a face that would have made Botticelli weep.

"So they began to pick off the Tuatha Dé Danann, silently in the darkness of the night, while the Tuatha slept, like the cowards they are. At first they disguised the kills as accidents, or the work of humans. Eventually, as they'd picked off the strongest that still resided in Europe, they became more blatant in their genocide, until they were killing off the descendants of the Tuatha, like you. They have killed nearly every Tuatha Dé Danann in Europe and the Middle East, every man, woman and child who possessed even a drop of Tuatha blood. When the earth was almost drowning in Tuatha blood, they found that we are no longer tethered to the soil of Europe, that we're now free to walk anywhere on Earth."

He suddenly sprang up and grabbed Azar's hand, clutching it almost painfully. The wind roared to life as well, the scent of the desert sands on the air as it whirled between Azar and Lorcan. Apparently, Bast didn't like the idea of anyone manhandling his girlfriend.

Lorcan looked up at the roof, small debris scraping his ageless face. "Please, my elemental friend, I mean your lover no harm. I still adhere to the old ways. I believe that the Tuatha Dé Danann are necessary to the survival of all the inhabitants of

Earth. That each one holds together the world in a small way, to help it continue turning. Your lover is a goddess, I would harm myself before I would harm her." The wind died down a little and Bast harrumphed in her head, still on edge.

"Jack is one of the last original children of Danu left. It is incredibly important that he survive. I do not know what would happen if he died, but I predict that the Earth will die with him. Already since the death of so many of Danu's children; natural disasters, famines, wars amongst the humans and Fae sects alike, have increased tenfold. The demise of the Green Man would be our final act of hubris." He looked her square in the eye. "But you are just as important. The small amount of power that the descendants possess is still integral in maintaining our world." He knelt in front of her, his head bowed in subservience. "This is why I must ask a great favor of you, if you will accept?"

Azar felt a bit shell-shocked really. It had been quite a tale, and a hell of a lot to absorb. She shook her head. "I will try, but I make no promises."

Lorcan nodded eagerly and motioned again for the guard, who disappeared out of the hut.

"It is of great importance, or I would not ask this of you." The guard returned, and his hand was on the shoulder of a boy who looked about ten. Lorcan stood and motioned the boy to his side. "This is Prince Neyvn, heir to the Golden Crown, the Seelie throne. He is also the last of Dagda's line."

"Not quite the last," Azar murmured. "I guess that makes us cousins," she said to the boy, who appraised her with intelligent eyes in a cherubic face.

The boy bowed his head. "Greetings, Sister." His voice was clear, but it had the depth that promised he would have quite a deep voice when he grew into maturity. Azar bowed her head and returned the greeting, glad she was sitting down.

The last three days had been the weirdest of her life, and after the events of the last six months, that was really saying something. Lorcan motioned the boy away, and he went to swing on the hammock, like the child he was.

"I need you to take him, protect him. Living with a battalion of soldiers is no place for a child or someone who is to be revered in all things. He does not need to see the blood and the death any more. I rescued him from the Seelie Fae, but I was too late for his family." He let the statement hang there, and Azar knew what it meant. They had been killed during the Fae genocide.

Azar felt an overwhelming sadness for the little boy with the intelligent eyes. There would be no soothing lies to help him forget the bloodshed he'd seen. In that moment, Azar knew the answer would be yes. The irony that she'd been in this situation twice in a month didn't pass her by.

Maybe we should put out an advert. Foster care for supernatural entities on the run from assassins. No recompense needed. Bast's words were light, but she knew that he too would be sickened by the murder of children.

We could take him to the Sterling Forest Pack, they would protect him.

We would owe them big time. You used up your favor with Freya. They aren't supe equivalent of an unwanted baby drop bin at the fire station you know. You can't treat them as such. But he didn't disapprove of the plan.

She looked at Neyvn, swinging gently on the hammock, like a babe in a cradle, and she melted. She was getting soft, but she knew she would do what she could to protect him. He was safer with her than he was with his own kind. She looked at Lorcan and then at the boy. Maybe her hormones were on the fritz or something.

"We will care for him." The boy was returning her gaze intently. "After all, what is family for?"

CHAPTER 21

"You know, when most tourists come to Amazonia, they leave with mosquito bites and sometimes dengue fever, but I've never seen anyone come out with a pasty white kid before," the boat driver yelled in heavily accented English above the roar of the boat's engine.

Azar waved her hand in a non-committal gesture but her silence didn't slow the man down. He prattled on about his wife, boasted proudly that his son had gotten a scholarship to a college, much to his relief. His dog had puppies to that no good mutt who lived down the road. Azar had eventually tuned him out. Neyvn was pressed rigidly to her side in the small confines of the boat. The man's chatter was relaxing in its inaneness, completely oblivious to the rumblings of change in the paranormal world. To him, genies, fairies, and werewolves were children's tales, not potential overlords.

Neyvn shifted uncomfortably on the bench seat next to her and she resisted putting her arm around his shoulder. The kid had the cool royal etiquette down. He'd barely said two words to Azar since Lorcan left that morning, off to track down Jack and the rest of her party. He also promised to make sure there were no other Fae lurking on their tail. Before he left, he told her the only way Bast could regain his physical form was to get a poultice from a Fae healer. If the healer was strong enough in power, the poultice would break the spell that was embedded in Bast's body by the dagger. The real grind of the whole situation was that there were few healers left with that kind of power, and none that were opposed to the current Fae campaign of Djinn subjugation and Tuatha annihilation that Lorcan was aware of. Plus, there was a small chance that the necrosis had eaten away too much of Bast's body and he would never be able to regain his human body without dying almost instantly. Bast had been very quiet after that conversation.

They'd been on the boat for hours now, and the sun beat down on them unrelentingly. The glare off the water was starting to sting her eyes. At some point the boat driver had even fallen silent. She knew she should be trying to build a rapport with the kid, but she didn't know what to say to a child who had seen his whole family slaughtered, that had been amongst a small army for months, and had now been dumped with a complete stranger who had no idea about his culture or people. She thought her childhood had been rough. Her mind scrambled to think of what little boys were even interested in, let alone Fae children.

"Do the Fae have pets?" She said in a normal level over the wind. The boatman wouldn't hear from the back of the boat, plus he would probably write it off as a mishearing. Humans were very good at seeing and hearing what they wanted. Neyvn's head whipped around, and he looked at her like she'd lost her mind. She guessed it may have been a rather random first conversation to have with someone, but hey, she was working under duress here.

"Yes, most Fae have an affinity for animals, and the royal families have Weres as companions and servants." Azar grimaced. That wasn't going to go over well with the Pack. She made a mental note to have a long conversation about the expectations of the paranormals outside of Europe when they got back to the States.

"Did you have a pet?" she asked, keeping her tone light.

"I had a companion since birth, a Werefalcon named Tino. He was killed." He looked out over the water, so he missed her horrified expression. This was the conversational equivalent of the Titanic.

"I'm really sorry to hear that. And about your family. And the fact that the two Courts turned out to be such dicks."

Neyvn cocked his head to the side and stared at her, like a child would look at a crazy person on the street. Completely non-judgmental curiosity. Azar tried to keep the conversational ball rolling. After all, she'd come this far. "When I was a street rat in Madrid, I shared my box with a mangy dog. He stunk, but he was warm. Every night at dusk he'd come and lay with me in the box, and every morning he was gone when I woke up. He saved me from some bad situations more than once. Sometimes, we'd share food, if we found enough that day. One night, he didn't come back, or the next night, or the one after that. I moved on after that. It just didn't feel as safe to be in that alley without him." She cleared the lump in her throat. She hadn't thought about the mutt in decades. "That's probably the closest I've ever come to having a pet."

Neyvn stared at her with his round child eyes. "Where was your family?"

Ah, this isn't how she wanted to bond with the kid, over mutually horrific childhood stories, but she answered anyway. "My mother died when I was five and I lived in an orphanage until I was too old and they kicked me out. But I survived, and eventually I got to a place where I was happy. I only met my father this year, by accident really. Now, I have family coming out my ears." She gave the boy a smile, and he returned it halfheartedly. She patted his knee. "So tell me, what is your favorite thing to do? I like to fly now. When I switch forms, I have fiery wings." And as she knew he would be, the boy was impressed.

He had a million questions about flying, about changing forms, and she in turn asked him questions about hunting, which apparently a lot of Fae children did, about his magic and the rituals of the Fae. Turned out, it was Neyvn who sensed her essence in the Faery circle, a gift from his Tuatha heritage. He asked her what her gift was, but as far as she knew, the Tuatha blood in her veins was far more watered down than Neyvn's. She didn't have any talents other than those of the Djinn, she told him ruefully. The boy shrugged it off, like only kids can do, and continued to chatter. Now that she'd brought him out of his shell, she enjoyed his conversation long into the afternoon, before the boy yawned, and his head nodded to his chest, his eyes closed.

Azar gently pulled him onto her shoulder so he wouldn't crick his neck, and sent out her thoughts to Bast, who was floating around in the atmosphere ahead of them, searching the jungle for any more unwelcome surprises.

Any more of this babysitting business, and you'll want one of your own, he joked, although there was a hard edge to his words.

Not likely, I'll be too old once the servitude is up. Plus, I thought there were rules about interracial procreation. She unconsciously rubbed the spot where the Anadari Bracelets should have been. It wouldn't happen if the love of her life was unable to become corporeal either, but she kept that to herself.

Bast didn't reply, and she felt him leave her mind. The loss of his physical form was hard on him. The sooner they got everything sorted and bribed a Fae healer to unspell his wound, the better. The physical weight of his sadness was crushing them.

She knew they were coming back into civilization, as the bank of the river exposed more tiny pontoon docks, and simple huts. She reached into the side pocket of her pack and pulled out her cellphone. They'd finally be coming into some service soon, and she wanted to call the compound as soon as she could. There was a sense of urgency riding her, and she knew better than to argue with her gut.

The boatman, who's name she'd discovered hours back was Luiz, guided them into the dock next to his hut. It was on the outskirts of Lábrea, on the poor side of town. Their Jeep was still parked next to the dock, and Azar felt her muscles cramp as she stood up in the boat. She checked her phone, but this far out of town there was still no service.

Neyvn stood up and shifted Bast's pack onto his back, and it all but dwarfed him. If it wasn't for his preternatural strength, she was fairly sure the kid would have tipped backwards and landed in the river.

She'd bargained for a lift to town with Luiz for another handful of US dollars, which he was happy to accept. She also gave him a couple of hundred more to keep making the trek down the river every couple of days.

Luiz had merely laughed. "If you come back with a white kid, I can't wait to see what souvenirs the others came back with." The guy was being paid well, in US dollars at that, and Azar knew that he would happily make the trip up and down the river for the rest of his life, if the money kept rolling in.

Azar knew when she'd reached cell service, because her phone notifications went nuts, pinging every second. Most were missed calls and voicemails from Oliver, a couple from Donovan and several from the Sterling Forest Pack. Her stomach knotted with dread, but first she had to call into the compound, report the attack, and relay Danu's premonitions.

She called Killian's number, but it rang out. Then she called Mira's cell, and got a recorded message that the number was unavailable. A cold sweat broke out on her skin as she called back Oliver.

"Thank fucking God! I've been so worried," Oliver's strained voice came over the line, relief pouring out in waves. Azar felt relief too. A little bit of her anxiety ebbed away at the sound of his voice.

"What's up? I've been away on a mission, remember? I have to come back early but I can't get a hold of anyone. Bast needs help," she choked out.

There was an eerie silence at the end of the line. "I have to tell you something, Az." He drew in a deep breath. "The New York Adel compound was attacked yesterday. The whole place was set on fire, and collapsed. The Weres have rallied trying to find any survivors, but so far we've only been able to drag out remains. The Fae somehow sealed the doors and windows with magic. No one could get out, they're just there, crushed against the glass," his voice broke a little. "I knew you were on a mission, but I thought you might have been in there. You didn't say how long you were going to be gone, and then I couldn't get you on the phone…" he trailed off, his voice gravelly with emotion.

The premonition from Danu surged into her mind. People trapped behind glass doors. They were the Djinn. Her friends and her enemies. Her family. Bile rose in her throat as she thought about the other piece of Danu's predictions. Dead wolves in the forest. Fuck!

"Oliver, listen to me. You have to get the wolves to leave the forest. I don't have time to explain, but please, get them to find a safe place to lie low or they'll all die." She shot a look at Luiz in the driver's seat, who was listening in intently. "The others broke their word, they are coming for them before the week of grace is up. Try and get the word out to the other clans. Please Oliver, I can't lose you too." *Not like she'd lost Bast*, a small part of her mind filled in the gap. She clenched her jaw and pushed the thought down. She hadn't lost Bast yet, and she wouldn't. She refused to give up on him without a fight.

She reached out for Bast with her mind. *Did you hear all that?* She pushed down the rising panic, her training, both from being a firefighter, and with Killian, kicking in. There was time to panic later.

Yes. We must get back to the States as quickly as possible. Apparently, a lack of body didn't make you less of a commanding presence. She had her orders.

"*A menina*, you are awfully pretty to be a spy." Luiz gave her a hard look from the driver's seat.

Azar shook her head weakly, still trying to take in everything Oliver had told her. "I'm not a spy."

"What are you then? Black Ops? *Os militares?*"

Azar gave a hard laugh, imagining Luiz's face if she told him exactly what she was, better yet, showed him what she was. Instead she gave the old man her most innocent smile.

"I'm a firefighter," she said simply. Well, at least she was once, in a simpler time. Luiz gave her a skeptical look, and she wondered if he would continue to go up and down the river, to collect Jack, Cy and Vivian.

She got Luiz to drop them off at the post office,

and thanked the man. She scrawled a letter for the rest of their group and left it in the care of the postmaster. She called the airport to harangue the operator for the soonest possible flight to Porto Vehlo. The tired sounding man on the other end of the phone said he could call up some dude called Marc, and if he wasn't drunk in the bar, they could fly out at dusk. But she couldn't book a flight from Porto Velho without a significant complication.

The kid doesn't have a passport, and there's no one at the compound to forge one, Azar explained to Bast, the frustration of being a continent away really grinding her down.

It's okay. I know a few people in the Sao Paolo compound that owe me a favor or two. Enough to get us a private plane back to NYC and I can take care of customs. But we'll have to keep the kid out of sight. If any of the Adel come upon a Fae, it'll be shoot first and ask questions later, regardless of their age.

AZAR GAVE Marc the last of her cash as she got out of the sardine can he called a plane. There was rust showing through some of the peeling paint, and she had never been so happy to alight a vehicle, ever. She wasn't the best flier, but landing in that squeaking tin tube had been a harrowing experience she hoped never to repeat. She'd rather fly herself transatlantic than do that again.

Azar hoped Bast's contacts came through, because she had no more funds left to get them out of Porto Vehlo. She stepped out on the tarmac in the private aircraft section of the airport. Bast had left her before they'd boarded in Lábrea, to call in his favors. She thought perhaps he didn't want to board the death trap, even in his incorporeal form.

She sent out her mind to the familiar thread that was Bast. The freaky Vulcan mind-meld thing they had was becoming more and more natural to her, as if she could feel around inside her brain like a map.

Did your guy put up the goods? Azar asked, and wondered if he was in hearing distance. A light zephyr swirled around her, dipping inside her shirt. She laughed out loud. Definitely in hearing distance then.

I forgot the perks that came with being incorporeal, he giggled like a high-school boy, before he sobered. *Yeah, he said it was in hanger twelve. Apparently it's his private plane. He reminded me not to drink all the champagne.*

You didn't tell him about... our problem? What was the politically correct term for the fact that a man couldn't take a physical form? Male projectile dysfunction?

No, when I got there, the whole compound was in lock down. It took some serious fast talking to even get inside. The place is like a madhouse. The Jann Councilor hasn't returned from the States. None of the Councilors are able to be contacted. Killian is MIA also. They are in serious panic mode. I don't think they would have listened or cared about my problem, except for the fact that we had gathered another Great Weapon. It wouldn't be a priority. There was bitterness in him now, an acceptance that this was the way he would always be.

You know me, I stubbornly stick at something until it yields. We will fix this. You're a priority to me, she told Bast. A soft wind touched her face, and she could almost feel his lips touch her skin

Azar's stomach dropped when she thought of Killian and her father trapped or dead below the rubble. She'd only just gotten to know them, care for them. She wasn't ready to lose them again. Not to mention Mira and Danian, who had become her friends, and even Joia. The leaden weight of despair settled around her heart. She wasn't ready to acknowledge they were dead yet.

She carried both packs and walked towards the hangar Bast had indicated, Neyvn trailing along closely. A stewardess stood at the top of a set of silver stairs, a welcoming smile on her face. She ushered them into the plush interior of the plane.

Boy, how the other half lived. The seats were all buttery leather recliners, a polished mahogany side table between each set of two. A long matching mahogany sideboard ran up one side of the plane's interior. Little TV screens flipped out from the walls, and top of the line headphones hung on hooks next to them. It was all very lush to say the least.

"Please take a seat," the hostess crooned. "Can I get you anything to drink before we take off? The Captain has informed me that we'll be in the air in fifteen minutes now that you have boarded." Both Azar and Neyvn ordered a coke, and she made sure Neyvn was properly secured into his belt. By the way the boy was looking around in wide eyed wonder, she was going to assume this was his first time flying. Though, this level of comfort was new, even to her.

That was quite a favor you were owed, Azar commented to Bast, sensing his presence close to her.

I saved his life once. It's how I got the scar on my face. Her hands ached to stroke that pink line that ran from his eyebrow to his jawline, as she had done hundreds of times before. She shook off the melancholy like a too tight coat.

In that case, you should have gotten him to throw in some caviar, she joked, but even to her own ears, there was a sense of loss in her voice.

A part of her couldn't wait to return home, to abandon all the turmoil that had happened in the Amazon to the past. But she had a feeling that it was only just the beginning and the worst was yet to come.

CHAPTER 22

Azar knew she should have gone straight to Sterling Forest, to beg them to take Neyvn, and to double check that they had followed her advice to leave the forest. But when she hopped into the taxi, she found herself giving the driver directions to the compound. She had to see the damage for herself. She wanted to know if it was as bad as her premonitions from Danu. It was something she both feared and hoped. If the premonitions were true, then she had a chance to stop them. If they weren't, then they were all going to be flailing around blindly in the dark. It would be a horrible blessing.

No matter what, she was glad to be out of the

jungle and back in NYC. Azar cast a look at Neyvn, and could see that he wasn't faring so well with all the concrete and iron.

"Are you okay?" She asked as she patted his arm.

From what she knew, the rumors about the Fae not being able to tolerate iron were fairly over-exaggerated. They found it uncomfortable, and if cut with it, they would heal mortal slow, but it didn't cause them excruciating pain or mean instant death. Still, at Neyvn's tense nod, Azar felt guilty about going to the Compound first. She should have gotten him back into the forest, amongst nature, where his kind was happier. She pushed the guilt down. She just had to see. Then she would take him where he needed to go.

The traffic congested as they got closer to the compound, and every moment dragged on like an hour. She didn't try and make conversation; she just sat in silence and prayed to whatever deity would listen. She prayed they'd made progress in the rescue attempt, that her father and Killian, and her friends, had all been rescued from the wreckage.

She knew when they had reached the blocks around the compound because there was police tape blocking the area off. Azar paid the cabbie, and grabbed their packs from the trunk of the cab. Neyvn was half hiding behind her, but his gaze roamed around in awe at the towering pillars of glass and concrete. She couldn't see the compound yet, but her heart had started to beat like a bass drum in her chest.

Azar was in two minds about what to do with Neyvn. Should she hide him, and hope none of the Djinn came across him while she was gone? Or should she keep him with her, so she could defend him if need be. She rubbed her temples. Having a kid was all hard work and constant worry.

In the end, she decided to keep him with her, but got her cap out of the pocket of her pack and put it on his head. It covered his slightly pointed ears and the crazy big eyes that marked him as one of the Fae.

"Keep your eyes down and don't look at anyone, okay? They aren't going to be particularly overjoyed to see any of the Fae right now, and their usual code of moral conduct is going to fly out the window. So try to be as unobtrusive as possible. And stay close." Azar squeezed his shoulder and gave him a reassuring smile.

She walked around the corner, with Neyvn so close on her heels that he banged into her back when she stopped dead.

The old sandstone building that housed the public part of the Compound was now just a pile of steel and rubble. There were dozens of people walking around, and she could see Donovan amongst the Djinn she didn't know. She could also see Keenan Riley with Danian. Azar let out a little sigh of relief. Three friends safe.

All of a sudden, something ploughed into her side, two strong arms wrapping around her middle.

"Goddamn, it's good to see you," Oliver sighed next to her ear, taking a big breath to draw in her scent as his arms crushed the breath out of her. She squirmed until he put her down, and she could finally draw in enough oxygen to speak. She turned in his arms and he hugged her close. "I know I was talking to you, but I didn't stop worrying until right now, where I can see you for myself." His voice was thick and he gave her one more squeeze and moved away.

"I'm fine, Oliver. But this..." she waved her arm in the direction of the rubble. If she didn't look too closely, it was just like any other demolition site. But if she really stared, she could see the outlines of faces beneath the dust covered glass. People who were crushed against the doors and windows as they tried to escape.

Oliver let out an exhausted sigh and walked toward a shelter someone had erected, where they were running the rescue operation by the looks of it. "The Pack sent as many of us as it could. There were a lot more of us yesterday before you sent your warning. Now, most of us have gone home to help with the evac. We weren't doing any good anyway. We couldn't smell anything, or move anything. No one can hear even the faintest sound from beneath the surface. It's as if someone has put the site on mute and welded the debris together, and no matter how we lifted, or what machinery we had brought in, nothing could shift it."

Keeley saw them arrive at the tent, and she raced over, throwing her arms around Azar. She couldn't even imagine what Keeley was going through, having her twin missing, presumed to be beneath the rubble. By her red rimmed eyes and bright red nose, it was obvious that she had been crying quite steadily. Azar hugged her sister back tightly.

"I'm so glad you're here. Oliver said you were fine, but I couldn't take it if another one of my family was stuck down there, in pain or..." Keeley swallowed hard, "dead. I can't feel Killian at all. I know I'd feel if he died, or if he was alive, but I feel nothing."

Azar patted her on the back, genuinely wanting to soothe her. She had only known her family a few months, but Keeley had spent centuries with her father, and shared the womb with Killian. The not knowing would be enough to break a weaker woman.

"We will find a way to get them out. Don't worry," she said. It might have been a lie, but Keeley looked like she needed a few false platitudes before she broke.

"We've tried everything. Digging. Using our powers. Danian even tried his incorporeal form to get in. It's blocked to us all." Tears dripped onto Azar's shoulder. She didn't have any new ideas. She wondered if Bast was close by.

Have you tried to get in? There might have been a silver lining to his incorporeal form.

A light breeze ruffled her hair. *She speaks the truth. I couldn't even enter through the obvious gaps in the debris.*

She ground her teeth in frustration. *There has to be some way to get in there; maybe if they dug underneath, and then came back up through the bottom?*

Someone tugged on the bottom of her tank top. "They have bound the wreckage to the earth. I believe I might be able to be of assistance." Dread washed over her, as Neyvn's little voice piped up from behind her, and every set of eyes whipped towards him.

Azar's hands lit up in case of attack, and Oliver went into a defensive stance in response. Bless his kitty cat heart, he didn't know what she was fighting against, but he had her back.

Neyvn was looking directly at Keeley, his big Fae eyes a blinking neon sign espousing his heritage.

"Ah, Az, why do you have a little Fae kid with you?" Oliver stage whispered. He still faced off against the entire group of Djinn, and seemed more interested than accusing.

"It's a long story. But he's under my protection," Azar said loud enough for everyone to hear.

"You have a lot of nerve half-blood," someone growled from the back, "bringing the enemy onto our territory. Is he here to witness the destruction his lying people have caused?" There were mutters of agreement, and the group took a collective step forward.

"Maybe we should have an eye for an eye. Send him back to his people in pieces," someone else said, and she prepared herself for a fight she couldn't possibly win.

Damn the kid, why couldn't he have just kept his

mouth shut and head down like she'd asked? On the heels of that thought was guilt, and forgiveness. He was only offering to do something good.

Donovan came and stood on her other side, ready to fight with her. She threw him a quick, grateful look. Keeley was still standing in front of her, but she hadn't taken her eyes off Neyvn. The group tightened around them, like a noose.

She could really use Bast in his corporeal form right now. He had a little bit of authority. He may have been able to defuse the situation.

This is bad, she sent out to him. *I just want you to know that I love you. Even though I've been nothing but trouble, you've been a rock to me. If there were no other reasons, I'd love you for that.*

A wind picked up, like a tornado, under the awning. *It's not over yet, Jaanaman. Plus, I'm not completely useless in this form. Have a little faith.*

She had faith alright, faith that this mob would tear her apart to get to Neyvn, to exact revenge on whatever scapegoat they could find.

Keeley looked away from Neyvn, and gave a single nod to Azar before turning to the crowd. "Will you lot stop behaving like Neanderthals? If this Fae has offered to help, who are we to turn it down? Would you rather our loved ones, our kinspeople, rot beneath the rubble so you could have a little revenge? The boy is just that, a child. The enemy destroys one building, and we are resorting to mob mentality, like we are nothing but humans." She flicked a sheepish smile to her and Donovan. "No offense."

Sure, that wasn't offensive at all, she remarked to Bast, but outwardly she just waved a hand dismissively. "None taken."

Keeley didn't hear her response as she continued. "I'm sure Azar has a very good reason for having the child, but right now that doesn't matter. If the boy says he can help, then let him help. Let him rectify some of the sins of his people." Azar resisted the urge to applaud. Apparently, grandstanding was in their blood.

She rested a now flameless hand on Neyvn's shoulder reassuringly. She still didn't trust the crowd, but they'd stopped their ominous advancing.

"The boy lost his entire family to this Fae war. To kill him would be doing the enemy a favor," Azar added. The Djinn weren't generally known for their compassion, but they were known for their spitefulness.

There was some more muttering, and everyone

stepped back out of the menacing ranks they'd instinctively formed.

Keeley peered down at Neyvn. "What do you need to unbind the wreck from the earth?" she asked seriously. Apparently when she was having her stare off with the Nevyn, she'd decided to treat him like a very small adult rather than a child. Azar understood, there was a world of pain in the kid's eyes, the kind of pain that couldn't co-habitate with childish innocence.

"I just need everyone to move back, and I need a circle drawn in a clear bit of earth. And I need Azar." There wasn't a hint of nervousness in the boy's tone. From his strong, clear voice, you wouldn't think that only a moment before, a group of supernatural creatures had wanted to tear him limb from limb. Royal stoicism ran in his veins after all. Steadfastness in the face of adversity.

The Weres who were mingling around the site cleared away a spot for Neyvn, pulling up concrete so he could reach the dirt beneath. Neyvn went to the reddish clay ground, and stood on it, letting out a sigh of relief. It was probably the first natural surface he'd touched since they'd landed in NYC. He'd been a real trooper.

Neyvn beckoned her over, and then drew a circle

around them both. "I'm hoping that the Mother will help, otherwise I'm unsure if I have enough strength to do this, even if I borrowed some of yours. But I felt I had to try," he whispered so softly that even Azar had to strain to hear.

Azar wasn't exactly eager for a repeat of the last time she was in a Tuatha Dé Danann circle, but he was right. They had to try. Neyvn sat cross legged in the almost perfect circle he had drawn around them. Azar followed suit and sat. Neyvn took her hands in his tiny ones, an almost comical reflection of her and Jack only days ago.

He pressed her hands to the earth, his over the top, and they connected to the earth like they had been struck by lightning. It definitely wasn't as smooth as her connection with Jack. That had been like falling into a bath of molasses. This was like she'd been strapped to the electric chair.

Azar's body went rigid, as the time slowed and things became hazy. As she looked around, she could see the black film lying over the top of the demolished building next to them. That must be the binding. She looked at Neyvn and could see him glow luminous. Not quite the eye searing brightness of Jack, and nowhere near the ethereal light of Danu, but his Tuatha blood shone through nonetheless.

Neyvn's little brow creased, and sweat dripped off his nose onto the ground in front of him as he started chanting. His face was red with exertion, and Azar wished she knew how to help, to ease some of the burden. He was so strong, but looked so fragile in that moment.

Another hand cupped over hers, and she looked up to see Danu, one hand on each of theirs. Joy swept through Azar like a wave, as Danu's thoughts started running through her head. First, she was happy to be able to touch two of her children, two that had been lost to her. Then, deep disapproval at what had been done on this spot, though Azar couldn't work out if she meant the City of New York, or the binding on the destroyed building. Both would be abominations to the nature loving Danu.

The crease in Neyvn's brow eased as Danu put some of her own energy into the task. Azar tore her gaze away for a moment to watch a wave of light chase away the oily blackness of the Fae's binding. Her gaze whipped back to the ball of luminescence that was Danu, because it hurt to look away in her presence. Danu removed her hand and Azar felt an acute sense of loss. She wanted to weep. Danu leaned forward and pressed a kiss to her forehead, and then another to Neyvn's. The little boy was crying uncontrollably. Azar wanted to reach out and console him.

Danu sent her an image of Neyvn, with a crown on top of his head, surrounded by flames that didn't burn him, but kept the shadows away. Azar nodded earnestly; she got the message loud and clear. He was the crown from her premonition, and she was meant to protect him. It was a duty she'd already undertaken willingly.

Just as suddenly as the Mother had arrived, she winked out of existence again. The sense of loss stole Azar's breath, and tore a cry from her chest. She blinked a couple of times to recenter herself, then she took Neyvn's hands and the little boy shook with sobs.

She stood and pulled the boy into her arms. It wasn't until then that she noticed the crowd around them. Their expressions ranged from awe and horror, concern and disgust.

"The binding is gone. You should be able to move the debris," Azar said shakily. Still the crowd hesitated, until Donovan ordered the Weres in his employ to start moving chunks of sandstone and steel. That seemed to shake the rest of the crowd from their stupor and everyone started grabbing rubble and moving it to a pile away from the wreckage. Keeley came over and hugged Azar tightly. Then she looked at the boy, and hugged him too.

"Thank you," she repeated over and over.

A call went up from one of the Weres, "I can hear someone!"

Azar grabbed Neyvn's hand, and took off across the debris with speed and agility that would have showcased their otherworldliness to any humans who had sneaked past the barriers, but she didn't care. She felt the breeze pick up, and knew that Bast was rushing ahead of her. She pushed her way through the crowd around the Were that had called out, Keeley in front of her and Neyvn sandwiched between them.

Everyone hushed to listen as a voice, barely more than a hoarse shout, reached the surface.

"Down here!" croaked out a voice she recognized, and her knees went weak.

Killian. Thank Danu.

Keeley knelt on the ground, the jagged steel cutting her knees as she wept. It was a small hope, but Azar knew that the probability of them getting many survivors was slim.

Her father, Mira, Joia, dozens of other Adel, all the Council members were all in the building when it had exploded, and the ones who hadn't died in the initial assault had been trapped below the earth for almost forty-eight hours. But she took this one little ray of hope, and started to dig with the others. She could only hope and pray, and she did both fervently. No matter what the outcome was, she knew that the world would never be the same.

Thank you for reading. None of this would be possible without you wonderful readers, and I am so thankful every day I get to share my stories with you all.

I love hearing from readers, so you can find me at any of these places below:

Facebook Author Page: https://www.facebook.com/GraceMcGintyAuthor/

Instagram: @gracemcgintyauthor

Website: www.gracemcginty.com

Twitter: @McgintyGrace

Email: gracemcgintyauthor@gmail.com

And now for the battle cry of all indie authors. If you liked this book, or any book, leave a review, or recommend it to a friend, or write the Amazon link on the wall of a bathroom stall.

Anything helps, and it keeps indie writers creating the stories you love so much.